NEWBIRD

Tyler David Rigdon

FISHER BOOKS

New York | Michigan

Second edition, 2026
First published by Amazon KDP in 2024
This edition published by Fisher Books in 2026
ISBN: 979-8-9943970-0-8
Published by Fisher Books

Ebook published by Indy Pub in 2026
ISBN: 979-8-2955-1501-9 (Ebook by Indy Pub)

Cover design by Sara Velasco
Author photo on back cover by Nick Rigdon, taken along the Colorado River.

For more writing or to contact the author please visit:
https://linktr.ee/tylerrigdon

Newbird

prologue

Spring, 1599

THE wigwams stood like leatherbacks all in a row. The stillness of the morning was a painted stillness, delicate and precious, not to be touched. It was broken by a dubious squirrel in search of a nut. He pattered across the village alone with muddy claws, slashing through clay all wet from dew, ash-colored and void of food. Empty-handed, he raced up a tree and woke a mess of birds who called out their morning songs. Soon the little village was buzzing with life. Racoons and mice and other vermin scavenged for scrapped bones and puddles of grease around the fire-pits. Birds assaulted the ground, pecking holes in the soil and pulling from its depths a hundred worms, swimming in the air, dangling to death. Insects made skeleton noises in the open air.

One of the wigwams shook with the gentle urgency of an egg and it birthed a man, tall, dark, and nearly naked, who stepped across the ground to the firepit. The birds retreated to their high homes at the sight of the giant. Soon other men populated the fire. Food was being passed around. The thick steam of hot beans rolled off the bowls. Patamon ate with the men at the fire. He wiped his eyes with the backs of his palms and whispered with the men next to him. They smoked, and ate beans and fish and when they finished, Patamon stood and continued on through the village. He peered into the open door of a wigwam and saw a family still asleep, laid about the floor on hide rugs and blankets. In another home, a couple made morning love quietly and plainly. Patamon smiled at the sight of their love. Racing from a third wigwam, two boys were in chase over a toy and their laughter woke their neighbor who crawled from his home in the anguish of the dawn. He saw Patamon and they regarded one another with a lift of the chin and both carried on.

Back at his own home Patamon stood patiently with his hand on the viney bark that framed his door. He breathed the clean air of the forest and smiled. From his door, a boy stepped with sleepy feet. Forest dreams still shone from his brown eyes. Patamon gathered the boy in his arms and brushed the sleep from his face. He reminded him of the journey ahead. It would take them two days to reach the ocean and Patamon was not content to travel at the speed of the sleepy child. Patamon rose and set forth for the trail. His son followed him. He held with him a satchel and a small bow, fit for a boy.

Book I

Franklin's Fort and a Band of Young Men
Fall, 1836

N
WYOMING
SOUTH DAKOTA
Missouri River
Iowa
La Ramee's Rendezvous, 1815
North Platte River
Sandhills
NEBRASKA
Villasur Expedition, 1720
Lake McConaughy
Bourgmont, 1714
Stephen Long, 1820
Platte River
Fort Vasquez, 1835
South Platte River
James Purcell's Trading Post, 1803-1806
South Park Basin (Purcell, Pike), 1806
Franklin's Fort, 1835
Colonel Dodge, 1835
Platte Canyon
COLORADO
KANSAS
Royal Gorge (Pike), 1806-1807
0 25 50 75 100
miles

one

THERE was water. Bell was soaking in it up to his belt. There was also sound. It was the wading of the water. It washed upon the bone white banks as they stepped. Fifty of them, hungry and tired with slow swollen legs in unison under the iron weight of the night up and over each ripple of the South Platte River. The October mosquitos had not taken to hibernating quite yet. They feasted on the men merrily. Unseen for the darkness, each man was covered in red blots like plumrashes where they had slain full, fat mosquitoes on their faces and necks.

Above the men a river of stars was stitched into the sky, carved out by the tall red walls of the canyon. The sky mirrored the river below, each star a reflection of a pebble that sat heavy at the bottom of the river bed. Bell remembered walking into the canyon some hours before the sun abandoned them and lifting his heavy head straight up the walls to try and find their tops. He slipped and slid in the water, gawking at the rustic colors of the walls and their contrast to the blue sky and the water. With each misstep he was scolded by the sergeant in front of him, but Bell didn't mind the scolding. He smiled and decided that this was the most dramatic and magnificent place he'd ever been.

They were achingly ancient walls he concluded—he'd learned that anything so tall had to be ancient—which put him in the heart of an ancient place. He'd heard someone say that Platte Canyon was some millions of years old. He didn't know that things could be so old but when he looked at the walls he sure believed it. The canyon was thin and steep and it was starkly naked save for a dusting of birdless trees, dumb with loneliness. The banks of the river were breathtaking in their nakedness. The roseblood walls swallowed most of the flora. Wicked vines and webs of weeds tried to come free from the cracks of the rocks that hung from cliffsides like stone chins—mandibles clenched shut by time. It was hardly touched by humans.

It had been since noon that they bisected the canyon and there was no sign at all of whom they were pursuing. Now it was so blindingly dark Bell wasn't sure he could even see the man in front of him to whom he held on. Occasionally, Captain Flete, at the head of the column, had stopped the march at the sound of a running racoon or the sight of some game between crows in the distance. When he started up again, the groans of fifty men filled the tight canyon behind him.

"You ugly bunch'a sorrys," he called to them. "Get ahold'a yerselves."

But now it was dark. Bell did all he could to occupy his mind during the futile march but the feeling in his legs had long left him and the column as a whole had slowed down considerably. The march they ensued on now was one of convention, something to protect the captain's ego, who had lost track of whatever or whomever he was tracking. Bell's exhaustion came to overwhelm him and his tired weight fell on the pack of the man in front of him.

"Cut it, Bell," said Murray in his soft Irish. "Yer yankin' me down. Stand up now, woul'dja."

"Sorry," Bell said. He shook his head trying to rattle himself awake. "How much longer do you think we'll go, Sergeant? We're not going to continue like this all night, you don't think."

"No use in complainin' lad, this is no leisure march."

"There wasn't hardly ten of them, Sergeant. They've got to be five miles ahead of us by now."

"Can't do much 'bout it anyhow, lad. Why don't ye just keep yer bloody mouth shut so they don't hear'ye. These walls will canoe yer voice t' Mexico and back."

Bell sighed and marched on as his mind began to wander off into the night. He worked to conjure up the fleeting colors of the canyon, attempting to distract his uncomplicated mind from the misery of the cold river and the insects. He wondered how many cold rivers he'd crossed since he'd left the barracks outside St. Louis. Or even more yet, since he left New York. It seemed to him that the whole country was just rivers separated by leagues of green grass and corn. Occasionally there would be a town, but it had become hard to tell it any different from the last one. Mostly it was just rivers. He was always walking in a damned river.

He imagined himself skipping stones on the Hudson with his brother. That river was so wide that Bell never saw his stones die and thought that perhaps they would skip forever. New York seemed like a lifetime ago, he thought. It had only been three years, but in that time he'd lost the memory of his brother's face. When he thought of him, he saw some featureless shape of a man move like oil paint—gleaming and wet like nothing in fractured light—like bits of dreams or a haunting that was identical each time but not necessarily true. He could close his eyes and watch his brother skip stones or cut wood or smoke his pipe out along the waterline, and he wondered if those pictures ever happened at all.

He remembered the docks and the days they spent together burnt and blistered, battered for nothing on the waterfront and swearing they'd find a way to put it all together one day. Bell laughed to himself as he thought this. Three years later and he still hadn't put it together much. In fact, with the water in his underwear and the mosquitos in his ears, he wondered if his work was more meaningful on the old Hudson, stocking ships. It wasn't a great job, but it was steady. He remembered the day he started. It was snowing in New York and he could hardly move his mittened hands to button his coat, let alone to work. He was only fifteen and shivered under the silver snow. His father introduced him to the dockmaster. "This is my youngest son, William. This will be his first job. He won't let you down."

It was only two months after that that his father caught the violent fever that buried half the neighborhood that winter. The boys took to sleeping under trees in Battery Park just across from the docks until his brother got smart and disappeared with something plump and golden-haired. It was then that Bell wandered into a recruiting office and begged that he be taken anywhere but Manhattan.

A crash of rocks fell from the top of the canyon to the river. At the sound of the water, the column halted.

"This should do it," said Murray. "I bet Flete turns us 'round here." The men waited patiently as they could hear their officer moving about in the water.

"You think we're turning around?" Bell said.

"Sounds like it, ole' boy. Yull be back at Franklin's sleepin' like a farm pig anytime now."

"I'd sooner pitch camp here than make that march back tonight."

"I reckon we would do jus' that if it weren't fer the cavalry waitin' fer us. I'm sure Lockhart's already inna frenzy. Ye know how he gets."

"Something tells me the dragoons have been sleeping for hours now."

"Ye might be right 'bout that, lad. Those girls certainly do need ther beauty sleep." Murray laughed a toothy laugh. "Don't ye know, I heard Lockhart is havin' a Tudor bed and wardrobe brought in on wagon train."

Bell laughed hard and then from down the way he heard the captain speak.

"Quit your chumming down there, boys!" Flete's voice was deep and commanding. It echoed between the dull walls of the canyon. "We're going to turn the column around. Wait your turn and then move it."

As the column began to turn, Murray spoke in a whisper. "I guess it's not a half-bad life, wouldn't ye say, Bell? The dragoons that is." His continuance of the conversation was an admittance of his boredom.

"How do you mean?"

"Well ye sit down all day fer one." He already burst with laughter before he could make his next point. "Fer two, ye get sent out t' mountain country and when it comes time t' meet the mountains ye just make the poor infantry do it."

The two of them laughed together. Bell thought it felt good to laugh.

"Make more money than the damned infantry too," Murray added on.

"How much do they make?"

"Hell if I know but it's a lot better than me and you, lad. I don't even want t' know what you make, Bell, poor bastard, 'cause I'm not exactly livin' right on me sergeant wages. I betcha ole' Lockhart makes as much as Jackson or more. Ye ever seen that black horse he rides on? That's no issued horse, no sir. That's a good family horse, it is. A good battle horse. I reckon he's had that beast since its birth, don't ye think so, Bell?"

"I suppose," Bell said. The column began to bend where they stood. Bell felt the wake of the river at his knees. "I don't know horses too well, I never really spent time with nice horses."

"Lockhart's has to be some rare Arabian colt, ye understand? Ye ever look it in the eye, Bell? Sometimes, when I'm passin' by, I look at these horses, yes. And ye can see when ye look at Lockhart's horse that he's not like the odders. He won't even feed nor shite near the odders. He knows he's better than them and that's why Lockhart rides'im, don't ye know, Bell?"

"I never took much notice. I suppose when we get back I'll take a look."

"You take a look at that horse, Bell. That horse probably had family in Alexander's army. It is a warrior. Ye can tell when ye look it in the eye. Big black eye like black marble. Stern eye."

Bell left a space for Murray to continue on about the horse but he was silent. They walked at a steady pace through the water for some minutes when they suddenly stopped again. At the head of the column Bell could hear men whispering but couldn't make out the words. Then it became apparent that everyone was listening. They listened in the mountain air. They listened to the river and to the rocks and to the sky. The low hum of the moving water sat in the canyon with them. The water listened too. Bell took his hands off of Murray's pack. He bent slowly and took from the river with his hands and drank from his hands like a cup.

"Oh hell," he cursed. "My spectacles. Look out, Sergeant, I dropped my spectacles."

"Oh, hell, Bell," Murray said in a throaty whisper. "Hurry up or we're goin' t' have t' leave'em." Murray took a short step to let Bell dig around the water at his feet. Bell took handfuls of sand and gravel from the bed of the river. It felt good to pull out soft sand and feel it through the cracks of his hands in the cold river.

"I can't find 'em. Hell, Murray, help me look, would you?"

Murray bent down without saying anything and stuck his hands in the water. They both felt around in the darkness for a moment before the column began to march again.

"Come on, Bell, leave 'em behind."

"I can't see anything!" He reached into his pocket and pulled out a box of matches. "Permission to light a match, Sergeant?"

Murray was still in the water.

"Just for a minute," Bell said. "The water is clear, I'll be able to see them."

"Damn! Yer goin' t' get *me* rung up, lad. We're in pursuit."

"We're in *retreat* now."

The column was slow but it began to pull away from the two men. Still a line of soldiers waited behind them. Bell heard Murray scratch his head in the dark. He sighed too.

"Make it quick, lad. One match. We'll take a look and if we don't see the devils, we've got t' go."

Bell dried his hands in his armpits and found a match. The two men were bent down over the water. Bell pressed his finger against the box and struck a match hard against the striker. The flame erupted with a pop and startled his blind eyes. He saw the orange, glowing figure of Murray in front of his face.

"Good to see you, Bell," Murray said smiling, and then came the shots. Bell dropped the match and even in the thunder of the musket fire he heard the spit of its end touch the water. Screams like death splintered the walls and the infantry spread to the sides of the gorge. The sound of downed men filled the gorge. They could hear what sounded like a thousand beetles crawling over cold stone at the top of the walls—the clatter of musketry. Another volley poured down from the sky and the infantry answered the muzzle flashes with scattered shots of their own. Bullets sparked off the high walls and sang before falling back down and dying in the water. Another round of men were hit. Under the reports of the guns was that dull dead sound of lead finding wool over and over. Bones cracked and animal sounds lit the dark. Men spoke tongues into red water—Hail Marys and bloody penance. The entire column was in pandemonium, men collided in the black of night, bodies fell and broke the riverglass. Stones and arrows and lead rained Revelation down into the gorge.

Bell began to run but he was punished by branches, bushes and bodies. Stones tripped his feet and sent him flailing into the chaos of the fight. Another round of guns cracked off from the top of the wall. The muzzles looked like exploding stars high above his head.

"Fire! Shoot something!" Flete yelled.

Bell's breath was fast and shallow. A dizziness moved him to the ground. He couldn't tell if he had been hit or if it was a sickness that was taking him. He reached for his gun, which he just remembered he had, aimed to the top of the canyon wall and fired a lazy shot into the unending blackness. He attempted to move again but each muscle was still. He had no thoughts—they were swallowed by the disorder. He heard the cracking anvil of the moon and then the lights went out.

two

THE histories regarding post-Columbian expeditions along the main bodies of the three Platte Rivers are a long and complex collection of factual written documentation, oral tradition, exaggerations, propaganda, folklore, mythologizing, and general misunderstandings. Additionally, there are a number of characters who act as heroes, villains, martyrs, geniuses and tragic figures that populate the inner-workings of such stories, as well as an endless list of names of men who have been forgotten at the bottom of the deep well of history. While it is difficult to connect and present each and every mountain-man, trader, Indian chief, and brave army colonel that spent the prime of their lives traversing the North American Frontier along the Platte Rivers, there is a general historical acceptance of the perceived order of events that directly affect the story being told henceforth.

***

The geographical nature of the three Platte Rivers is as follows: The North Platte River flows eastward, starting in the highlands of eastern Wyoming where it is fed by its largest tributary, the Sweetwater River. The North Platte meanders slowly, downslope from the high hills of

Wyoming until reaching the town of Douglas where it is redirected to the southeast, passing through Guernsey about forty miles west of the Nebraska border. Just south of Guernsey, the North Platte is joined by the Laramie River before it finally cuts into Nebraska, rushing steadily to the southeast before flanking the city of North Platte, Nebraska to the north where it joins its southern sibling and forms the main body of the Platte River.

The South Platte River begins its life deep in the heart of the Colorado Rocky Mountains high along the Continental Divide where several strong creeks, fueled by the mountains' runoff cycle, converge into one glorified puddle around the basin of South Park, Colorado. From the basin, the South Platte runs slowly southeast until it is redirected northward around Springer Gulch. Here it runs along seemingly endless beds of green-needle pines and luscious red rock for about one-hundred miles until it reaches the foot of the mountains, the place where the great divide of the continent kisses the Great Plains. The rocky corridor that marries the river's mountainous terrain to the plains is called the Platte Canyon—a brown and red ravine of majestic height and awesomeness, cut grain by grain by the ferocity of the South Platte over millions of years. After exiting the canyon from the mountains, the river continues northeast where half a dozen small creeks and streams rush from the Rockies to meet its body near present-day Denver. These small tributaries include Boulder Creek, Big Thompson River, St. Vrain River, Deer Creek, and the immortal Clear Creek (once called Vasquez River). Just south of Fort Collins the river turns its attention dead-east for some time before finally settling northeast again for a few hundred miles where it meets with the North Platte River in North Platte, Nebraska. The Platte River is born at this confluence.

The Platte River itself is a slow, shallow, and sandy river that flows to the southeast in a long, inverted arc across the dry, empty plains of Nebraska for hundreds of miles before emptying into the Missouri River. The Platte River being long, wide, and steady, became a popular and important mainline for New World and American exploration, becoming not only the means by which the mountains were discovered, but also the first highway in which the Rocky Mountains could be reached from the Great Plains.

The first European known to have seen the Platte River was the French trapper Étienne de Veniard, sieur de Bourgmont in 1714.[1] Bourgmont was a convicted felon in the French mainland who escaped his country at nineteen years old to New France and quickly became the commander of Fort Pontchartrain in present-day Detroit, Michigan. After several bouts of violence with Indians, Bourgmont deserted the fort and spent some years aimlessly exploring the Great Lakes region, including a brief stint living on an island in Lake Erie, before he met the daughter of a Missouria chief and traveled with her to her home village on the Grand River in present-day Missouri. Thus ensued a period of avid exploration and consistent residency along the plains of the Mississippi River for Bourgmont. It wasn't long before Bourgmont had fathered several children with his Missouria wife, and had gained a great amount of respect from her tribe. He used their knowledge of the land to map and document his explorations in the West. He and several other French trappers living among the Missouria people gained access to the Platte River by way of the Missouri River either by watercraft or by foot sometime in 1714, per Bourgmont's published reports. He named the river, *Nebraskier*, an Indian word meaning "flat water." In 1721 Bourgmont returned to France, not only pardoned of his previous crimes, but *celebrated* for his unending reconnaissance, and was

---

[1] See page #253 for all endnotes.

eventually officially commissioned to return to *Amérique* to lead a group of soldiers into the plains once again. He and his men quickly established a French fort called Fort Orleans, on the Missouri River at the mouth of the Grand River near his Missouria wife's village. Departing from Fort Orleans, Bourgmont and his men set off to explore and map the land westward, where they soon established a small trading post in northern Nebraska along the Niobrara River. Over the course of several months they were involved in numerous bloody engagements and ambushes by Pawnee Indians that left only sixteen of Bourgmont's original fifty-six soldiers alive to return to Fort Orleans. By 1726, an exhausted and battleworn Bourgmont had returned himself to France and subsequently, his fort's garrison was reduced to only eight men. It was attacked, burned and abandoned later that year at the hands of the Pawnee.

Beginning in the middle of the 16th century, the Spanish had unofficially "claimed" all of the land known as the Great Plains for New Spain. However, due to the sheer amount of land there was to explore and govern, it was unrealistic, if not impossible, for the Spanish to maintain any sort of consistent patrol of their still mostly unprobed claims. Still, news of Bourgmont and his French soldiers mingling on what the Spanish *legally* considered "Spanish soil," provoked the Spanish government of Santa Fe to commission a counteraction deep into the Great Plains.

Lieutenant-General Pedro de Villasur[2] of New Spain organized a voyage of over one-hundred men to march from New Mexico Territory to the Platte River in June of 1720 to forcibly remove any French presence—military or civilian—who had taken up trapping or exploring along its banks. Villasur marched for several weeks through southern Colorado, Kansas, and Nebraska, making no contact with the French. As the Spanish came upon their destination at the confluence of the Platte and Loup rivers, they were attacked in the night by Pawnee Indians resulting in the loss of forty-seven men.[3] Immediately after the attack, Villasur retreated back to Santa Fe which he reached in September.

***

Later in the century as the Seven Years' War raged on and the fighting carried over from the European theatre to the New World, the French interest in the land west of the Mississippi River dwindled considerably[4] as they fought incessantly to maintain their claims around the Great Lakes region. As a result of the French defeat in the war in 1763, they ceded all of their claims along the Mississippi River, including New Orleans and St. Louis, to the Spanish. This extended the Spanish Empire's borders officially from the Mississippi River to the Pacific Coast—an unimaginably vast amount of land that was still significantly unexplored and would remain as such as a result of Villasur's disastrous confrontation with the Pawnee earlier in the century, which greatly discouraged Spanish explorers from venturing north.

Simultaneous with the French defeat, the Spanish were seeing a period of uprisings, revolts, and rebellions in support of colonial independence in the more civilized regions of New Spain. The sheer chaos of maintaining their volatile empire left Spain completely inundated and literally incapable of colonizing any land further north than Santa Fe. With the French defeated and the Spanish distracted by domestic affairs, the area of the Platte Rivers would be all but forgotten in the entire second half of the 18th century.

In 1800 as Napoleon's sudden political and military dominance strangled monarchies and wreaked havoc on the diplomatic status quo of an unstable Europe, he took advantage of a financially bleeding New Spain and regained control of the former French colony, Louisiana, in exchange for a number of regions in Tuscany. He turned to the Americans just three years later and sold Thomas Jefferson the entire lot of land, which stretched roughly from the Mississippi River to the Rocky Mountains, for just $15 million, an incredibly favorable price to the Americans.

With the purchase of these western lands, Jefferson immediately commissioned the well-known voyage of Meriwether Lewis and William Clark, who relied mostly on the Missouri River as their guide.[5] The pair of men and their party would reach the Pacific in 1805 and return to St. Louis in 1806 in what would become one of the proudest and most mythologized expeditions in the history of man. Their contact with dozens of native tribes and their stories of prolonged, freezing, mountainous hikes were immediately immortalized in the American canon of art and literature for all of time to come. What is lesser known, however, but perhaps equally as important, is the voyage by an undecorated, Kentucky-born trapper named James Purcell that occurred concurrently with that of Lewis and Clark's.

Purcell penetrated the Louisiana Territory for the first time in 1802 with two friends in an attempt to establish hunting relations with the Osage people. After incidents of violence with the tribes of the area, his companions left him and he continued hunting alone until he encountered another explorer who was drifting up the Missouri River. The two men continued northward together until they reached the Platte River wherein Purcell continued onward alone. At the fork of the North and South Platte Rivers, Purcell chose the South and found himself settled and hunting in present-day Brighton, Colorado at the foot of the Rocky Mountains. He befriended several local tribes in the area and eventually was asked by the Kiowa people to go south to Santa Fe and gain permission from the Spanish on their behalf to trade on their land. Purcell agreed. His journey to Santa Fe began with a deep excursion into the Rocky Mountains, likely via the South Platte River, marking the first time an American had ever breached the Continental Divide, and likely the first time any man of

European descent had ever traversed the mountains in such a fashion. After several months he and his Indian guides found themselves inside a vast, flat basin surrounded by various shining, silver peaks in every direction. This was modern-day South Park, Colorado. In this basin, he met the French-American explorer, Jean Baptiste Le-Lande[6], who had entered the basin from the south—the direction of Santa Fe—with a Spanish expedition headed north on a diplomatic mission to a Pawnee settlement. He assisted Purcell in his journey to Santa Fe, which he reached in 1807. Purcell chose to settle in the Santa Fe area, flaunting his renowned skills as a trapper and hunter to entice the Spanish into employing him rather than arresting him.

Later that year, his path would cross with Zebulon Pike, a twenty-seven-year-old U.S. Army Lieutenant and leader of a commissioned military expedition that had gotten lost in the depths of the Rocky Mountains in the winter of 1806/1807. The expedition wound up captured by Spanish forces and brought to Santa Fe for imprisonment. Pike's Expedition was the U.S. government's first act of further reconnaissance following the return of Lewis and Clark to St. Louis. In June of 1806 Pike led his men from St. Louis through Kansas and west along the Arkansas River to the eastern plains of Colorado, and eventually to the foot of the Rockies by the fall. Approaching the mountains, Pike spotted for the first time the ever-famous peak that is now named for him and led his men into the depths of the range making an attempt to climb the peak, believing it would provide him with the greatest vantage point of the area. His attempt failed, as the temperatures at the high elevation quickly became sub-zero and his party, starving and not equipped for the winter, abandoned the idea and spent some time recouping in the Royal Gorge, a deep ravine cut by the ancient force of the Arkansas River. Pike then made an attempt to exit the mountains to the south where he intended to find the Red River and follow it east to the Mississippi, but he became turned around in the arduous terrain and marched along the South Platte River—believing it to be the Arkansas—following it north as far as present-day Fairplay, Colorado. This would make him just the second American to ever reach the South Platte, after James Purcell. After realizing his folly, he marched a cold, hungry, and grueling one-hundred miles back to the Arkansas River before finally finding his way south and exiting the mountains via the Medano Pass on January 27, 1807. At least five of his men were dead or left behind. A few days later, Pike and his remaining ten men began construction on a fort, later known as Pike's Stockade in present-day Sanford, Colorado—Spanish Territory at the time—where they decided they would wait out the winter. It is unclear if Pike knew that he was raising an American flag on Spanish soil or not, but regardless of his intent, he and his men were arrested by a squadron of Spanish cavalry on February 26 and brought to Santa Fe. Here, Pike and Purcell met, forged a friendship, and exchanged stories and maps of their exploration through the plains, mountains, and South Park basin. Several of Purcell's findings and observations made their way back to the U.S. government by way of Pike—most notably Purcell's report of gold at the headwaters of the South Platte River in South Park. Pike later published these claims though they were initially ignored due to the perceived hardship associated with a civilian's excursion to Colorado.[7] After spending several weeks in Santa Fe, Pike and his men were then transported as prisoners around New Spain for a number of months before being released to the Louisiana border on July 1, 1807. Pike would return to Washington with a dozen notebooks worth of reports and findings on the South Platte River and the Rocky Mountains. James Purcell would spend the rest of his life in Santa Fe.

***

Though the South Platte River began to accrue a wealth of notable activity much earlier than the North Platte, it would ultimately be the North Platte River that would prove its value and importance more immediately to the United States government, becoming a more lucrative region of activity in the Western Frontier for the century to come. This was generally due to the North Platte River's geography on more navigable land than its southern sibling. While the South Platte River terminated in a series of dizzying loops deep in the heart of the highest peaks of the Rocky Mountains, the North Platte gave birth to several helpful tributaries across plateaued land that would lead to the discovery of such iconic American wonders as the Yellowstone river and geyser systems, as well as the Oregon Trail.

Between 1810 and 1834 there would be several important and remunerative voyages by way of the North Platte River including Jacques La Ramee's many trade expeditions around the confluence of the river that now bears his name,[8] William Price Hunt and Robert Stuart's initial discovery of South Pass in 1812,[9] Jedediah Smith and Robert Campbell's rediscovery and national publication of South Pass in 1824,[10] Lieutenant Benjamin Bonneville's famous utilization of South Pass in 1833 to reach present-day Idaho, Utah, Nevada and California, and finally William Sublette's 1834 founding of Fort William.

All of these fearless and adventurous tales of exploration would greatly influence the routes, motives, and conduct of the later generation of mountain-men to come. Names like Jim Bridger, Kit Carson, and John Frémont are still timeless in the history of American folklore and they all forged their way by literally following in the footsteps of those who walked along the North Platte River in the early part of the 19th century.

During this period of magnified interest in the North Platte region, the South Platte River had fallen into complete obscurity. Zebulon Pike's stories of starving winter nights wandering aimlessly at 10,000 feet in the Rockies were only made worse by the miserable scouting reports of one Stephen Long. Between 1810 and 1834, Long and his party made one of *only two* known visitations[11] to the South Platte River.

Stephen Long was commissioned by the U.S. military to embark on a scientific excursion of the Louisiana Territory and to survey the country's southern border with Spain.[12] He set off from St. Louis in June of 1820 with a team of geologists, botanists, zoologists and illustrators. They spent the first two weeks along the Platte River traversing Nebraska, until they ultimately connected to the South Platte River which they followed to the edge of the Front Range of the Rocky Mountains. Long's voyage was relatively productive in a scientific sense, as his party discovered and documented dozens of unknown fauna, vegetation, insects and rock formations for the use of the U.S. government. The men attempted to follow the South Platte deep into the mountains but turned back towards the plains after much of the party became ill with altitude sickness. Back on the plains, they turned south and walked along the Front Range towards the Arkansas River. In July, a group of Long's men climbed to the summit of Pikes Peak, becoming the first white men, and perhaps the first people to ever do so. One explorer called the mountain, "a region of astonishing beauty." The temperature on the peak was under 40° F while the temperature at the base of the mountain approached 100°. For weeks after their descent from the peak the temperature continued to scorch the men as they made their way through southern Colorado along the basin. They hiked without water for up to thirty miles each day for several days before finally reaching the Arkansas River. Upon reaching the river they rested and hydrated in the Royal Gorge—the same place that Pike and his man had holed up during the winter of 1806—an experience that one of the scientists found to be "the grandest and most romantic scenery I ever beheld." On their subsequent voyage eastward to the Mississippi River, the party had run out of food and water again as they had eventually abandoned the Arkansas River in search for the Red River, which they never found. The streams and creeks that they did find were nearly dried up by sand or polluted with manure. Long and his men force-marched with empty stomachs and suffering from severe dehydration at risk of death for several days before they finally reached Fort Smith, Arkansas on September 13. While it was an important and scientifically productive expedition, Long was left skeptical of the land due to the lack of water and provisions during the second half of the voyage. He later wrote in his reports that while the regions he explored were of immense beauty in nature, the land between the Mississippi River and the Rocky Mountains was "a Great American Desert, not suitable for cultivation," and that "the scarcity of wood and water—almost uniformly prevalent—will prove an insuperable obstacle in the way of settling the country." In short, he greatly discouraged the government from wasting any time or resources on the West, especially before the land east of the Mississippi River had been settled fully. It was his suggestion that the Great Plains and Rocky Mountain regions be used as a buffer between the United States and the Spanish. The American public took Long's advice as it would be another fifteen years before anything resembling a permanent settlement showed up on the South Platte River.

***

It would be Louis Vasquez, a renowned fur trader and future business partner of Jim Bridger, who would set up his little outpost, Fort Vasquez, on the South Platte near its confluence with Boulder Creek in 1835. Vasquez was no stranger to the trapping industry and although the fort's beginnings were slow, within a year he had a dozen men working out of his post from a plethora of differing descents—American, Mexican, Spanish, Indian, English, Irish, and French. Vasquez had been meddling in the area for over a year. He would be the first American trapper since Purcell to run business off of this land, although by 1836 at least three other companies would join him along the South Platte River, becoming links in the chain that would later be known as "Trappers Trail," a trail that ran from Fort Laramie, Wyoming to Santa Fe, New Mexico.

The first trapper to be drawn to the South Platte River after the success of Vasquez was a man by the name of Jim Franklin, a self-proclaimed descendant of Benjamin Franklin—a claim he supported by his uncanny resemblance to the Founding Father. Franklin himself was a fat and jovial man nearing old age. He hailed from New England, and looked the part. His thin, white hair seemed to just fall off the back of his bulbous pink head as if it were in danger of vanishing into the air with the next good gust of wind. His rose-pink cheeks and round, piggy-nose earned him the affectionate nickname "Porky," a name he championed and often used for himself in the third person. He was not known as the greatest trapper of his time, nor the smartest businessman, but he was kind, selfless, and kept good company. He was known to break even the most stoic of men into a fit of belly-aching laughter. With a modest inheritance and a band of young men, Franklin built his fort on a gentle hill in present-day Denver where Ruby Hill Park stands today.

In the summer of 1835 while his fort was still a camp, he was joined briefly by the likes of the 1st U.S. Dragoons led by Colonel Henry Dodge. Dodge was leading an expedition from Fort Leavenworth, Kansas to the Front Range of the Rockies by way of the South Platte River—the first government sanctioned expedition to the area since Stephen Long's scientific endeavor fifteen years prior. The expedition contained several young and enthusiastic men who would go on to achieve their own fame in a variety of ways including one Jefferson Davis, future president of the Confederacy.

Dodge's dashing troop of mustachioed cavalry in deep soldierly blues and brass buttons and ornate hats floated upon perfect stallions as they approached Franklin and his men along the South Platte. Ordinarily, Franklin would have been displeased with the presence of the military on the grounds of his personal operation, but during the summer of 1835 he was actually relieved to see the army on account of an ongoing problem: since his arrival to the area a year prior, Franklin and his men had fallen victim to a series of silent burglaries in the midst of the night. On some mornings, they would awake to find guns had been stolen or the food chests had been raided, pelts had gone missing, and on one occasion, the disappearance of a horse. None of the trappers ever caught more than a glimpse of the perpetrators and even then, their silhouettes moved swiftly and weightlessly through the cover of the night and could not be caught or identified. At first, Franklin placed the blame on the Indians, but after confronting his friends of the Ute, Crow, Snake, Cheyenne, Arapaho, Apache, and Kiowa tribes—who took genuine offense to the accusations—he became convinced that it was a band of Mexicans who must have ventured too deep into American territory and took up living somewhere in the foothills of the Front Range. Franklin began to employ sentries and patrols at night but men often fell asleep drunk or exhausted and proved to be of no use. Only once did a patrol catch a thief in the act, but before he could fire a shot, the perpetrator had disappeared from sight behind a curtain of darkness. With the arrival of Colonel Dodge, however, Franklin suffered no such burglaries and on top of that, the soldiers even purchased from him and his band of trappers a season's worth of furs, hats, clothes, and meat. Business had never been better. Franklin asked the colonel if he would be kind enough to leave behind a squadron of men for the rest of the summer to protect his post and deter any adversaries from encroaching on his land, to which the colonel denied. As a rebuttal, Franklin requested that his concern of lingering Mexican forces in the area be relayed to St. Louis upon the colonel's return, and if possible, a small scouting force be sent to sniff out the area for soldiers or hungry deserters. Dodge informed Franklin that the possibility of any permanent military presence in Colorado was very little on account of most dragoons being on active duty in Florida fighting the Seminole War, but he promised to take his concerns to his superiors regardless. Before departing, Dodge led his men through numerous valleys at the foot of the Rocky Mountains as a conciliatory gesture to Franklin, but found no traces of hostile camps.

After over a year of playing cat-and-mouse with a still invisible enemy of the night, Franklin was surprised to see a column of dragoons approach his fort on October 20, 1836. The fifty soldiers on horseback were part of the 2nd U.S. Dragoons, fresh from Jefferson Barracks, Missouri, on their first patrol mission in the West. The platoon was led by Lieutenant Samuel James Lockhart, a prim and proper man of the East Coast with considerable wealth and a reputable family lineage in the United States Military dating back to the Revolution.

Marching beside the dragoons was an additional platoon of fifty men from the 7th U.S. Infantry, a unit that had seen considerable field time in the War of 1812. The 7th was led by Captain Jonathan Flete, a bold, yet compassionate and thoughtful commander whose style of leadership differed vastly from that of his cavalry analogue. These two units were sent to Franklin's Fort (named as such, *Franklin's Fort*) on the basis of national security, tasked with performing deep excursions into the river canyons and valleys of the Front Range in search of renegade Mexican units who might threaten the peaceful activity of American citizens along the western border. It did not take long for the 7th Infantry to encounter action, as on October 23, while on patrol along the base of the mountains, they became involved in a skirmish with a small force of irregulars outside the Platte Canyon. There were no initial casualties on either side, but after a series of passive volleys into the boulder-laden hills that the insurgents occupied, Flete ordered his entire force up the river to pursue what he believed was possibly a small Mexican detachment of a larger unit holed up inside the canyon. He vastly underestimated the difficulty of the terrain and the length of the canyon and soon found himself several miles in, practically trapped inside its steep walls in the middle of the night with no dead Mexicans to show for it.

There are several differing accounts as to the exact order of events that led to the fighting inside the narrow throat of the Platte Canyon that night, but what remains factual is that the 7th Infantry were ambushed in the night by an unseen force and when they emerged from the canyon back onto the plains the next morning, they had suffered a detrimental loss of fourteen dead, and twenty more wounded. When Lieutenant Lockhart of the 2nd Dragoons was made aware of this atrocity, he immediately assumed command of the entire mission. Captain Flete, usually possessing something of a backbone when it came to matters such as order of command, was wounded himself and encouraged Lockhart to do whatever he felt necessary to avenge the dead of the 7th Infantry.

three

WHEN Private Bell came to, he was at first surprised that he wasn't dead. He might as well have been; he would have never known the difference.

His ears woke first to the frail voice of a medic counting able bodies.

"Sixteen…seventeen…roll him over, is Kelly alive? Alright then, eighteen…nineteen…"

After his ears, he could feel the aching of his legs like stiff logs under his hips and he tried to move them from side to side. They barely budged. He'd never had legs so sore. He took notice of his tremendous headache. When he finally opened his eyes, he scoffed at that rude blaring sun and immediately covered his face with his forearm. The metallic light sent a stabbing pain into his eyes. That thin line of nervewire behind his eyes ached like a moaning hinge under the white light.

Through this initial assault of the senses he gathered that he was sitting in the courtyard of Franklin's Fort again. The last thing he remembered was a devilish suffocation, not from a lack of air, but from the fear that overtook him like a paralysis in that demon's nest of a canyon. As he thought longer, he remembered fragments of images, though he had trouble placing the order of them. He remembered the sound of several men getting hit and falling into the river. That sound came to him first and it made him shiver. He remembered discharging his musket. He remembered the voice of Captain Flete cutting through the sound of the gunfire. However, he didn't remember feeling any pain, and for that, he decided to brave the taunting of the sun and open his eyes to conduct an assessment of his person. Had he been shot? It didn't feel like it. He drove his fingers sternly into the meat of his arms and then down his legs. He opened his shirt and saw that his chest was filthy with black grass and debris, but his skin was pink and fleshy and without wounds. His head began to manifest an even greater pain as he attempted to focus on these matters. Finally, Bell ran his fingers up his neck and to the bridge of the U-bone at the knoll of his skull where he felt blood. A whole mess of blood had clotted and halfdried in his hair. It didn't *feel* like blood to him, it was more like mire—a gel of mucus, plasmatic and soft to the touch. Under the blood he could feel the source of his headache. It could only be described as a hole and simply a hole.

"Rock fell on ye," said a voice from behind. Bell turned slowly and saw a shirtless and bloody corporal. He boasted his own hole where a tooth used to be. "Buncha' rocks came down in the canyon. Found yous under one. Lucky yer alive, really." He spit blood from his mouth and sucked on his cigarette some. "Divine luck that any of us are alive the way it seems to me."

Bell took a moment to feel his head again and worked to remember how to talk. "A lot of guys dead?" he asked. It was all he could really muster.

"Think it's ten right now. A lot more wounded."

"Who was it? Mexicans?"

"Hell if I know—I went down rolling around in the water and blacked out. Woke up on Rudolph's back bleeding out the shoulder. Hell, I don't know if Flete even knows who it was. Sounds like they busted us up pretty bad though. Don't think we even saw'em."

Bell pondered the corporal's words for a minute and looked around the camp again. In the distance he could see Captain Flete, a bandage around his own arm, talking to a group of men. He looked to his right and saw another mass of wounded men sleeping, curled up around each other in precarious shapes like old volcanic deadrock. He saw the remnants of other men strewn out across the browning grass. Men laid face down, bloody and dying around him. A private next to Bell was wrapped in four places with bandages and he slept like a corpse, breathing up a tempest—the only indication that he wasn't one.

"Where's Murray?" Bell asked.

"Murray? Irish sergeant? Didn't make it. I mean, he's 'round here someplace if you'd like to say goodbye, but he ain't in a state to say nuthin' back. They might'a started buryin'em already. I saw'em diggin' holes out north of the fort."

Bell's breath sunk into itself and he laid down on his back, looking up at the open blue sky. It was all very blue. It was a blue day. Out past the plains there were low clouds draped between the troughs of the granite peaks, and a powdered daymoon hung mountainwise unfinished and receding between two caps. A breeze danced across his face and it felt good. It was a very old autumn breeze. His veins were very hot and the breeze cooled him. He took dirt in his hands and let it go slow out the bottom of his curled palms like an hourglass. He thought hard about his last memory before the fighting happened, the last thing he actually *saw*—Murray's big, red, smiling face in the light of that match, just a breath away from his own face. *Oh, the match,* he thought. He felt a lump in his throat.

"Corporal," Bell choked out. "Corporal, does anybody know what happened? It all seemed so sudden."

"The hell do I know. Like I said, I got hit. I only know what I overheard and the people I overhear it from don't know much either, but Flete reckons they were followin' us on top of the canyon walls damn near the whole way. Musta got up there quick 'fore we even made it onto the river. Stubborn bunch of devils."

Bell's mind moved back to the match. Who had seen him light the match? Murray. Anyone else? Who was behind him? He figured it was only a matter of time before some wounded private up next for the legsaw sold him out or blackmailed him out of his wages. Bell laid there on his back, filthy and bloodbathed under the ancient autumn breeze wishing that he had been killed.

***

Several of Franklin's trappers were put to work. They made bandages and wrapped wounds, fed ravished soldiers, and even dug graves. There were men of all shapes and skills working for Jim Franklin. There were old, grizzled, veteran trappers who remembered when the frontier was young. When they were starting off, "going West" meant Ohio or Kentucky. In more recent years, they'd already spent a decade up and down the North Platte River in Wyoming. Some of them had even worked for the likes of La Ramee and perhaps even John Colter before him. There was a former Mexican slave who escaped from Santa Fe and wandered the plains until Franklin picked him up somewhere in Kansas. He was a most talented tracker and knew the terrain well. There was also a Fox Indian who hailed from Michigan Territory and fought in the Black Hawk War. He had fallen in with a band of white traders along the Mississippi River who eventually led him along the Platte where he met Franklin at a rendezvous.

Among all of these men with their storied pasts and masterly skillsets was a young man who, despite his young age, knew the river valleys of the Front Range better than anybody, including Franklin himself. His name was Russell

Clark. The young trapper wore a clean beardless face of soft cotton skin and bright, straight teeth like Greek columns. His blonde hair was thin, and often fell in front of his face with each movement of his curious head—a nuisance he would combat with the constant push of his hand across the top of his scalp. He dressed in a buffalo hide and thick coon cuffs as he carried canteens of water through Franklin's Fort.

"Fresh water, soldier," Clark said, approaching the ragdoll man. Bell opened one pathetic eye and looked at the trapper.

"Set it down next to me, please," Bell said.

Clark bent and set the water near Bell's head. "Ye got quite the wound there, sir. Yer hairs a mess of blood. Ye seen a doctor yet?"

"No need for a doctor, friend. If I'm lucky I'll just bleed out anyhow," Bell said. Clark was still crouched and ran his hand through the soldier's hair, feeling around the hole.

"We got t' get ye patched up here or this thing is gon' keep leakin'. What happened t' ye?"

"They say I got shot by a rock. I don't remember it."

Clark pulled out a roll of bandage from his bag and began to work it around Bell's head.

"It was a mess in that canyon," Bell said.

"I heard that," Clark said. "I been talkin' t' the soldiers all mornin'. I can't imagine who it was that snuck up on yous like that. It's not like Injuns t' be so organized, I 'spose."

"You've been talking to the other soldiers?"

"Well yes. Naturally. We don't get action like this out here much, ye got t' understand. Porky and I been trying t' get t' the bottom of this thieving bidness for months now. We asked the Injuns 'n ever'body. Porky even went up and asked Ole Vaskiss and Lupton too. Lupton was gettin' stole from this winter just like Porky."

"Lupton?"

"'Nother trapper. Lupton's fort is up on the South Platte by Vaskiss. He come out here two summers ago with yer ole Colonel Dodge. Liked it so much I 'spose, he came back. Anyhow, they don't know nuthin' 'bout nuthin' either. It's the damnedest thing." He finished the tight wrap on Bell's head, tore the bandage with his teeth and remained sat by his side, taking a long drink from one of the canteens. "Ye see, we been havin' these thieves for ages in the night, but we can't get t' the bottom of who they are. We tried ever'thing. When we're ready for'em, they don't come. We set up six or ten men with guns at the gates and they won't come. When we aren't ready, they take us for quite a loot. Finally the army shows up t' give us a break and before ye know it, yous are gettin' cut down in Platte Canyon." He spit and wiped his mouth with the back side of his bloody hand. "Listen, I been in and out of Platte Canyon a dozen times. Ain't nobody livin' in there. Not even the Injuns have a reason t' be in there. Most the Injuns are either up around Grand Camp Crick or south of the range. On the other hand, none of us ever seen no Mexicans up here neither. They ain't come 'round in years, I hear. Tho, the border out here is pretty disputed. Gray. I wouldn't be surprised if some Mexicans got lost up here thinkin' this is Mexico. I'm thinkin' bout ridin' out this afternoon and see if I can't get to the bottom of all this."

Bell was finally drinking from his canteen. He lifted his head and looked at Clark. "You can't go out there alone. What makes you think that's safe?"

"I go out there alone jus' 'bout ever'day, thank you, sir. Ye see, yous boys jus' arrived here t' do a job that yous was told to do. Yous can go back home anytime you'd like, rather that job is done or not. Yer doin' us a favor the way I see it, and I do thank you, but me and Porky live here. This is my home, and I want t' know who's millin' 'round in my backyard." Clark waited for a minute to let Bell speak but he just sat nervously under the weight of his headache. "Anyhow, it sounds like one of yers lit a match in the canyon last night and got everyone kilt. A few of the boys I spoke with say it was some mick named Murray. Well, he turned up dead so if it's true, you got nobody t' blame for yer head there, sir."

"Poor Murray," Bell muttered.

"Poor Murray is right," said Clark. "Hell, if he was the one who lit the match, he was probably the first t' take a bullet. I bet he didn't even know what hit him. Shot by a bunch of nightstalkers from the top of Platte Canyon. God Damn! Sometimes I really can't believe what goes on out here. It's another world, ye know…the people back home would never believe it."

"Not in New York they wouldn't."

"Not in Kaintuck neither, no sir."

"How long have you been out here?" Bell's brain was asking questions he didn't care to know the answers to.

"Huh," Clark said. He thought about it as if he'd forgotten that people keep track of time. "Goin' on two years, I guess. Just after Old Vaskiss got out here. His fort now is up on Cannonball Creek—well, now we call it Vaskiss River—but he used to have a little fort down here closer to Porky's. We spent a lot of time with Vaskiss too back then. He's a helluva trapper. He taught me a lot when I first come out here."

"You know these trails pretty well then?"

"Sure. We done some trailblazing with Old Vaskiss and his band last summer. Good trappin' out in these foothills. Ye jus' follow one of the rivers or streams and you start makin' yer own way in any direction ye want. I can't tell ye the 'mount of trees I touched or hills I stood on that I looked out and said, 'Damn, if I ain't the first man t' ever touch this pine, God strike me now.' I mean, y'all saw Platte Canyon yesterday and that ain't even the best one."

"It's really something when the sun is up."

"Well, think about that canyon and try t' make yerself believe that there are another hundred thousand of 'em just like that in this here mountain range. I could choose a different trail ever'day and it would take me a thousand years 'fore I saw half of 'em. It kind of bothers me to tell ye the truth. Do ye know what I mean by that? Ye ever walk by a trail in the woods that ye can't go down and it bothers ye, like ye have to know what's down there or yull wake up in the night thinkin' 'bout it? I can't stand that. I'll be walkin' my own in the trails and I'll see some dirt I don't recognize—some clear path—and I'll stop and ask the listenin' pines, 'I wonder what the devil it leads to. I can't imagine what it leads to.' Sometimes it ain't nuthin. But sometimes you find somethin' worth walkin' for."

"That's why you became a trapper, I suppose."

"*Hah!*" Clark slapped his knee. "No sir, I became a trapper because I ain't good at nuthin' else. Seein' this country is just a little extra blessin' I get for doin' good."

"Sounds like you found the right line of work, friend."

"My apologies, sir. Name is Clark, please. Russell Clark."

"William Bell."

Clark's face widened with a smile like a child's. "Bill Bell! Well if that ain't the most English name I ever heard. Bill Bell! You sure are from New York ain't ye?" Clark had himself another hardy, boyish laugh. Bell watched him, amazed that one creature could have so much fun entertaining itself. "I'm sorry, Bill. I know yer likely in some pain and here I am laughin' at yer Christian name. I don't mean t' offend ye."

"I've just got a headache."

"Well just tell me to scram if you need me to. Just be careful about going t' sleep, Bill, 'cause my pa once told me t' never go t' sleep angry and never go t' sleep after ye hit yer head hard like you did. Ye probably won't wake up. Stay awake 'till the pain goes. If it don't go, ye gotta go see 'bout that doctor, Bill." Clark pulled a flask from his coat and dangled it in front of Bell's face. "Maybe a little whisky'll help, huh Bill? Go ahead, don't be shy, I'll share with ye."

"No, thanks."

"Suit yourself, Bill Bell. I oughta move like a rabbit anyhow. I got some traps t' check out on Deer Crick. Figure I'll go out and do a little roamin' 'round myself, see if I can't get t' the bottom of who's out there causing trouble for Porky and ever'body."

"I really don't suggest that you go alone," Bell spoke urgently, finding himself concerned for the trapper. Bell had misperceived Clark's whimsicalness as immaturity and cast him as a juvenile, or even more accurately, some go-lucky breed of dog. "A boy can't go out alone after what happened last night. Why don't you stay here where it's safe, Clark."

"Boy? I don't see no boy 'round here! I got twenty-seven long dirty faithful holy years, thank you much Bill Bell, and how 'bout you?" Clark spit and looked straight on at Bell, smiling and waiting for his answer.

Bell turned red and his head began to hurt even more. He felt sorry and dumb to say what he had to say next and thought for real this time that he'd rather be dead than sitting here with a hole in his head next to Russell Clark. "I'm sorry, Clark. I didn't mean to offend you," he said.

"No offense taken, Bill Bell. Now why don't you tell me, how old are ye?"

"I'm twenty-one."

"Damn, I woulda guessed older. Anyhow, get feelin' better, I'm gointa check my traps. If ye ever need a slug of whisky, jus' call my name."

Clark stood up in a fluid motion only using his legs, and walked off into the courtyard whistling away.

four

OUTSIDE the fort the 2nd Dragoons patrolled the sprawling sea of earth that washed upon the eastern foot of the mountains. Each man was grand and tall on top of his horse and his back was straight and his saber was polished and ready in its sheath. The horsemen were proud, and their pride protruded with a sort of feigned bravery that could convince even the most observant man that they were fearless. In reality, dragoons were not unafraid of death because they were brave, they were unafraid of death because they did not believe they could be killed. Let it be known that a man who lived his life with such confidence and sureness of his fate would later become a dragoon, not the opposite manner—that is, becoming a dragoon did not install an immortality complex in a typical man, rather, each dragoon was born a God.

Lieutenant Samuel James Lockhart embodied every aspect of this unwavering superiority. His chin was always high and straight on his handsome stone face as he bobbed atop his handsome horse. He wore his dark curly hair long down his neck and he had a square shaped body, strong like a fighter.

In his veins his blood combusted with that primordial temptation of power, that Biblical stuff—monkey-moving tongue, master of the bluff, master of the proposition—a long trained perceptive eye far too all-knowing to be of any goodness. He carried himself almost like an American Murat, basking in the glory of *what it means to be* a cavalryman in the purest essence; Quixotic, romantic, cold, and correct. Under him, he harnessed the wild majesty of the vessel that lived between his knees—that beast of burden who had been evolutionarily slated to obey him and to be brave for him and to kill for him even when facing death. Lockhart and his horse pursued omnipotence together—to quite literally become one, both of them operating under the same mind and instinct. Their object was divinity, their method was mercilessness.

His reputation preceded him among his men as he was a successful Indian hunter in the wars of the east. He served in the 1st Dragoons during the Black Hawk War and saw considerable combat for an officer. His ability to improvise strategically under fire earned him praises from none other than General Winfield Scott during the conflict's final offenses. Additionally, President Jackson singled out Lockhart due to his shared ruthless disposition on matters such as Indians and westward expansion. After the Black Hawk campaign, Lockhart was one of those who accompanied Colonel Henry Dodge on his expedition to the Rocky Mountains in 1835. Upon his return to St. Louis, he was transferred to the newly formed 2nd Dragoons to help raise and train a grass-roots unit of soldiers at Jefferson Barracks who would follow him west. Presently, he trotted through the open fields that stretched from the mounds of Franklin's Fort to the far foothills of the Front Range.

Lockhart was going from man to man, commanding vigorously with each limb in every direction. He stood on his stirrups and cursed and laughed and shouted under the blue sky, blue sun with blue light, the silky autumn breeze bending dead strings of wheat and browned maize into windshapes along the near plains all around him.

He entered the fort, poking his head back and forth in search of something. In the fort there were clusters of men like small mountains laying around sleeping or dying. He paid no notice to this scene. The long, white tail that birthed from his hat dripped down his back and swung slowly like a pendulum as he moved. In the courtyard of the fort he spotted Jim Franklin, fat and pensive, overlooking the bivouac that had consumed his home.

"Mister Franklin!" Lockhart called. He snapped the reins of his horse and the beast moved to the side of the fat man.

"Oh, Lieutenant," Jim Franklin said, "you must believe me that I did not know it would be like this. This is awful, awful trouble, sir. If I knew it would be like this—"

"No time for apologies, Mister Franklin, we must heed progress, not remorse."

"It's just that we've never had anybody killed out here, sir. I didn't mean for your men to come and get killed dealing with our trouble."

"*My men* are just fine, Mister Franklin, it is Flete's men who went and got killed. But there will be no more of that, my good man, I assure you." Lockhart stiffened his lower lip and turned his head straight and away from Jim Franklin.

"I...I have spoken with Captain Flete, sir," started Franklin. "He thinks it is a poor idea to pursue this band of...whoever they are—deeper into these canyons without more men. He suggested sending a distress message to Fort Leavenworth where there may be some spare soldiers and I would happily—"

Lockhart snapped loudly, "With all due respect, Mister Franklin, I will speak to Captain Flete myself about what we should and should not do about this canyon business. You are a trapper, I am a commander, let us address each other as such."

"Of course, sir, I didn't mean to offend you. I only desire to help."

"I'd be happy to use your help in another way, Mister Franklin." Lockhart dropped his gaze down at the trapper while still keeping his chin stiff. "Put blatantly, I need to ask you for volunteers. It is my opinion that it would be advantageous for me to open an investigation into this mountain range myself. It is *clues* that we need, not more men. I would aim to search for tracks, tools, anything that may indicate signs of life in these trails. Anything that could give us an idea as to what exactly is going on here. Your men's knowledge of this terrain is invaluable to the United States military at this moment and I implore you to elect a few selfless souls to guide myself and the dragoons into this wilderness. Their duty and bravery will surely be looked at as honorable service in the eyes of Washington, and they will certainly be compensated for their cooperation. Do you have any men in mind who would take on such a task?"

Jim Franklin's red face became redder which made the size of his round cheeks look rounder. His eyes batted almost in a pretty way, like a woman's. "Oh sure, Lieutenant! My men would be honored to help in any way! They are brave, alright. I have some of the bravest and most willing men in the West. Perhaps you'd have to exclude a few of them—namely the negro and Indian fellows…their willingness to sacrifice their, erm…*safety* for the army may be somewhat muted. I hope you understand, sir."

"With no qualms, sir."

"Otherwise, eight or nine other men would be happy to assist your endeavor. This is our home, Lieutenant. We'd like to exterminate whatever pests may be lurking in the cracks, so to speak. My men, they earn their keep in these mountains and they must be uninhibited in assuming their assets are safe here in my fort. I built this fort, Lieutenant. It is a fine fort. You know it."

"I do, sir."

"I will not stand for my trappers to be driven away from such a fine fort. Nor will I stand for them to be apprehensive or untrusting of the security of my fort. I refuse to have my name tarnished at the hands of these measly weasels who spend their days in cowardice and their nights in my pockets. It is only a matter of time before my men begin to distrust Porky all together. I cannot have these men playing tell-all to Vasquez and giving him the impression that Porky's fort has been overrun with thieving swine. I touch wood that the word is not already on its way up to the North Platte. Sir, I'm sure you are aware that *this* is my livelihood; providing a place for men to trap and to trade and to sleep is how I earn *my keep*."

"I am astoundingly aware, Mister Franklin, and I refuse to let you or your men down. Though, I cannot proceed without your help. From here, I will speak with Captain Flete and get a count on his able men. You are doing very good work, Mister Franklin! Very good work, indeed!"

Franklin was tickled pink by this opportunity to help the charismatic lieutenant. He had not considered the irony that his men were now being enlisted to help the man that he enlisted to help him. He had not exactly been *duped* by Lockhart, but the lieutenant surely took advantage of Jim Franklin's impressionable personality. Nonetheless, Franklin would spend his afternoon excitedly approaching each of his men like an evangelist sharing good news. To say the trappers were enthusiastic about the proposition would be an outright lie, but to say they were uncooperative would be in itself untrue. The men took the prompt as an unavoidable duty——the army had no knowledge of the canyons or waterways that bled from the Rocky Mountains. The previous night when they attempted to probe one on their own, catastrophe occurred. The mountain men had already spent months—some of them years—digging around this land and making a home of it. It was only natural that they led the excursions.

Lockhart stepped down from his stallion, passed a hand through its mane and tied it to the stablepost. He walked across the courtyard commandingly, stepping over the bodies and medical instruments left across the plain in an attempt to reach Flete who now sat alone in a tent. Flete's face was desperate. He was in pain, although he would not admit it. When Lockhart approached him, he did not move his head. Only his eyes lifted towards the dragoon and back down towards the ground.

"Twenty-four," Flete said.

Lockhart's thin, European eyebrows soured on his forehead. "I regret to hear of your losses, Captain."

"No. It is twenty-four able. My losses are greater. Twenty-six. Wounded and dead. And I myself would be a liability on the field. I don't even have enough NCOs to lead three squads."

"My condolences, Captain. Truly. While I respect your period of reflection, I ask for your attention regarding my own morning musings. I have considered your losses already and have devised what I believe to be a temporary remedy to our predicament."

"A remedy to our predicament would be to wait here and send for help, Lieutenant. We have no business doing much else."

"I disagree, Captain. We were sent here for a reason, and with your inability to command on account of your wounds, I will see that we perform our duty. Or at the least, leave here with more information than we came with. I request that you hear what I have come to sell you."

"Go on."

"I propose that we embark on a series of excursions into the Front Range with hybrid units guided by the local men. Your infantry will pair with squads of my dragoons,

commanded by my sergeants. I understand you don't prefer to hear that."

"And neither will the infantry."

"Five or six of yours to every fifteen or so cavalry."

"That is nonsense, Lockhart!" Flete held his aching
arm as he got excited. "I don't have near enough men to
be of use. Besides, they've never marched formation in a
cavalry unit before."

"They won't have to, don't be frivolous. These squadrons are going to have to act as reconnaissance units.
They'll march at ease, each of them following one of
Franklin's scouts. I've already spoken to Franklin and he is
going to deliver to me a group of men to guide these squadrons. The idea is to not engage immediately. We're not
looking for another fight. We're looking to find *anything*.
Perhaps by the time we do, you'll have recovered some of
your wounded and we can play sport with whoever it is we
are dealing with in these mountains."

"I wholly oppose such a plan, Lockhart. We should
rest here and send for more men. If we tell Leavenworth
or St. Louis that we were ambushed, they would happily
send us a hundred, two-hundred more men. If we told
them it was Mexicans they might even send us a brigade.
We could undergo a proper campaign of the mountains."

"Unnecessary, my friend. There is no Mexican army
hiding in these mountains. I suspect a band of deserters—
maybe even Americans—perhaps thirty or forty of them
making due in a cave somewhere. It is a job we can handle
ourselves as long as we don't go on marching into Hanni-
balistic traps in the darkness again."

Flete turned his scruffy, weathered face towards the
shadowed side of the tent. He had contemplated his mistake enough; for an officer of inferior stature to taunt him
with it was a redundant embarrassment.

"My dragoons will continue to patrol the plains for a
few days while you and your men recover," Lockhart said.

"You can hardly move yourself, Flete. You're sick with fever and who knows what is in store for your bad arm. Until you are feeling yourself again, allow me to do the thinking, for I have seen this sort of thing before."

"What *sort of thing?*"

"These armed nomads, these wayfarers of war. I musn't remind you, Captain, I have a decorated history with handling irregulars such as this. I have chased break-off units of Indians for scores of miles in rain and snow and returned victorious with their scalps. I have hunted defunct sailors through marsh marathons and watched each of them rot to their ends in a prison cell. I've hung deserters and shot traitors. This is nothing but a bunch of poor trappers and halfbreeds lost and desperate. They tricked you, Captain, but I will not suffer the same fate."

Flete bore holes in the dirt with his black, stale eyes. His bad arm shook with fever and his face, flush and sweating, fell tired with the work of conversation. He breathed hard and with very much pain. "So it must be, Lieutenant. I will tell my men that they are to follow your command."

Lockhart cracked a lipless smile. "In no more than a week shall we dispatch into these hills. I would love to see you on the field, Captain. Rest up, ole'boy."

He turned with one foot back towards the courtyard. He walked with brash steps through the canyons of casualties, his long hair, his hat's tail, and his saber swaying in unison. Private Bell sat alone, wrapped in gauze, watching the officer walk. The sun reflected off Lockhart's black boots and into Bell's eyes, provoking his headache. He threw an arm across his face and groaned.

"Keep your head up, soldier," Lockhart said to him. "There is work to be done!"

five

ABOVE the crystal clear water like diamond clear water with its blues and browns and sandy drift at its bed, there were red rocks like rocks after a rapture's red rain. The rocks jutted out from the earth and they looked like the faces of Indians and they had Indian names and voices and wide stone chins like Indians. It was Deer Creek, and it was thin and shallow and it ran for miles across Deer Mountain until it split, and its monozygotic twins raced to their deaths which they achieved together in glory somewhere deep behind Legault Mountain in a land that Russell Clark had never been before. Unlike the other tributaries of the South Platte, Deer Creek was seldom trafficked. Grand Camp Creek to the north held a great band of Indians—Indians of several tribes who gathered together and lived together and protected each other. At the mouth of Grand Camp Creek where the water spits out into the plains, the Arapaho and Comanche and Apache and Cheyenne and Kiowa and Ute and Crow and Snake all lived together and traded together in the same powwow and looked out ten miles east and saw the fires of the white-man burning at Franklin's Fort. North of that still, there was Vasquez River and Mt. Vernon Creek that the Kiowa and Arapaho had known and hunted for hundreds of years. Louis Vasquez had begun to trap them just a year ago. But further south at Deer Creek, just above the South Platte, there were no Indians, and there was no sign of them. Clark had chosen this creek as his trapping grounds when he first arrived at the range and he hardly permitted anyone to accompany him.

The first great summit along Deer Creek is Pyramid Peak, a modest sized hill with a great overlook of the eastern basin. The previous winter, Clark had gotten stuck under a snow bank on Pyramid Peak. He had finished a day of setting traps and diverted from his faithful guide—the rushing water—up to the peak where he set his eyes out over the land. The view of the Front Range from the top of the peak was enough to warm his freezing insides on a day as cold as that. He marched up the peak across a bed of leather snow and there were dead branches that froze and snapped at random from the pines that hung over him. The other leafless trees were anatomical and astral at once, moving lazily in the wind and imitating a million bloodways or boneways or brainways or starways across the backdrop of a frozen blue sky. That sky was deep and oceaness at its core, at the apex of the earth, but it froze with the curvature of the planet and at its horizon it was the color of transparent polar ice like white dressed up as blue. The tops of distant mountains shone like needles that froze the sky and some few clouds swirled like white blood around their tops.

When Russell Clark reached the top of the mountain it greeted him with a swift blow of wind that ensured that his face had indeed frozen. Next to him was an old pine that grew wrong and deformed and had twin trunks that twisted like rivers and in the center of each trunk was a seat, horizontal and naked for which Russell could sit. He decided, unknowingly, to climb the trunks and to sit on the limbs of the old pine. The climb was a novice effort and before he'd even realized he was in the tree, he was smoking his pipe some twenty feet above the ground. He wondered what he had done to deserve such beauty—Kentucky's brown mountains were no comparison to even the youngest peaks of these Rockies.

Suddenly there was the cracking of wood and just as quickly as he had climbed the tree, he had fallen from it. He and the old, dead branches landed together at the shoulder of the hill and rolled towards the bottom. He tried to grasp with thick gloves at the earth but came up with handfuls of snowdust that disappeared into the air above him. He tumbled like a circus accident into a mound of snow and he watched with horrified eyes as another mound chased him down the hill and swallowed the bank. All went dark and for nearly an entire minute, Clark sat still and quiet and thought about how long it would take for him to die.

It took him fifteen minutes to dig enough room for each of his arms to move at his side. He cleared out enough space to breathe, patting at the snow with his paws. Once his lungs and his arms were free, he reached into his coat pocket and produced his flask which he proceeded to finish there on his back in the darkness of a collapsed mountainside. Drunk and unafraid of death, he cut through the snowbank. He punched the wall of the bank from the inside and stuck out his head to the dark canyon. As he breathed in, he was filled with all of the greatness of the earth and the splendor of conquest that sits brewing in a man for a lifetime waiting to be ejaculated in mortal ecstasy. He called a primal call to the elements. Birds scattered across the starry sky. His face was all shades of red as it poked out from its snowshell. When he emerged, he rode twelve frozen miles half-dead back to Franklin's Fort where he slept by a fire for two days. Franklin was adamant that his hands had been bitten by the frost and were in urgent need of amputation, but his concerns proved to be rash.

Today Clark rode his horse along Deer Creek looking up at Pyramid Peak and could see at the top, the broken corpse of the tree that sent him on his battle with death on that winter day. He smiled at it and a dozen magpies exploded from its grasp and into the October sky.

Along the creek, he had a chain of traps spread apart by about a quarter mile each. He tied his horse to a long ponderosa, the same long pine to which he always tied his horse, and set off against the run of the creek on foot. He came to the first trap, a shallow water trap that laid just under the surface across from the osteolytic dam. Clark held high expectations for such an advantageously placed trap, but his optimism was dulled at the sight of a squirrel inside its jaws. The squirrel was fat from the water and laid upside down and its buck teeth shone from its open mouth and it looked funny like a child's drawing of a squirrel. Something about its death seemed sentient to Clark; they never die like an animal, he thought, they always look like they were in the midst of doing something very human before the jaws come down. Clark pulled the squirrel from the trap and wrapped it and set it gently in his bag. Later, he would place the corpse elsewhere, away from the dam so the emanation of death did not tip his trap. He pulled his lure from the mud and coated it with a castoreum he had received from Louis Vasquez—said to be the most potent castor along the Platte. Once his lure was coated, Clark stuck it deep in the mud overhanging his trap. He cleaned and set his trap again and checked his stake, giving it a firm knock into the ground with his mallet and moved on to the next one up the creek.

Westward down the creek, Clark was puzzled to find the second trap as empty as he had left it. *That can't be,* he thought. There was an abundance of beaver along this creek and he knew that nobody else was trapping it. He bent down to examine his lure which was strong and well-oiled even after several days. Still, he coated it again with Vasquez' castor and drove it back deep into the mud. He tucked the open trap back into the creek and carried on again to his third trap. He looked around the rich ravine and took a moment to bask in its silence. Only the gentle roll of the water made any noise at all. Then he heard a woodpecker at work on some spruce to the west. It hammered the trunk in long dedicated phrases and stopped for a few moments to examine its work. In the tree beside the woodpecker he heard the squawk of a jay and then saw it stomping upon a wood branch, throwing a fit, arguing with the magpie below it. A fantastic cotton cloud rolled over the canyon and stole the sun from the earth and the birds and bugs cried apocalypse. He wondered about birds. He wondered how a bird could migrate on the same day each year, taking the same route to the same tree and yet, scream as if the end of the earth was upon it every time the clouds swallowed the sun. Clark laughed aloud at the randomness of God, or so he called it. Perhaps he didn't have the eyes of a hawk or the ears of a dog, but at least he knew that the sun would always return.

Approaching his third trap, Clark heard a rustle in the foliage ahead of him. He halted and looked sunward. There was a faint patter of footsteps, slow and very heavy. Clark awaited a bear or a moose to crash through the tall grass and he drew his gun from behind him. He cocked the hammer and looked down its bore into the trees ahead. The sun began to return slowly over the gorge and the trees cast massive, mangled shadows upon the creekbed. Emerging from the thick of the shadows was a tall, strong, white man with long, brown hair and a hat of beaver. He walked jollily and purposefully. Clark felt the cold iron of the trigger on his steady finger. He followed the man with the barrel of the gun. The man walked along the creek, peering down into its clear waters as he stepped. He was walking right towards the trap. Clark's throat was indecisive, twitching to shout several times before his mouth refused the words. He thought about firing his single shot and killing the man and burying him there under the trees in Deer Creek Canyon where he would never be found. The man stopped at Clark's trap, bent forward, and played with its mechanism. From its jaws, he pulled a good, fat beaver.

"Hey there!" Clark shouted. In an instant, the man stopped, startled at the sight of Clark. He reached for his own gun but Clark fired first. The report from the shot rang like a church bell through the depths of the canyon and Clark assumed that every soul in Louisville must have heard its crack. The shot sailed over the man's left shoulder. "Damn!"

The stranger answered with his own shot. Clark heard the wisp of the bullet hit the tree he stood at, sending splinters of wood to his face. Clark reached to his belt for a cartridge but there was no time to reload—the man had started towards him. He could see by the maddened look on his enemy's face—dogeye rabid and scared too in his small soul—that there would be no negotiations; he was going to attempt to kill him. Clark pulled his knife from his pants and braced himself to fight. The man drew a saber. Out-armed, Clark turned and fled towards his horse, nearly a mile down the creek.

Clark ran along the water where he knew the terrain well. He anticipated each bush and each foxhole on the bank. He hurdled branches and wild tree roots that came out of the ground and looped like lassos at his feet. He turned only once to gauge the speed of his pursuer. Clark was faster than the stranger, but there was a desperate animal alive in the eyes of the man. Approaching the second of Clark's traps, the idea came to him in a flash to lure his pursuer into its mouth. He crossed the creek with a leap and set his sight on the trap. He could see the stake protruding from the ground now just thirty yards ahead of him. He could feel the man gaining on him as his pace changed. Clark stepped over the trap into the water and back onto the bank and waited to hear a shriek. He had missed it. He needed him to follow even closer. He began to slow his pace more so that the stranger was nearly right behind him. Clark would need the man to be an arm's length away to follow him directly into the trap, then he could have his way with the stranger.

Inside of his chest Clark could feel a burning. His lungs began to betray him and he searched for a buried courage to continue. He remembered being consumed inside the womb of the mountain the previous winter and how he was sure that he would die. He remembered the glory he felt when he birthed himself into the cold air of the range and how God overtook him and how after he succeeded in freeing himself from death he felt that he would never die.

Ahead of him, he saw his last trap—his last chance to free himself again. He slowed his pace even further, coming to a jog. He heard the jangle of bone jewelry and loose bullets and tools that hung from the man's belt. He was just a step behind him. The two of them stomped in unison, shaking the river—shaking the earth beneath them and sending birds about their path. As Clark could feel the breath of his enemy upon the back of his naked neck, he stepped over his own trap and closed his eyes in what he realized was a prayer. A heartbeat later, he heard the spring of the trap set and then a deep, muted *thud* and then the sound of his man crashing into the water. Clark turned and saw the man emerge from Deer Creek and try to pull away from the trap. The tall stake wouldn't budge. He was stuck. He bent over himself to free his foot with his hands but before he could reach it, Clark picked up the fallen saber and stood on the man's shoulders.

"I should kill ye now," Clark said sharply. His own animal came alive inside him. He taunted the fallen man with the saber, waving it slowly at his nose. "But I won't, 'cause I got a feelin' ye been playin' wit' my traps. I also got a feelin' that ye know somethin' 'bout them federal boys who got licked in Platte Canyon. Don't be shy now."

The man stared blankly up at Clark. They both breathed heavily, still in unison, but Clark had forgotten that he was breathless. "Ye don't speak no damn English do ye? Aw, hell. *Habla* Spanish? French?"

"I speak English," the man muttered. His accent was bent, old.

"Well I'll be damned, we got a Britisher out here in the West. I almost feel too bad for ye to kill ye, friend," Clark said laughing. "Where did ye come down from? Kanada? Ye lost out here?" The man laid on his back silently, blinking at Clark. Clark's face soured again and he reminded the man that he held the sword. "I ain't kiddin' though, friend. What are ye doin' this deep in Deer Crick?"

"Trapping."

"Don't look like it t' me. Looks like t' me yer pickin' up the beavers that I'm trappin'."

"I have traps along the water here, honest, sir. I can show thee where they are."

"Not interested, Your Majesty. Where do ye camp at? Ye got friends here?"

"No, I am here alone."

Clark smiled, "Aw hell, I know these mountains, friend. I know that one man—a damn dumb Britisher at that—don't wander on up here 'lone and start trappin' on Deer Crick. Where are yer friends hidin' out?"

"I am alone. On my honor, sir."

"Tell me one more time yer alone and I'll slit yer throat, friend." Clark raised his voice. His eyebrows darkened down his boyish face. With the sun behind him, he looked more menacing than he really was.

"I have got some companions up the stream that way," the man said. "We are only trappers. We are merely looking to make a living. We will stop trapping this stream if thou allow me to go free, sir."

"I don't really plan on lettin' ye go t' tell ye the truth. But now that I know ye been lickin' my traps, I want ye to tell me what yer doin' down by Franklin's Fort stealin' all our pelts and food and horses?"

"I know not about Franklin's Fort, sir. Really, I am a trapper and—"

"And what are ye doin' rainin' hell down on those Washington boys?" Clark was shouting now and he brought the blade of the sword down to the man's chin. He poked at his flesh and a river of blood ran from his lower lip to the bottom of his chin. The man squirmed at the pain of the blade on his face. He looked up hopelessly at Clark, a boy with a boyish face and a boyish voice who was strong and stood on his shoulders.

"We…" he began regrettingly, "we thought yee were Spanish. We didn't know yee were English, we would have never stolen anything if we knew yee were English, sir. We have been in these mountains for some months now. We thought the Spanish were moving in."

"Spanish?" Clark said. He cast a skittish look at the man. "The Spanish been gone from these mountains for fifteen years. What ye have'ta look out for are these Mexicans. Ye thought we were Mexicans?"

"Yes, sir…Mexicans."

Clark pulled the sword away from the man and stared at him long and hard with skeptical, squinted eyes. The man was panting for air. A pale fear took over his body. The blood on his chin was smeared along his neck and pooled in the bowl of his throat. Clark saw the confusion on his broken face. His face looked like an Indian. His skin was white but his nose and his eyes were Indian. His hair was a dark Indian brown with sides that ran down his ears and covered an Indian jaw. His eyes were a deep, wet, human hazel like some of the Indians that Clark had known.

"Somethin' ain't right here, friend." Clark stepped off of the man and stood at his side. The man did not move. "Let me ask ye somethin' of a riddle. It's the easiest riddle I can think of: If I ain't Spanish, and I ain't Mexican, and I sure *as hell* ain't no English, what am I?"

The man's mouth opened to say something but nothing came. He shook his head slowly and his eyes swelled a bit. He breathed a cold speaking breath but his tongue fell silent.

Clark was fascinated by his silence. "I ain't goin' t' kill ye, friend," he said. "Let's put all that beaver trappin' business behind us, all right? Now I'm goin' t' ask ye a couple more questions. If ye answer me truthfully, I won't kill ye. If I think yer lyin' t' me, I'm goin' t' put this sword through both yer hands and leave ye stuck on the bank of this crick till the vultures start to rippin' out yer tongue. Maybe if ye scream loud enough, yer friends will hear ye and if they hurry, they'll come get ye b'fore ye bleed to death. Understand me, friend?"

The man nodded his head yes.

"What is yer name?" Clark asked.

"Mohan."

"Got yerself and Indian name, Mohan. Have ye ever heard of a place called Kaintucky?"

"No, sir."

"Can ye tell me where Boston is?"

"No, sir."

"What river did ye take to get here?"

"I would not know, sir, I have been lost in these mountains for some time. I...I could not say with certainty..."

"Well ye had to take some river, din'tcha? Can ye give me the name of one river that runs through these mountains?"

"Cold Wind River, sir."

"I've never heard tell of that one, Mohan. Where is it?"

"That is the river thy fort lies on."

"I see. Well, we don't call it that. We got another name for it. That must be the English name for it."

"That's right, sir."

Clark looked at Mohan. He shook his head with a slow, pensive stare. "Somethin' just ain't right here," he said again under his breath.

"Sir," Mohan finally muttered, "what be thy name?"

Clark smiled a slow, reluctant smile, showing his big teeth. "My name is Russell Clark. I'm a trapper. I was born in Kaintucky in the year 1809. I'd be happy to tell ye anything else ye'd like to know. But tell me, who in God's name are you?"

six

CLARK sat on his horse while Mohan walked. The latter was leading Clark westward along Deer Creek. They did not speak. As the creek thinned, Mohan turned south into a quilt of pines and they climbed endless shelves of ridges until they reached the middle of a mountain where a well-worn trail wrapped around its winding body. Clark had never been this deep in the range before. Looking out over the side of the mountain he saw what looked like one-hundred-million blue butterflies sleeping on grass and moving their silk wings, breathing as one and drifting a slow sway to the east. Then with a gust of wind they overtook the grass and the whole of the blue came to life before Clark's eyes like a tidal wave and he could see their lifecords underneath them, feeding the dripping blue wings and at once he knew they were columbines. "What flowers," he said.

For hours they climbed. They closed in on a hollow corridor of trees. Dozens of pine limbs joined at a soft arc to form a ceiling over a trail stained orange by dead needles and pineseed. There were tree stumps all along the ridge, chopped by hand. He saw a system of trails that stemmed from the one he walked. Little trinkets and markings and tents were scattered about the forest floor.

"It's just through here," Mohan said.

It was nearly nightfall by the time Clark and Mohan had finally overcome the final ridge and looked upon the wide green valley before them. Clark was astounded at what he saw. All along the valley there were houses and wigwams and teepees. There were fires all throughout the land. Most surprisingly, there were people—hundreds of them. People bustled inside the valley like a hive, mindless and infinite to their tasks. There were families and wood and food and horses and dogs and guns and graves and young and old and boys and girls. Women carried children on their backs, boys played ball in the open fields, and men hauled lumber and sacks of meat and beans and maize all across the land as far as one could see. There was a smith doing work alongside a busy butcher. Down the path from the butcher was a sort of mill and stacks of timber sat along its side. In the center he saw what appeared to be a schoolhouse, old and English with that triangular mood and high tower above. All of these buildings were contained inside the weathered walls of a fort which mirrored a colonial standing. It had massive pine beams standing upright from the ground flush with each other. Four sentry towers—one to each corner—rose tall above the ground and men kept guard with guns and bows in each tower. On the western wall of the fort some dozen men wrought repairs on a section of beams that looked dilapidated and black with rot. They raised new, flesh-colored wood to fill in the old wall. They sweat, even in the cold of the early evening and Clark could see that they cared about their work. Near them a small stream ran down from the mountain and through the valley and into the fort, dividing it almost perfectly in half. A careless orange sky backlit the hundreds of black mountains that silhouetted the western horizon.

Clark and Mohan descended the mountain together as the moon opened up above them. It was a full moon and Clark could feel it shine like iron on his eyes. Its whiteness was slowly brining, soaked by the fog, and the melt of the moon morphed to wet brass by the time they stood at the foot of the fort. A crowd of creeping eyes watched him walk the path to the center of the village. There were white men and there were Indians and there were men who seemed to be both or neither. He saw what looked like Indian women in silk gowns and silver jewelry as well as white men in furs and hides. He heard whispers in English and Spanish and Indian tongues all about him. Some men clutched their guns and others smiled and winced in curiosity at the young, handsome stranger. Mohan led Clark to a door. It was a good door of a humble cabin made of unfinished cedar and stone. A torch hung and burned at the door. Behind them, a mass had gathered and watched in shadows and whispers under the fog-soaked moon. Neither Clark nor Mohan moved to knock before a dark man of great stature opened the door. He was middle-aged and strong. He looked at Clark with a long, folded face. He towered over the boy by nearly a foot.

"Greetings, boy. I am George," he said. "Would thou like to enter?" And then he sent Mohan away with the wave of his big hand.

Clark sat down and set his hands on top of the table. Around the room there was furniture and art both European and Indian. George sat in the chair across from Clark and the entire cabin moved as he sat. He pulled a knife from his belt and set it on the table, holding its handle with one hand.

"Thou must be lost, traveler," George said.

"No, sir," Clark said. He was frightened and very still.

"Thou come to mine own home with purpose?"

"Well, no sir. I was in the crick valley, sir. I found yer friend there, Mohan, by my traps."

"Mohan is a fine trapper." He spoke each word finely and clearly. His mouth hardly opened when he spoke and the words came slowly straight from his throat.

"I'm sure he is, sir. But when I come across'im, he was lookin' as if he been takin' my furs."

"Was he then?"

"A lot of my furs have come up lost recently, ye see, sir. Me and Mohan wrestled for a while and well, we got t' talkin' too."

The red flame of a candle on the table shone at George and cast his feathering shadow on the wall behind him. It was even bigger than he and darker than he and it moved with him as he spoke.

"I am grateful for thou did not kill him."

"Well, I wouldn't do that, sir. I'm not the killin' type. And t' tell ye the truth, sir, I been lookin' for the mens that's been stealin' my furs for some time now. I live down at the fort on the South Platte—Franklin's Fort—though ye probably don't know who Franklin is…well we been havin' thieves lately Mister George, sir. When I found yer friend Mohan, I thought maybe he's the man I'm lookin' for, sir, but after we got talkin' it seems t' me that Mohan don't hardly know nuthin' 'bout nuthin', sir. I asked him all sorts of questions and well, sir, a lot of things he said dint make much sense to me so I made him bring me here."

"What is thy name?" George asked.

"I'm Russell Clark, sir."

"Russell Clark, thou come armed?"

"I have me a musket outside on the horse. With me now, just an old knife. I don't mean no harm, sir. I'm just a trapper," he said with a tremor. "I…I come from Kaintucky but…but I live out here on the plains now."

"Thou art not a soldier then?"

"No, no, no sir, I'm not a soldier. I'm just a trapper and I don't mean no harm. I live in a fort down on the South Platte River. All we's do is trap beaver and do a little huntin' and fishin' too. We been havin' thieves for some time though, sir. Thieves in the night, takin' our horses and food and furs and such. So we asked the army t' come and give us a hand and a buncha' them went and got kilt down in Platte Canyon—"

"I do not know anything about that, Clark," George snapped.

"I...I don't mean to *accuse* ye of nuthin' Mister George, sir. I wasn't implyin' nuthin'."

"Is it a matter of importance to thee, boy?"

"What's that, sir?"

"Is it important to thee to know who killed your companions in the canyon?" George pronounced each syllable with care. He had no accent. His words were square and his slow voice droned above the candle flame. He moved the knife so the blade stood straight up and the flame cast a black monolith onto his long face. "Thou sayeth thou art a trapper, nothing more. Well I am the very same. Mine own home here was built by good trappers."

"Very well, sir. We are alike, then, somewhat, sir. But about the canyon—"

"I have heard of the killings last night, Clark. Though, I have no inherent interest in what thou may know about any business in any creek or canyon. Does it matter much to thee what I know about a skirmish in the night?"

"Well it does a little, sir, 'cause I have a feelin' that...that whoever kilt the army last night is the same people who keep stealin' my furs. And Mister George, sir, I'm a hardworkin' man, I can't allow people stealin' my furs in the night, so I'm just wonderin' who might be takin' away my work, ye understand? And today I found Mohan playin' with my traps, so I don't mean to accuse nobody but—"

"That's enough, Clark." His voice echoed in the space and then dissolved like mist in the air. In silence they looked upon one another. George's black eyebrows pulled the weight of his forehead down so that his eyes were impossible to see. His hair was black and full like an Indian's and he pushed it back behind his ears. "I regret to inform thee, Russell Clark, that I shan't permit thy departure from this valley." Clark began to stand but George brought his fist down like a gavel on the table and shook the cabin. "I know the habits of you Englishmen. Yee art relentless in thy thirst for conquest. It is only a matter of time before yee start to probe and rape each and every river, valley, and canyon in these mountains and I do not have time to wait for the army to arrive at mine own door before I do something about it."

Clark looked long and hard at the man across from him. George was calm and huffed through his big nose into the air like an exhausted dog. He was quite satisfied with his own words.

"Are ye plannin' to kill me then, sir?"

"That is to be decided later. But the risk to mine own people is too great to allow thy return to thy home. My greatest, sorrows to you, Clark."

Clark thought hard, looking at the giant man painted in darkness against the shade of the cabin. The dark wood about him enclosed him, shadowed him in even greater gloom as the candle strained for life between them. They tore into one another with sharp eyes as one does in a game of wits. Clark feared to speak, but he knew he must.

"Sir," Clark started slowly, "I'm sorry fer comin' here and makin' ye feel like this. I can see ye care much about yer land. I can see yous have built somethin' nice here. It's a charmin' valley sir, really. Ye have the right to feel ye want to protect it. I really don't mean ye no harm, and I wish ye'd see that and that ye'd let me leave. I won't care to ever come here again if that's what yous want. But still, somethin' is odd here, sir. And nobody 'round here seems to understand me when I say this: *I am not English.* I am an American. I'm from Kaintucky. The United States is my nation, sir. I's been thinkin' that *yous* are the English. Or Injun. Or whatever yous is. Hell, I'm not understandin' so good, so won't ye stop with bein' so secretive and please tell me sir, what is this place?"

"What such nation?" George laughed. "I know thy origin, boy, do not riddle me."

"No sir, I feel that *yous are riddlin' me.* Nobody wants to tell me who they are, and everybody keeps callin' me English. If ye ain't goin' to make this easy sir, I'll try and learn ye. This valley that yous live in is property of a nation, sir. This is the United States of America. All of it 'round us. From here t' the Atlantic Ocean there are no English, sir. Been decades since we rid of 'em. There was a war. We raised an army of farmers and trappers and smiths and merchants and even boys and women. Our people were made into soldiers, sir, and our land was made into battle-fronts. My father fought in that war and when it finished, he was given some land in Kaintucky for his service. I was born on that land and I learnt t' trap on that land. I come out here two years ago t' make my own livin' and find my own land just like hundreds of other men. And as we speak, there are thousands more on their way."

"Nonsense! These are lies. Thou art a lying jester."

"It is all true, sir. I have no reason to lie."

Clark saw that George was shaken. And at once, he understood where he was. He did not know how, or why, or when, but as he watched the horror wash over the giant's face, he knew just what he had done. He felt the confidence to speak again.

"Ye see, sir, ye can steal all the beaver and kill all the soldiers ye want, but this is somebody's land. There is a lieutenant back on the plains, a mean ole' cuss, who is preparin' t' send soldiers into every crack and crevice of these mountains lookin' for the men who hurt the army last night."

"Silence, Clark!"

"And if ye kill them, they'll just send for more. There's thousands of 'em. Really."

"I will have thee killed, Clark!"

"I would not do that, Mister George, sir. If ye kill me, they will find ye."

The two men stared at each other for a long time. Clark was leaning across the table now, his hands trembling, his face flushed. The man across from him was speechless.

"I can help ye, sir," said Clark. "Do not kill me. Please, just listen."

"Of what help do you speak?"

"Yous have been here for a long while. I can see in yer village that it is old. I know that ye are proud of it, sir. Ye can kill me if you want to. I 'spose I have no choice in that and I'll face my death honorably, sir. But on the contrary, I think that I am yer only hope of survival."

George's fingers were restless at the table. He stood again which frightened Clark. His head nearly touched the cedar beam that floated across the ceiling. His shadow exploded through the entire cabin. He looked back at Clark with black eyes. "Well, speak if thou want to speak!"

"Mister George, sir, the army is here to find ye. There is a man named Lockhart who ain't gon' stop till he does. I happen to know that I'm goin' t' be asked to help guide the army through the trails of these mountains. I heard'em talkin' 'bout it back at the fort. Now sir, I blazed most'a these trails myself, and I am the only one who knows how t' get here to yer village—or rather, I know *how not to*. Without me the army is goin' t' keep pushin' westward no matter what. At first, it'll be fifty troops, and then one-hundred. In a month from now another two-hundred, and a year—hell, I could see them buildin' their own fort on the South Platte. They're goin' t' send men down every which waterway there is; Grand Camp Crick, Turkey Crick, ole Vasquez River, Boulder Crick, all the same. But I could deter them from gettin' too close t' yer village, sir. I could tell'em that I've been down this way already. I could tell'em that there ain't no people, just bears and wolves and mountains ye can't climb and rivers ye can't cross. I can send them down another way till they get so bored n' broke they decide to give it all up. I can stop'em from findin' ye, and believe me when I say, I am the only man who can."

George had begun pacing. It seemed to Clark that he was contemplating whether to kill him right then and there.

"I might add, Mister George, sir," Clark stood up from his chair, "the army knows which direction t' look if I don't come back by tomorrow. They won't stop lookin' either, whether they find me dead or alive."

"And tell me for what reason I shouldst trust thee, boy?"

"Because, Mister George, sir, *I don't care* if the army finds ye or not. I don't care about yer village or how long yous been here. I don't care about who owns what. I don't care about the army. I can't wait to rid of'em, in fact. I came out t' these mountains t' get away from all of that. I care 'bout trappin' and makin' my livin'. I ask ye this one favor beyond sparin' my life, sir: If ye stop sendin' men to steal from my fort and my traps, I will stop anybody from comin' down here lookin' for ye. I'll dedicate my whole poor life to it, sir."

The flame of the candle danced wild as George strode past it and then suddenly it went. The room was nothing, black with diseased silence and choked air and then the nervous yellow of the moon came through an old window and struck George as he spoke. "I suppose we can make a deal, Mister Clark," he finally said. "I will allow thy departure if thou shall turn these men from my valley as thou has't sworn. I do have eyes all about these hills, Clark. I should not regret this."

"I do not take yer trust for granted, sir."

"Good," George said commandingly. "For if I never see thy face for all my days, I will know thou art a good fellow."

"Aye," said Clark.

"If thou causeth me to regret mine decision, thou shall be dead before it's been realized. Leave me now, Clark."

"You won't regret it, sir. I swear it to you." Clark shook the giant man's hand and made towards the door. As he opened the door, he turned. "Though another thing, George..."

For the first time George lifted his chin so that Clark could see his bright blue crystal eyes under the shadow of his forehead.

"This country of mine, it moves fast. It moves fast as the whippin' wind. Perhaps they will not find ye tomorrow. Perhaps they will not find yer children, or perhaps not even their children, but one day somebody will find this place. That is not a threat, sir. It is a warning. One day, they're goin' t' cover this land from east to west. Trust me, I'm runnin' from it."

seven

A flock of birds performed in perfect formation flying over Franklin's Fort as a reformed infantry stood at attention. The sun shone bright on the fort but the air was deceivingly crisp and the soldiers shivered an October chill. It was beginning to smell like winter. Despite his wound, Private Bell had been identified as "able-bodied" and was to be reorganized into a mixed reconnaissance unit consisting of a few of the other surviving infantry and fifteen dragoons, all led by one of Franklin's guides.

Bell's blue coat was stained, smeared, unwashed, and torn at the left pit. His nose ran down his face in the autumn air and none of the infantry felt proud or brave or glorious to be standing there broken and disheveled across the courtyard from the haughty cavalry.

Standing between the infantry and the cavalry were Lieutenant Lockhart and Captain Flete who talked amongst themselves quietly and turned their attention back and forth from the foot soldiers to the mounted troops. They whispered and pulled papers from their breast pockets and wrote with fine pens and finally began to divide the men to separate corners of the fort creating the reconnaissance squads. It was a long and decidingly uninteresting drama that played out between the officers. When the alarm of his name was finally sounded, Bell was directed to walk to one corner.

"Private Bell you'll be assigned to Squadron A, under the command of Lieutenant Lockhart here," Flete said. "Assume your position with the rest of the squadron and wait for further orders."

Bell held a mild disdain for Lockhart though he barely knew the man. All the way from Jefferson Barracks across the plains he had watched Lockhart walk and speak with his upper-class snarl. He knew who he was, of course—nobody could spend much more than a day around him before the stories began to spill out either from the man himself or the little sewing circle that was the United States Army—but beyond his distaste for the man, Bell didn't trust him much either. He knew that Lockhart was a gifted officer, but he also pinned him for a vain one. In Bell's mind, the lieutenant was just as likely to lead his men to fame, glory, and riches as he was liable to lead them straight to a row of pine boxes constructed by hastily drawn plans and insatiable ego. There was no room for mediocrity; it was always death or glory.

It was in this moment—the moment Bell was assigned to Lockhart's squadron—that he realized he would leave the army at the end of his service period. Joining the army three years ago had been an exit solution to his meandering indecisiveness as a young man. He knew that he was not a talented smith or cobbler or butcher or much of anything at all. He could not read or write. His father was long dead and his mother deader, and he had no hobbies of his own. He had worked the docks in New York so that he could eat, but even then he barely ate and his housing situation was inconsistent at best, non-existent at worst. He knew plenty of men his age who fell into unfortunate circumstances and pulled themselves out of poverty or into glory through tenures in the army. A man could be fed, clothed, housed, and paid and all he had to do was build stables, dig ditches and walk for hours—until he didn't. That is, until some Indians tore up an armory or some thieves raided a trapper fort a couple of times. It took Private Bell just one skirmish to realize that the money was no good if it couldn't be spent. Eight nights ago in the black eternity of the Platte Canyon under a harrowing lead rain, Bell wished he would have never joined the army. There in Franklin's Fort as he was assigned to Lockhart's reconnaissance squadron, he decided to quit it. He stood in his designated corner, overcome by melancholy, and he thanked God that at least he hadn't been sent to Florida to be skinned by Seminoles. What he was doing now in the West was hard enough. It was as much as his fragile heart could handle.

Russell Clark had been quiet since his return from Deer Creek some days before. Even Jim Franklin noticed his change in disposition, asking him if he had come down with something. Clark guardedly answered that he was frustrated by his own trapping of late. He told Franklin that Deer Creek had run dry and he was thinking of taking his traps elsewhere.

In the previous nights, Bell had tried to signal to Clark to join him for the sake of conversation at supper. At each attempt, Clark feigned a smile or waved with a lazy hand towards the private. He did not fraternize with the other trappers as he usually did. He left his bed in the morning, and in the evening he returned; sometimes with beaver, sometimes without. He was consumed by worry and found himself alone and praying for sleep each evening before the sun had even set. He had thought to run away but had nowhere to go. He couldn't run off to Vasquez or Lupton or William Bent for he didn't have the heart to let Franklin down. He loved Jim Franklin and he knew that not only was he his best trapper, but his closest friend. *Porky needs me,* he thought. So he wrestled with himself as to what to do next. His trepidation grew worse each day. He appeared to sleep but he did not. He appeared to eat but he merely chewed and swallowed. He appeared to trap but he often walked laps along his trails without ever checking to see if he'd caught anything. All he had really done since his parlay with George, that peculiar, massive, indomitable man, was think. And the thinking was beginning to hurt his head.

At the dividing of the squadrons, Jim Franklin offered up Clark to Lockhart as his most trusted guide. Clark, of course, had no choice but to agree to assist Lockhart.

"Russell Clark at yer service, Lieutenant. Ye ask any one'a these fine men at Franklin's Fort and they'll tell ye that nobody goes through these hills b'fore askin' me fer directions first. I blazed quite a few'a these trails my-self…others with the help of Porky or Vaskiss up north. I ain't never had no problems with the Injuns er no-body…And yer in luck, sir, b'cause I like t' walk."

"Very well, Mister Clark!" Lockhart said delightedly. "You'll accompany me in Squadron A then. Perhaps this evening the two of us can join Mister Franklin and Captain Flete in private and go over a number of maps together. I have an abundance of questions for you."

So it was that evening that Russell Clark revealed nearly everything he knew to Samuel James Lockhart. The four men stood over a table in the dim light of a lantern, filling the tent with seething smoke and words like *incursion* and *obliterate*. Clark explained what he knew of the Indians in the area. He pointed to various river mouths on the maps that laid before him and briefed the officers on who lived where. He identified Fort Vasquez and its proximity to Grand Camp Creek, where a colossal settlement of In-dians lived. He explained that the northern range was pop-ulated by the Arapaho and Cheyenne. He told them how the Ute had once held a home where the South Platte met the Front Range but they had already made a swift move to the north since the whites began intervening. This left Platte Canyon indisputably bare. Inside of Platte Canyon was the bended gorge where the infantry had been ambushed. Lockhart had begun officially referring to this bend as "Flete's Graveyard" to the dismay of the guilt-ridden infantry officer. Clark assured the both of them that the canyon was bare.

"I don't think the people yer lookin' for are anywhere near Platte Canyon, Lieutenant," he said. "It's just not a practical place to live."

Lockhart nodded his head in contemplation.

"But ye got t' accept that there is life all over this range, Lieutenant. Just 'cause ye see a few Injuns inside Platte Canyon or down on the red rocks don't mean they're the men yer lookin' fer. There are camps and Injun villages all over this range and men like t' walk from place t' place t' trade and t' hunt and t' fish. Even the gorges and valleys where there ain't no settlements might have life inside'em from time t' time…camps, hunters, those things. This terrain is unpredictable sir, to try and understand it is a task that requires patience and a tolerance for surprise, I 'spose."

Lockhart smoked and smiled at Clark. "I don't have a very high *tolerance for surprise*, dearest Clark. But I will do my best to adapt to your suggestion."

"I'd just hate t' see somebody get kilt that don't need to get kilt. Ye understand."

"Yes, boy. What a pity that would be."

The meeting carried on well into the night with each map marked and pinned as Lockhart saw fit. Franklin had fallen asleep in his seat a number of times with a bottle in his lap. Flete, still nursing a wound and reluctantly submissive to Lockhart, stayed quiet and small at his corner of the table. Clark's eyes burned in his head and sleep sought him, but with each going of his mind he packed his lip full of tobacco and sprung awake long enough to answer Lockhart's ceaseless questions. It was in the wee hours,

Lockhart broached the subject of the nearly forgotten Deer Creek.

"Well sir," Clark said, "I can count on ten hands the 'mount of times I been down ole' Deer Crick, sir. I got most'a my traps now along Pyramid Peak which is right here." He pointed with his middle finger to the crudely drawn mountain. "I been far down the crick some dozens of miles and there ain't nothin' or noone down there. I ran into all sorts of trouble down there before, in fact. Wolves like hellhounds and bugs that'll suck the life right out'ya. Once ye get past here," pointing again at a scaly ridge atop the columbine fields, "you've gone too far fer a fair ride."

"You don't believe there to be any rogue Indians that deep in the range do you, Mister Clark?"

"I ain't seen'em. There's rogues down here, south'a Platte Canyon. They probably fell off the Arkansas somewhere and tried scaling the mountains t' git t' the Platte but decided on stayin'n'huntin' instead. Plenty to hunt down there." Clark spit tobacco juice to the ground and pushed his hair from his face. "I seen some rogues back here too behind the first row of peaks. Gotta take Turkey Crick t' get there. Some rare Injuns back there. Look funny, talk funny, smell funny. Not sure who they belong to. They been there a lifetime. I trade with'em sometimes but they don't hurt nobody. Hell, there's only twelve or thirteen of'em. Mostly men, couple squaws and little ones. I suppose they could be the one's stealin' from us 'cause they're a little desperate, but they ain't the ones who shot down Flete's boys. They ain't smart enough. And they don't even got guns, them."

"Now tell me this, Clark," Lockhart said, "this area between the South Platte and Deer Creek. All of this open green? What lies there?"

"Uninhabitable treachery, Lieutenant." Clark looked up at his peers and a spastic sleepless quiver moved

through his face. "Mountains. Bears. Trees. Ain't nothin'
in there for us, sir."

eight

IT took Lockhart just over one month to penetrate each pass of each mountain along the Front Range according to his plan. He was still dissatisfied. His squadron acted as the primary scouting unit, spending days at a time in each and every clearing of trees, poking around looking for artifacts, clothes, bullets, human excretion, anything that would indicate the presence of his foe.

Clark had first led Lockhart down Grand Camp Creek where the princely and well-armed cavalry was received with silence and resentful passivity by local Indians. The sight of the lordly officer in their village signaled an end of times for many of the chiefs who had already relocated from their homes in Kansas, Nebraska, Wyoming and the Dakotas. They sat masking their anger with fear as Lockhart refused to give them even the respect of his eyes. He barked orders at his sergeants and had Clark provide a translator who hesitantly interrogated the Indians. Only when the Indians refused to cooperate did Lockhart speak to them directly, by raising his voice with threats of violence in search of a weak soul that would crack under the pressure of the saber. No such soul existed. Lockhart would work Grand Camp Creek for two days. He even went as far as forcing the men of the village to display their weapons, taking count of what they possessed. When he finally departed, the Indians celebrated.

Days later in Platte Canyon, Lockhart asked the infantry to lead him to "Flete's Graveyard." He wanted to study the land in an attempt to understand any sort of directional incentive of the evasive attackers.

Private Bell loathed the canyon. He looked up again at the brown and red and silver walls of the rocks and tried to make himself believe that it was Manhattan. He pictured himself on the course silt of the Bowery walking north, boxed in by the tall red buildings. He looked off a hundred yards in the distance and saw the tops of the buildings combining into a thin black ceaseless line that ran to the ends of the earth. His illusion left him when the night began to fall and they had entered the bend of the massacre. With the twilight still overhead, the men could see the fossils of their skirmish littered along the banks of the South Platte. Brass buttons and cartridges and ornaments and single shoes and teeth and guns had already begun to merge with the clay of the canyon, becoming the canyon, immediately ancient and sacred and storied like the stones of the old canyon. In an overtly cruel display of leadership by Lieutenant Lockhart, he commanded that the men pitch camp along the banks of the river that night. They were to sleep atop the blood-stained ground of their dead.

That night in an exhausting quarrel with restless sleep, Private Bell dreamt that he was swimming in the East River overlooking the docks of south Manhattan. The ships arrived at an abominable pace and his father stood on the dock shouting Bell's name, commanding that he finish his swim and help him unload the ships at once. The water was warm and Bell laughed as he twirled like a fish in the river, ecstatic that he wasn't working and well aware that he had no intention to. His father was furious. They shouted back and forth at each other over the roar of the ships. As he swam, he felt a tug at his leg from underneath the water. He dove under the sheen surface and opened his eyes to see a stranger there. The stranger was homely with a long, inconclusive face that Bell had never seen before. It looked pale and amphibious under the water. The stranger stared back at Bell with his arms stretched in front of him, holding his spectacles. Bell took them from the stranger and thanked him and asked for his name. The stranger replied that it was Russell Clark, and that he lived underneath the water. When Bell emerged from the surface of the river, he wasn't in New York at all. He was in Franklin's Fort. He sat alone and in his dream he wore his spectacles and in his dream his vision was refined. He could see the dense wrinkles of the adobe walls. He could see the nats and mosquitoes doing battle in the cool, light air around his face. He turned and saw the mountains and they made him smile like he did when he first saw them all those weeks ago. He decided that he would go into the mountains alone and that he would follow the South Platte into Platte Canyon and set a camp along the river. As he stood up from the floor to step towards the west, he awoke. He shivered on the riverbank and thought for a moment about his dream. Several men snored around him and he lay awake for some time as the sun rose. As he laid, he thought how nice it would be to be anywhere but Platte Canyon. With the sun, Lockhart awoke and sent them back eastward down the river.

Over the next weeks, Russell Clark led Lockhart down Vasquez River, Ralston Creek, Mt. Vernon Creek, and a second excursion into Grand Camp Creek because Lockhart swore that "one of those young Apache boys is going to break soon." His second arrival to the Grand Camp was met with jeers and cursing. Chief Bear Tooth, the leader of the Indian conglomerate, threatened to wage war upon Lockhart and his men. Bear Tooth had no objections to trading with the world of the white-man—what he would not tolerate was to be patronized by him. As the soldiers walked the grounds, they were made targets for stones, sticks, rotting foods, and meal scraps. Reluctantly, Lockhart withdrew. Embarrassed and infuriated, Lockhart began to press Russell Clark on the issue of Deer Creek, the only trail they had not yet run.

"It's not that I don't trust your judgment, dearest Clark," Lockhart said, "it's just that I would feel so much better if I laid eyes upon the land myself. You understand that, do you not?"

"We can go on down Deer Crick if ye want, sir, there jus' ain't much t' see."

"That is all I want to do, Clark. Just to *go down* and see what there *isn't* to see. It would make me feel all the better. It has been a month now of searching for this lost band of imbeciles. My men are tired. *I am tired.* I expected to be back in Missouri two weeks ago, Clark. I have to admit that I am aghast by the situation at hand, but I also believe that our mere presence may have scared our adversary off in any cardinal direction but east several weeks ago. With a successful breaching of Deer Creek, we can say that at least we've made an attempt at each and every point of entry to the range. With a peaceful return to the plains, I will close the book on this chore and write our enemy off as having abandoned its mischievous behavior in favor of migration or death. My men and I will leave you and your trappers to work just as you did months before. I just want to be sure we haven't overlooked something."

Clark finally did lead Lockhart, Private Bell, and a squadron of twenty-five United States soldiers up Deer Creek and past Pyramid Peak. They walked on the path that Clark had blazed himself. Concealing his nerves, Clark busied their march with several stories of his time along the creek. He pointed out his favorite rocks and trees and overhangs along the path. He told the men of his fight with Pyramid Peak on that cold winter day a year ago and how he drunkenly pawed himself out of sure death. Lockhart remained unimpressed, but Private Bell's eyes were as wide as his mouth listening to Clark tell the tale with such animation and narration like a floundering Homer of the wilderness. Who needs Greek epics when you have America, thought Bell.

They walked for an hour at a steady, soldierly pace. As they approached the bend where Clark's first beaver trap lay, he scanned the distant hills, praying that Mohan or any of the other valley strangers were not on the move in the tall grass.

"This is nearly as far as I ever go," Clark said. "Look here, this is the tree where I tie my horse." It was a tall, strong ponderosa branded by a dull halo where the bark had been burned by the rope over time. The raw muscle of the tree was red and agitated. Inscribed in the yellowish wood was *R.C.* "I got t' b'lieve I was the first man t' ever touch this tree. A holy feeling fer a man t' have."

As they followed the creek to the west it widened. Strong, white stones lined its clear body and the trail narrowed, only allowing for a single file line of men to fit along it. The horses walked beside them in wild grass and high ferns, grunting and complaining in dismay. The men were able to pick out the small beginnings and ends of beaver dams on the overgrown banks. Clark pointed down to his trap. It had a beaver in its teeth.

"Damn!" he shouted. "I ain't been up this way t' check my traps in so long, that beavers no good no more. Probably been swimmin' like that fer two weeks." The beaver was bloated with water and its fur was black and miserable like oil. "Lockhart ye old pistol, ye owe me a beaver."

"I'll be sure that you're compensated for your loss of capital, dearest Clark," Lockhart said in his unironic, humorless way.

"Hey, you said it, Lieutenant, not me."

When the party arrived at the bend in the creek where Clark had first met Mohan, Clark pointed up at the towers of stone before them and warned Lockhart of their contents.

"This here is the farthest I'd go if I were you, Lieutenant. I been up further a couple'a times but that's 'bout where the trouble starts. It's animal country. Them wild cats up in them ridgelines will stalk us up and down and tear through this squadron like a coyote in a chicken coop. In fact there used t' be a young kid that Porky brought up from Santa Fe t' trap with us 'bout this time last year. Mexican kid. He come up here by himself one day and come back t' Porky's a week later missin' half his face. Said he got in a fight with a lion. Them cats and wolves take t' the high ground and this crick only gets higher from here."

"Very well," Lockhart said. He dismounted his horse and began to walk up the creek alone looking high into the caves of the ridgelines above him. He took out a telescope and studied each and every hill and tree before him.

"There ain't no Injuns or Mexicans or nobody livin' up here, Lieutenant," Clark said. "They'd be fools t' do that. Besides, I'da seen'em by now anyway."

Lockhart collapsed his telescope and gently placed it back inside his jacket. He removed his gloves, pulling off each finger preciously and hid them in his pocket with the telescope. He produced a pipe and a pouch of tobacco. "It appears you're right, Clark. It really is just a quaint little creek, isn't it?" he said smiling. "I see why you like to trap it. It is perhaps my favorite trail of the lot we've explored." He lit his pipe and looked out over his men, making sure not to acknowledge the likes of the infantry too intentionally. Two tails of smoke spun from his nose like white tusks. "Let us pitch camp here for the evening men. I'd like to experience the land overnight. In the morning we'll make our way back to Franklin. After that, we're headed back to Missouri."

That night as the men tossed and turned and the fires cracked with dead pinewood and bristle, Private Bell saw Clark awake and alone sitting upright, tearing meat from a bone and licking his fingers. He focused solely on the meat. His blonde hair fell in front of his face and his hands were wet with grease but he had no concern for how he looked or who was watching. He spit the fat of the meat into the fire. In his ferocity of eating, he was calm and content. He had a center about him that he had not possessed in weeks. Bell was restless and walked on light feet to Clark, hoping he'd be in the mood to talk. Bell had grown to admire Russell Clark in the month that they had worked together. He took him for an eccentric, but he also thought he might be the only sane person in the West. He was impressed by his encompassing conviction in each step he took and each word he said. Clark knew that he was a trapper and he refused to fight God on that fact. Bell was tickled by his confidence and his lack of regard for Lieutenant Lockhart with his medals and his saber and his long, lavish hair. Clark ate when he was hungry and he drank whisky when he was dry and he never complained. Bell sat down slowly and quietly at Clark's side.

"Hi there, Bill," Clark said first. "Can't sleep?"

"No. Hard for me to sleep outside like this."

"Ye federal boys do a lot'a sleepin' outside in the elements, don'tcha?"

"We're supposed to. I never got good at it."

"Hell, I been sleepin' outside nearly my whole life." Clark pulled his flask from his chest. He took a slug and his face clenched for a moment before he stuck it out to Bell. "This will put you right to bed. Go on and have a drink, Bill." Bell looked at the flask and then turned and looked behind him. He could see Lockhart asleep under a tree thirty yards back towards the creek. "Lockhart ain't gon catch ye. It'll help ye sleep, Bill."

"Hell, alright," Bell said. He took the flask and took a long slug and pulled off the nipple of the bottle with a deep breath like he had come up from underwater. The whiskey built a fire in his gut and he smiled.

"What happens if ye get caught? They kick ye out of the army?" Clark said, taking another slug himself.

"Much worse than that!" Bell squealed. "One guy back in St. Louis got stuck digging ditches every day for two weeks when they found his bottle," Bell said. "Another guy they dunked in an ice river for an hour a day for a month because they found out he was buying liquor off Indians and selling it to the soldiers."

"Goddamn."

"Yeah. I'd prefer they just kick me out between me and you."

"Well hell, Bill Bell, I'll go wake up Lockhart and let him know yer sneakin' whisky if that's the case," Clark said laughing. Bell laughed too. After they laughed they didn't talk for a while and the snap of the fire kept their attention and then Bell spoke.

"Let me ask you something, Clark."

Clark's eyes shot over to Bell with a calmness.

"How long do you think you'll be out here? At Franklin's Fort I mean."

Clark looked out to the distance at nothing in particular and thought. His eyebrows gave way and he pushed his hair back on top of his head. "Couldn't say, Bill. I figure 'nother couple years if things keep going well fer us. Lotta' competition out there though with Vaskiss and Lupton. St. Vrain been out here too. Hell, I miss Wyoming too. But Porky's a good man and this land is good. I'd like t' work with Porky fer a long time. I like these mountains—the mountains in Wyoming ain't the same."

"You think you'll always stick with Franklin then?"

"Fer now, I 'spose. He's given me a home. He trusts me like a son. No reason t' leave unless business gits t' goin' bad. I figure we resolve this situation with the thievin' and we got nuthin' else t' worry 'bout." Clark tore back into his meat and threw the ravished bone out to the sticks. "What makes ye curious?"

"Well," Bell started, lowering his voice, "I'm thinking perhaps when my contract is up this winter maybe I'll come out here and learn how to trap. I don't know. I've just been thinking about it. I like this country out here. I could go back to New York, but I just don't know if I have anything there for me."

"Ye wanna trap?"

"I don't know. I've just been thinking about it. I don't want to do this anymore."

"Aw, hell you weren't kiddin'! Here take some more whisky, I'll go get Lockhart!"

"Shh!" Bell hit Clark in the chest with the back of his hand. "Don't talk so loud. And give me that." He yanked the whisky from Clark's hands and took another hearty slug.

"Well," Clark started, not really knowing how to finish, "how much longer ye got?"

"Four months."

The two sat silent again. They each listened to the men behind them, making sure they were still asleep. A few men snored and the fire was loud too.

"I don't know how t' say this, Bill, but a man can't jus' come on out to a fort full'a lifelong trappers and decide he's gon' learn how t' trap. Ye might be a liability t' the rest of us. We're trying t' run a successful post out here."

"Well maybe I can just help with selling the stuff."

"Ye ride a horse?"

"Well," Bell said, blushing, "I don't have to get my hands dirty, I can do some administrative work for Franklin. Keep inventory, count money…"

"The hell ye want t' do that kinda work for, Bill? Yer from New York, go back and get a real job."

"I *can't*," Bell said. "I can't be a lawman or a clerk or nothing like that. I've never worn a suit. I don't know how to do that sort of stuff. I like it out here. I feel better out in this air, under these stars, between these mountains. If I wasn't sure they'd hang me, I'd leave this ratpack right now. I think I made a mistake, Clark."

Clark looked out again into the night. Bell could see his eyes and his lips really considering what he had said. Clark's face was funny and seemed to argue with itself as he thought.

"It don't seem like ye got any real skills, Bill," he turned and looked at Bell. "But hell, if ye come out here this winter, I'll show ye a little somethin' 'bout trappin' and maybe we can see if we got a place down at Porky's for ye. Ye seem like a good kid. I can tell by yer face that yer a good kid."

Bell's cheeks turned red and he looked down at the ground. He was feeling the whisky now.

"Ye gotta start somewhere I guess," Clark said. "Ye come see me after you get done in the army. Me and Porky'll take care of ye."

"I'll show you I'm a hard worker. Even if I can't trap, I'll show you that you guys can use me. I'll make it worth it for you."

"Hell, if we can't use ye, ye go see old man Lupton. He's an old army man, he'll put ye t' work." Clark laughed and opened the cap of his flask. "You'll do jus' fine, Bill. You'll do jus' fine."

***

Lockhart readied the troops for the day by stepping between their beds and denting a tin cup with an iron rod. Bell rolled over awake and cursed Lockhart and the whole army all together.

Clark awoke easily, standing up and packing his sack. Some men sat along the creek, dipping their hands and feet and heads in the cold running water. Lockhart was smiling and delighted to see that Clark had risen.

"We have a change of plans, gentlemen!" Lockhart said. He walked to Clark and took the scout by the shoulders. "Russell Clark, I've made a discovery this morning that I would like to show you. I trust you will be as fervent as I with the will to continue. Come, come!"

Clark put on his hat, pulled a cigarette from his pouch and followed Lockhart to a sparse treeline that ran above the water. A nervousness took him as he followed the delighted lieutenant. As they approached the treeline, Clark spotted what it was that Lockhart had found. It was a tall white aspen tree, dimpled by Mohan's bullet the day Clark had exchanged volleys with him. Lockhart approached the tree.

"This morning I awoke before the sun and decided to stretch my legs along the line of these trees. When I am stuck on a problem, I like to walk, Clark. Benjamin Franklin always said, 'The legs are the engine of the mind.'" The lieutenant smiled smugly as he said this. "The problem nagging at me of course is that of the men we are currently pursuing. I have stepped in and out of every one of these river valleys, trailheads, canyons, and clearings over the last six weeks and not only have I not found the men we seek, but miraculously—besides some Indians here and there— we haven't found any sign of human life at all. *That* my friend, is what nags me. The fact is this: we have reports from Franklin, yourself, and my own counterpart, Captain Flete, of these assailants retreating into the depths of this range. 'Tis not a fairytale—these are facts. However, when we probe this range, we haven't seen as much as a cufflink astray on the ground. Perhaps these men are particularly gifted at covering their tracks behind them. In fact, I would say they are certainly gifted at such a task, as they've left us completely in the dark for the duration of our pursuit. That is, until today." Lockhart removed his gloves proudly and took the girth of the aspen tree in his hands. His face erupted into a maniacal smile. "Just as the thought began to torture me this morning, I passed by this tree. This miracle of a tree. This tree, Clark, is my sign from God that our search is not in vain! Do you see here what I see in this tree?"

Clark took a drag from his cigarette and nodded his head slowly, "I think so."

"This is a bullet wound. The tree has been shot, Clark. Now let me ask you, son, did you shoot this tree?"

Clark shook his head no, biting his lip. He had no time to lie, to produce some story that would be believable and cohesive to the stubborn lieutenant. He had no strength to invent a tale. "No, sir," he said. "But are ye sure that is a mark from a musket ball? Could it not be the work of a bird? A stag?"

"Nonsense, Clark! Look at the way the wood splits. This tree was shattered by a ball. I've searched the grounds all morning for the lead, but to no avail. You must trust my judgment here, son. I have fought enough engagements around enough trees to know what a trunk looks like when it's been wounded."

"I trust yer judgment, Lieutenant."

"This gives me hope, Clark. It should give you hope too. I would like to continue west, along the creek for the day. I don't want to hear any of your legends about cats and wolves and bears and dragons that lurk in these woods. We have enough firepower to drop any beast. Gather your things, I do not want to wait."

Clark began to sweat. He felt his fingers begin to itch. He was choked by helplessness as he stood before the smiling lieutenant. He tried for a moment to deter Lockhart once more, but Lockhart snapped at him with a throaty curse and ordered him to alert the others. "We are going to continue! There are men with guns along this creek. They have given themselves away!"

The skies were gray and a prewinter breeze froze the air, chilling the soldiers all day long as they hurdled rocks and climbed ridges, forging their own path up the mountainside. The horses kicked and cried at the untreated terrain. As the landscape passed him by, Clark took note of each marker he had seen before. He remembered a bushel of thorns protruding from a cavemouth. There were odd shaped rocks fallen and stacked along the ridges. The field of purple columbines warned him that they were getting close to the valley.

As they ascended the side of the mountain, the wind snapped harder and froze the ears of the men. By noon, a frost had begun to fall from the sky, plummeting their morale. Their white faces turned red with hot blood. They looked up towards the peak of the mountain and saw that it was white with snow. With every step they took they felt the temperature drop. They groaned and slipped and fell and cut themselves all over the icy ridgeside. Several of the more stubborn horses had to be left behind, tied to trees, leaving a number of dragoons humiliated, marching side by side with the infantry on foot. Lockhart showed no emotion. He carried on upwards, following the natural incline of the ridge at the head of his order. Clark rode behind him with paranoid eyes, scanning each and every tree and bush for signs of life.

Private Bell marched towards the back of the caravan. His gun was slung over his shoulder and his hands were buried in his trousers. He panted up the ridge, his breath freezing in front of him. Seen from a short distance, the cold breath of the whole squadron could have been mistaken for a cloud as it was so thick and present and followed them like a fog up the mountain.

Towards the top of the mountain Lockhart led his men around a wide bow that seemingly hung off the edge of the earth. His men, frozen and miserable, couldn't help but gaze in awe at the vast land that they overlooked. For miles into the eastern basin they could see the prairies of the plains, flat and green and copper-colored like majestic pastures of heaven. It was the land they had traversed up and down every day for weeks. They knew it well, but for the first time, they were able to *see it*. They could see the veiny rivers cutting through the mountain passes like saws splitting stone. Above the land a dozen low clouds hung on strings just before their eyes. A lazy golden sunbeam dangled from the ether between two clouds, its jewels nearly reaching the green of the earth.

"My God," Lockhart exclaimed. "What almighty land is this place?"

Sitting alone on the seat of a pine that hung over the edge of the ridge was a chickadee. It sang its song into the open air, away from the mountain where it could be heard. Its lone voice cried out towards the east.

"That sure is strange," said Clark.

"What is it, boy?" Lockhart said.

"That chickadee. I never seen a red-beaked chickadee out here. I used t' see'em back home in Kaintucky when I was a boy. I never seen one out here. Not in two years have I seen one. It just looks outta' place, that's all."

"Perhaps it got lost. I wouldn't waste time contemplating the motives of birds, dearest Clark."

"It's time well spent, the way I see it."

At the end of the bend, Lockhart came to a halt. He poked his nose up in the air and inspected the land before him. Every man of the party saw exactly what he had discovered: dozens of tree stumps, cut by hand, awaiting them atop the next ridge. Just beyond the stumps, visible for the first time in front of them was the face of a second mountain, taller and grayer than the one they stood on. It looked down upon them like a God, like Olympus, like it was going to summon thunder and lightning to strike them down in their intrusion. The sight of the stumps and the great peak exhilarated the men. They all took hold of their guns and the color returned to their faces. They rallied with shouts and songs as they marched. Clark felt his breath leave him.

"Forward men!" Lockhart commanded. "It won't be long now!" The party climbed the ridge in double-time. In just a few minutes they reached the edge of the next ridge in front of the mountain whose wretched eye watched them. Lockhart hastily led them through thick brush, cutting down grass and stalks of tall weed with his saber. At the end of this brush, they came upon the same hill that Mohan had led Clark to, overlooking the great valley of the fort that sat between the two mountains. Lockhart and Clark stood together at the lip of the hill. Lockhart leaned his head over the edge and saw the valley move. Fires burned all around the fairgrounds of the fort. Men worked hard under the evening frost. Women led their children through the snow under the low eaves of old houses, their chimney's frothing with spinning smoke. Clark looked over the valley, his heart battered his sternum from the inside. He saw George the giant in a wine-red robe, his long black hair tucked behind his ears. He walked calmly and alone across the fairgrounds. Lockhart's eyes were black and wide like saucers. The corners of his lips were sharp as he smiled with a mouth like a bright crescent moon. He was gasping for air in authentic disbelief. He put a weary hand on Clark's shoulder and squeezed it tightly with excitement.

"It's just marvelous," Lockhart said genuinely. "It is absolutely magnificent. What in starry heaven is such a place as this." He pulled his telescope from his coat and put one eye to its end. As he looked, he erupted in a maddening laughter.

Book II

New Bristol: A Fractured History of The Going, and Additional Histories Regarding Colonial Exploration in North America
Spring, 1599

one

WHEN Patamon reached the coast he looked at the horizon over the sea. It was calm and blue. The sun was finally underground and the night sky was hoarding rays of light that glowed and laid a blanket of indigo over his camp. The ocean was easy and infinite. The rush of the tide breathed with him in sequence as he looked at the end of the earth. He never tried to see the other side of the sea; it was not important to him. He knew of its existence, and he figured, as anybody did, if he went far enough out, he'd end up around the same place he started. In one sense, he wasn't wrong.

He washed his hands and wet his face in the water and took another long look at the ocean's end. He'd seen it before, many times even. The first time he saw it, he was with his father. When Patamon was a boy, his father marched him from their little village to this very beach and it was here he taught Patamon how to fish and how to hunt and how to use the stars as a compass.

Patamon's village was on a river they called the Nanticoke. The people stayed close to the river and planted along its healthy banks and rose homes under the shade of strong trees with wide northern leaves. The journey from the village to the ocean took two days. Not many of the tribe had ever made that journey. Only Patamon made a routine of seeing the ocean. There was a holiness in that water that moved him in dreams and lured his soul from its home. He had no objection to braving the thick forest that separated his village from the coast—the same route that his father taught him all those years ago. It was always worth the trouble once he reached the ocean.

The land on the coast was green and full of food. Extravagant bird songs blew with the wind and ancient trees covered the water. He loved the land. It was untouched, unharmed and peaceful. There was another river, a much larger river, northward. Sometimes Patamon would travel to that river, and he loved that river too. The people there were friendly and traded with him often. Patamon's tribe would ask that he go to meet the people on the far river and he would return with shells with colors like starclouds and good smooth stones different from the ones they could find along the Nanticoke. On days of great importance, the two tribes would gather and feast and dance together. It was while serfs and servants worked in France and wars waged between England and Spain that Patamon and his people were content and efficient along these rivers. Patamon was perhaps the most content among them. He was fair-faced and sociable and he laughed often and he thought and prayed very often and he loved the land very much.

Patamon's son, Powa, was seeing the unabridged faultless ocean for the first time. Powa was short, even for his age, and had large brown eyes always deep and glistening. When he became curious or sad they seemed black. His hair was moppy and black and bounced when he walked. He had holes in his wide young smile, as children do. He had made fire at his father's instruction, drawing in the sand with the kindling, distracting himself from the work that needed to be done. He periodically looked up at the ocean. Its great emptiness stirred him. When he finally got a good fire burning, his father sat with him and the two ate fish and fruit. Patamon told Powa tales of the ocean's creation—the same stories his own father told him long ago. They sat on top of a dune near a mighty white oak. The father and son looked together at the big water as they laid their heads. They became tired counting stars on their backs near the fire. As the coals of small wood died on the beach and the light dimmed, the son blinked at the darkness of the water and he told his father that he loved the ocean. He thanked him for showing him the ocean and told him again that he loved it and then they slept.

When Powa awoke the sun was just rising over the ocean. He had awoken early from excitement. His father laid unbothered on the beach. All night Powa had been restless, for he knew that today he would kill and skin a rabbit and his father would be proud of him. He had been hunting with his father before, but only as an observer. He was graceful and skilled with his hands, but was timid to kill. He had not yet in his boyhood understood why men felt such pride in the exploits of their hunts. He didn't understand much at all of what other boys did. He did not like the games the children in the village played. While his friends played, Powa often took long walks through the woods, looking for creatures he had never seen or talking out loud to himself, creating stories and songs to occupy his busy mind. His memory was very good and he cared much for the stories his father shared with him. He cared nothing for winning. He found his joy in the sight of a beautiful strange bird or the sun over the ocean, but today, he knew he would make his father proud.

He had been looking forward to gazing out at the ocean while he waited for his father to rise. He walked to the foot of the tide and breathed in. He smiled with delight as the sweetness of the air and the brine of the sea woke his senses. The sun just teased the far edge of the water, melting the clouds of the horizon into a red stew. The breakers roared and were large enough to block the sun before they came down upon the tide. Powa was content. He thought of God as he watched the sunrise. He wondered about God. He had seen rituals and celebrations. He knew that God needed things from him and he did not know how to appease those needs. The worshiping of God seemed like something so serious, something only adults did with their time. As an eight-year-old who understood nothing of practical matters, he was curious and slightly afraid of God. He rarely associated his knowledge of God, or lack thereof, with love or happiness—God was mysterious and somewhat deprived in his mind—but when he saw the throbbing orange sun birth itself from the depths of the eastern ocean he felt the love of God inside him and it made him feel good. He was not fearful of God or of death or of disappointing his father in that moment. He was enlightened to be there.

He wanted to share this moment with his father and turned to awaken Patamon. He shoved his body a bit and whispered to him. Patamon rose promptly out of the sand. Powa wanted to ask his father about God and if the sun had anything to do with God, but he felt embarrassed and decided to stay quiet. Patamon took his son's hand and they walked together towards the tide. The song of the water was slow and gentle. It moved with the grace of the wind, rhythmically, lovely and convicted in its offering. It came and tickled their feet. The two stood together and watched the sun come from the underearth until its orange core ripened into its familiar hue. Patamon bent down and filled his hands with saltwater and washed his face. White seabirds flew overhead on top of a spring breeze and small crabs dashed along wet sand as they had on this beach for thousands of years. Powa felt that if he looked across the ocean glass long enough that perhaps he could see his own back, as if the end of the ocean was so far away he must already be standing there.

As he stared into the horizon further, he noticed something. He could not make out what it was, but it startled him and he felt his heart shutter in his stomach. He was seeing the silhouette of a figure between him and the distant light. He moved closer to the water and squinted his black eyes. For a moment he had convinced himself that what he saw was an illusion—a low, dark cloud sitting atop a pool of ocean a thousand miles away—but as he gazed longer, he noticed it move under its own volition. It was moving towards him slowly. His feelings of peace and God were replaced by terror. His sense of presentness left him. Patamon, not having noticed, turned around and marched up the hill of sand. He turned back and called to his son. Powa was paralyzed and said nothing. He was alone and he saw the figure. Patamon stepped and then looked at the sea and noticed the figure and he too stood still and watched it move. They were speechless as the shroud of the intruder grew larger and larger. Patamon's mind began reciting all of the myths and stories he knew about the ocean. At first he believed it to be a creature of the sea but as it grew closer, he noticed its giant wings that were filled with wind and he decided it must be a bird. He began doubting himself again when it made a wide, slow, sinister turn and he saw dozens of protruding spokes and unearthly limbs hanging from its body. At once, Patamon spoke and ordered his son up the hill behind them.

They hid in the thick tree line of the brush behind the beach. The land was elevated and they had a good vantage point of the figure. They stayed hidden, only letting their eyes poke out between leaves and branches. Patamon was calm as he closely followed each movement of the beast with his intense eyes. It glided naturally along the water. It turned with a calculated steadiness. He took his son in his arms. Powa's heart was fast and he did not feel well. A dizziness emptied him.

As it became closer yet, Patamon saw what disturbed him most. He saw people. He watched them as they manned ropes and wood about the deck. They carried crates and long tools. They hustled their belongings up and down steps and ladders. He saw children run along the top of the silhouette and into the arms of mothers—black shadows of children and mothers against the blazing sun. At once, Patamon understood what he was seeing.

They were close to the shore now. A series of moans and creaks sang from its hull as the ship settled. The sounds frightened Powa. The crew tossed anchors overboard. The water exploded as the iron anchors shattered its surface. Powa groaned at the sound of the breaking of the ocean. After the anchors, there were smaller boats which were filled with men. They rowed towards the shore and they moved very quickly. Patamon took Powa by the arm and they turned towards the old path and ran. The forest was dark and Powa feared every sound and shadow around him, sure that there was someone at his heels, though he dared not look back. As he ran he no longer thought of God. He thought that he wanted to be home with his mother. He wanted nothing more than to just be home. It would take them two days if they moved very quickly and slept little.

two

BETWEEN 1492 and 1598 England was irrefutably dom-
inated by their two primeval rivals in the race to colonize
the New World. Spanish colonies in the Caribbean and
South America were already three or four generations old;
France was finding success in the north developing the St.
Lawrence River into a self-contained trade-haven, all while
the English had yet to build as much as a church or a
schoolhouse anywhere on the American continents.
Though it was true that the 1,200-mile coast between New
France and Spanish Florida was called *Virginia* by the English, it was named as such long before it was permanently
settled. Throughout the entirety of the 16th century, England had made several attempts to settle the land they
called *Virginia*, but struggled to mature a colony beyond a
glorified bivouac. Some of their colonial hopes were
squandered by poor planning and feeble leadership, while
others were victims of circumstance; untimely weather, violence, or bad luck. By the end of the century, it appeared
that England would never lay claim on the New World.
With their enemies establishing transcontinental empires,
and a national anxiety washing over the English people,

Queen Elizabeth had no choice but to try again in the spring of 1599.

The settlement in question is one in a long chain of events that involved several world powers and over a hundred years of seafaring exploration. To best understand the historical gravity of this settlement, it is best to be aware of the related events that preceded it.

***

In 1492, Christopher Columbus departed Spain and sailed across the Atlantic, landing in the present-day Bahamas. Columbus initially set out in confidence that he could reach India—and eventually Europe again—if he just continued to sail west. He was correct. What he had not anticipated however, were the two continents in his way.

Galvanized by his circumstantial discovery, Columbus decided not to continue west and to instead study and map numerous islands in the newfound West Indies. Here he made first contact with indigenous populations and eventually sailed back to Spain with the news of his discovery. When Columbus returned to Spain, word of a newfound supercontinent quickly spread throughout Europe. A race to colonize this land began, and the Age of Discovery was underway.

Already before Columbus' return to Europe, England and Spain were locked in a cold war. At the time, the Spanish Empire was experiencing their own "Age of Enlightenment," a movement indebted to the national spirit and collective belief that Spain was to put all her financial, political, artistic, and military efforts into fulfilling a religious destiny: to spread Catholicism worldwide at virtually any cost. The newly Protestant English were determined to stop such an effort and quickly placed an embargo on Spain, threatening them in arms over land and sea territories all over Europe. With Columbus' news, Spain quickly moved to ensure Catholicism beat the Church of England to the New World and founded several settlements across the Atlantic in just a couple of years. England attempted to do the same, but had no such luck.

England's first hasty attempt at discovery was a voyage by John Cabot, who was dispatched by King Henry VII in 1497. Cabot was an Italian explorer who, like Columbus, gained financial backing and national sponsorship for an attempt at finding a new trade route to India and China. While Columbus' efforts became distracted, Cabot was obsessed with finishing what Columbus had started. Cabot insisted on departing at a latitude farther north than Columbus, convinced that the supposed passage to the Orient was nowhere near Columbus' initial discoveries in the Caribbean. Subsequently, Cabot struck land in what historians generally agree to be modern Newfoundland, Canada. An English merchant by the name of William Weston was present on Cabot's voyage, making him the first Englishman to travel to North America. By Weston's own account, the voyage encountered no native peoples, and they stayed ashore for several weeks only finding remains of fire and basic tools. Two years later in 1499, John Cabot's son, Sebastian Cabot, would man his own crew and land not far from John's original point of landbreak. Sebastian, however, would travel as far south as the Chesapeake Bay in modern Virginia, becoming very likely the first European to lay eyes on what would become the United States.

In the early portion of the 16th century, dozens of permanent settlements in modern day Puerto Rico, Dominican Republic, Venezuela, Colombia, Central America and Mexico brought great profit and pride to the Spanish Empire. While some relations with native peoples were peaceful, they were more often violent or characterized by the unintentional spreading of European diseases that natives had no immunity to resulting in mass death. This allowed the Spanish to acquire land incredibly rapidly, establishing cash crops, uncovering precious metals and treasures, and cultivating landmass that gave their military a great advantage over the other European powers who were slow to match their dominance.[13]

One nation that did the best at keeping up with the Spanish in the early years of the Age of Discovery, was Portugal. In 1500, a fleet commanded by Pedro Álvares Cabral, who too was searching for a route to China and India, landed in Brazil establishing the first Portuguese colony in the New World. This inspired the Portuguese born explorer, Ferdinand Magellan, in 1519 to explore even further south than Cabral's settlement in Brazil, and eventually circumnavigate the globe—the first voyage to ever do so—by way of a strait that separates mainland South America from Tierra del Fuego. That strait is now called the Strait of Magellan.

Magellan scaled the west coast of South America northwards, and then sailed dead-west across the Pacific. When Magellan's crew reached the Philippines, he attempted to convert the people there to Christianity. The native people of the Philippines responded violently to Magellan's missionary attempt, and he was killed. In fact, of the 270 that set out on the circumnavigation, just nineteen returned to Spain after this violent turn of events in the Philippines. After the death of most of the higher ranked seaman, the crew was taken over by Juan Sebastián Elcano who is credited for *completing* history's first circumnavigation.

After the momentous Magellan-Elcano voyage, competition in trade and land accumulation became more urgent than ever. Dozens of European voyages set out to replicate what Magellan and Elcano had done. King Francis I of France was under great pressure by French merchants and financiers to find yet another trade route to the Far East that would not require traveling below the entirety of the South American continent like Magellan had. In 1524 he tasked Giovanni de Verrazzano, an Italian, with finding a more direct route by way of the Atlantic Coast of

North America, a region that was still seldom documented up to this point. Verrazzano became the first man to explore the entirety of the North American East Coast from Spanish Florida to New Brunswick. On March 21, 1524, he reached present-day North Carolina, where he was convinced that the Pamlico Sound, the largest lagoon on the North American East Coast, was the Pacific Ocean. He followed the sound northward, but miraculously missed the entrance to the Chesapeake Bay and the Delaware River.[14] He returned to France believing and publicly claiming that he saw the Pacific Ocean, and that on the other side of that ocean, was China. Because of his failure to actually secure the intended route, King Francis discontinued their partnership. Later, Verrazzano would work for years to convince King Henry VIII of England of his newfound trade passage, but to no avail.[15]

Around this same time, Portuguese sailor Juan Rodríguez Cabrillo left his homeland to sail to New Spain. After several years in Mexico mining gold, he became an incredibly rich conquistador. A close friend and business partner, the forever famed Hernán Cortes, commissioned Cabrillo to sail up the Pacific Coast of the continent in 1542 as an official vassal of New Spain.[16] On September 28, Cabrillo became the first person to reach the coast of California as he sailed the coast of the San Diego Bay and eventually made contact with natives in present-day Santa Barbara and Ventura. It is thought he may have sailed as far north as present-day Washington; however, his descriptions of the voyage are vague and he died of gangrene while at sea.

***

On the other side of the continent in 1565, St. Augustine was established in present-day Florida as the first permanent European settlement in what would later become the United States of America.[17] As Spanish presence in the New World became overwhelming, the new monarch of

England, Queen Elizabeth I, began employing teams of privateers to disrupt Spanish seafaring missions.

Privateers were private sailors under the command of a non-military person that were hired by governments to engage in maritime warfare, which often included blatant raiding and pillaging of an enemy ship or settlement. Essentially, it functioned as government commissioned piracy. Over the next decade, tensions between the Spanish and English were at an all-time high, but both were unwilling to formally declare war on the other. Sir Francis Drake, an Englishman and perhaps the most famous privateer of them all, was hired by Elizabeth to circumnavigate the world in 1577, destroying any Spanish warships, trade vessels, or settlements that he could find along the way. Drake wreaked havoc in the Caribbean and along the coast of Central and South America. He followed the Magellan Strait westward, and on the Pacific Coast of South America he engaged Spanish fleets that protected the cities of Arica, Lima, and Guayaquil, decimating Spanish trade opportunities. His ship naturally took plenty of damage along his run causing him to stop in what is now Cape Arago, California to repair his vessel and rest his men. This would make him the first Englishman to step foot in California, and perhaps the first Englishman to step foot in what would become the United States of America. The native people greeted him with awe and enthusiasm. Drake's men maintained friendly relations with the coastal Indians for nearly a month and they often dined and celebrated together. Drake even followed them inland on several expeditions on foot, mapping their villages and taking note of their language and customs. He called this land New Albion, and laid a brass plate on its shore, claiming it for the Kingdom of England for all of time to come, though no further attempt at colonizing the land ever came to fruition.[18]

***

At this time, English stagnation and outright failure to establish meaningful colonies in the New World led to national embarrassment and unrest among citizens. The frustration of the ruling class was best summarized by a young English writer—a thirty-year-old man named Richard Hakluyt from London—who was described as being "acquainted with the chiefest captaines at sea, the greatest merchants, and the best mariners of our nation." Hakluyt published a pamphlet in 1584 entitled, *A Particuler Discourse Concerninge the Greate Necessitie and Manifolde Commodyties That Are Like to Growe to This Realme of Englande by the Westerne Discoueries Lately Attempted, Written in the Yere 1584.* In his writing, he argued that not only did England need permanent colonies in North America for the good of her economy, security, and cultural growth, but that God himself demanded such colonization, lest Spanish Catholicism would monopolize future lands, and English Protostantism would be at risk of extinction. His sentiment was upheld tenfold by his peers and eventually put heavy pressure on Elizabeth to make more serious efforts in competing with Spanish expansion for the good of England's people and the Church itself. Not coincidentally, this same year Elizabeth began a succession of unprecedented efforts at colonizing the New World.

Firstly, Sir Humphry Gilbert founded a small settlement in the area that Cabot discovered decades prior in Newfoundland. The settlement showed prospect of prosperity before Gilbert was suddenly lost at sea and his settlement abandoned.

The following year, Elizabeth tasked Sir Walter Raleigh to found the colony of Roanoke.[19] Raleigh's attempt was plagued by undersupply issues and logistic dumbfoundings leading to Roanoke's dissolvement in less than a year. All of its settlers would return to England and fifteen soldiers were left to guard the fort. In 1587, a man called John White was sent by Raleigh to resurrect the colony. Initial relations with the native population were friendly, but supplies again began to dwindle within the year. John White traveled back to England, under the premise that he would return with an abundance of supplies in a matter of months. Unfortunately, when he attempted to return to his colony, the Spanish had just launched the Armada—a massive and violent naval blockade of England—and White was trapped in England for over a year. When access to travel was again granted in 1590, White returned to Roanoke but found that the entire colony was abandoned and in a state of disarray with no persons found dead or alive. There was no explanation for their disappearance at the scene—only the eerie message, "Croatoan" carved into a tree.

Finally, in 1599 under great strain from ongoing conflicts in Ireland and Spain, and great scrutiny from her contemporaries in England, Elizabeth employed one Adam Stone, a former privateer, renowned Mediterranean trader, and one-time admiral in the Anglo-Spanish War (which had begun in 1585), to lead three ships to Virginia with ample supplies and the blessing of England behind him. This effort would be Elizabeth's final attempt at colonization of the New World during her reign.

In an encounter with an unusually treacherous storm towards the end of the journey, two of the three ships, *The Sealord* and *Sunprairie* were lost completely to sea. On May 12, 1599, Stone and his first mate, John Cobb, landed in present-day Delaware aboard the voyage's flagship, *The Rose Marie,* and laid claim to a piece of land they called New Bristol.

three

THE *Rose Marie* carried seventy-four people. It was a medium sized merchant ship, brown with blue and red lines painted across its smooth body. Two masts sat atop its deck, one of which was quite tattered. There was some damage to the hull at the bow of the ship as it sat atop the warming water. Women and children stood at the bow and watched the men step onto the shore.

"I by decree yond on this day, the twelfth of May, fifteen-hundred and ninety-nine year of our Lord, yond this seaboard and its subsequent wood and watershed, hencef'rth hath called New Bristol, Virginia, forswear parteth of Her Majesty's claimeth und'r sov'reign ruleth of Queen Elizabeth and the Kingdom of England."

With sword in hand, Adam Stone and his immediate landing party walked the cream-colored beach surveying the land. Stone was adorned in Arabian gems and Egyptian gold and Greek silks. He was dark-haired with a hint of gray in both his mane that rested on his shoulder, and his thick beard that curled along his neck.

He stampeded through gatherings of temperamental seabirds that populated his beach. They picked at the ground below the oak and maple trees that crowded the land. He strode confidently along the sand to the end of the beach where the soft sand surrendered to dirt and grass. The ground was wet and marshy. Behind the marshy land stood a tall hill. The hill plateaued into grassland and then into forest.

As Stone walked, he was tailed by John Cobb. Cobb was slender and younger than Stone though old in the face with sharp cheeks. He scribbled endlessly in his pocket-book as he stepped across the sand. He looked around and then buried himself in his book for a few moments, looked again and contemplated what to write, eventually making up his mind and going back to his book. He was clean shaven and weathered; his face eroded like cliffstone from wind, rain, and English winters. John Cobb had come to the New World as a renowned cartographer and like Stone, occasional pirate and privateer.

While Adam Stone was nearly peerless in his raiding of cities along Spain's north coast, Cobb had little to do with these things. Stone had the power to bring gold and precious things back to England seemingly on demand. He capsized ships and directed heroic maneuvers in the thick of battle. He executed prisoners and sold the gold from their uniforms in Africa and Greece for immense riches. He dreamed of a day that he sat at the head of the table in some elaborate London dining hall, sharing stories of his exploits to an audience of goggling girls. Cobb on the contrary, chose the sea for the sake of its anonymity. He sought a life that he could manage himself, without the meddling noses of neighbors, tax collectors, and soldiers sniffing out his affairs. When Adam Stone asked him to be his cartographer for his journey to the New World, Cobb could not think of a better way to disappear. The two men understood each other in these differences; Stone played to Cobb's nature. He knew Cobb was immovable and piously solace in his quest for novelty in the New World. And Cobb, considering the stature of Stone's exploits, understood the most important thing about him: Adam Stone was not a bad man; he was almost a good man.

On the beach, Cobb waddled behind Stone with his face to his book. A nearly divine rush of blood impelled his body. He could hardly believe where he stood. He felt with every step he took, the cosmic weight of such a discovery as this world, this New World, and this new Virginia. The scope of the present shook him with inspiration. He was overwhelmed with the urge to sketch the creeks and valleys and coasts in a sleepless marathon of discovery in search of the soul of the continent. He would make it his *life's work* to discover the soul of this continent, he decided there on the beach. What a privilege it was to stand before this barren canvas of earth, to see it in its natal holiness behind its linen swaddling with a lifetime to consider what it may grow to be. Would it be a shy and feeble world, this new Virginia? Would it lie in compliance like Europe, shaking its tail sat at the foot of its master? Or would it be a brash world; noisy and without shame, destined and wild to the ways of history. Would it be a muse to many men? Would it inspire great arts, songs, and poems? Who would come born from her sands? Who would be baptized in her rivers? He could feel lightning run from the soft stir of his step to his boney fingers, shaking with joy as he walked the coast. His imagination floating high above him, twirling tales of mystery in the new air. If there was any man ever born for the ways of this New World, John Cobb was he.

Some way down the beach, Thomas Stone, grown son of Adam, was the one to discover the footprints. Two sets—one smaller than the other—rushed up the sand to the grassland and into the forest. Near the footprints there were coals and scraps of provisions. The men gathered around and exchanged words over the scraps. It was no question to Stone whose prints they were. Stories from the Spanish and Dutch and Portuguese of a native people in the New World had been popular for over one-hundred years, especially among seamen, and England had not forgotten what had happened at Roanoke nine years prior—the disappearance of that colony was largely attributed to a massacre conducted by the native tribes of Virginia. As such, Indians had become a rather popular topic of dinner conversation in England. They had even been featured in cartoons and jokes concerning colonization. They were feared and belittled from folks who had never met them—folks whom the Indians themselves did not yet know existed. The war against the redman had begun in the mind of the English without having first fired a shot. It had been understood, though unsaid, from the first news of their existence that if England was to participate in the great colonization of the New World, the Indians must go. By 1599, England was on the outside of a snowglobe looking in, while those inside were still unaware of the glass around them.

***

The initial days in New Bristol were full of celebration. The tents were raised, the wine was shared, and music prevailed along the seaboard. Adam Stone, with all of his captain's charisma, kept spirits high, merrily mingling with his crew, his passengers, his new neighbors, giving glorious speeches and saying tender prayers, winning the hearts and minds of his companions with the grace of a prophet. John Cobb set off exploring each morning, returning in the evenings with various nuts, pinecones, weeds, leaves, and carcasses, all scribbled in his notes next to drawings of streams, trees, and hills. He was high with excitement of his new life. He felt the importance in all that he did.

Only a month removed from their arrival, Stone and Cobb oversaw a territory that reached nearly three miles inland by which their colony would continue expansion. Tents and supply nests were scattered all about the beach, almost resembling a town. The crude outlines of basic structures and the groundwork for a church were underway on the plateau overlooking the water. Bricklayers enlisted children to tread clay hour after hour, day after day, as they prepared to dry and fire the hundreds of bricks that had already been molded. The farmers had found relatively fertile land about a mile westward. They began the basic woodwork for a large farmhouse to keep the cattle, pigs, goats, and sheep that were brought on *The Rose Marie* to be bred and designated to a variety of fates. On the farmland, they moved up and down the clearing, digging rows and rows of planting holes—holes that waited to receive for the first time in their history, the seedlings of wheat, rye, apples, cherries, and barely. They built fences around their crops to limit the stomping of deer and intrusion of rabbits and field mice and other vermin. The young children, including Stone's twin boys, Simon and Andrew, were assigned to scout for trees and bushes that were starting to bud with nuts or berries. They marked them so that when harvest came later in the summer, they could gather such things and begin to cultivate those trees and plants themselves.

During this period, supplies within the colony were being used economically, spirits were fervent, and pride was rampant. For the first time since the beginning of the colonial age, England was actively nurturing a functioning settlement.

It was on June 14, 1599 that John Cobb first made contact with Nanticoke Indians when their paths crossed in the woods somewhere between New Bristol and the Nanticoke village. The Nanticoke were lead by the chief of the village, Machk, who in turn was led by a young man who had claimed to witness the arrival of the settlers some weeks before. The young man introduced himself to John Cobb as Patamon.

Upon their meeting, Cobb invited the Nanticoke to join him in New Bristol where at first the whites sneered and nearly took up arms against the tribe. Foul names were cast and some vague dramas arose between some men of the colony and some prideful Nanticoke warriors. It was Patamon who stepped forward first and offered his hand of peace. Cobb stood with him, representing his own people. When the commotion settled, Adam Stone ordered a feast be held to commence the union between the two distant worlds.

Over the course of several weeks, the Nanticoke slowly became a constant presence in New Bristol. Patamon and Machk left and returned to the settlement several times, each time bringing gifts and more people to meet and interact with the exciting strangers. There were always assorted Indian men helping to cut timber, raise buildings, and gather fish. After a month, a growing fondness for the tribe radiated between the circles of the English. Men began to praise the Indians for their impressive sense of intuition and natural skillset. They were surprised at their peaceful nature and willingness to assist in labor. The two nations dined together often and worked together constantly. The Nanticoke were a great help to the English farmers, helping them with everything from planting to identifying certain malevolent weeds and insects that would spoil their crops. They picked out locusts and worms and beetles that stunted the growth of plants, and helped to dig irrigation ditches to keep the soil moist and fruitful. They brought corn and sunflowers to the people of New Bristol. Machk often traded tobacco for wine, and took wine back to his village at the delight of the tribe.

The Nanticoke also helped the settlers to build wigwams. These homes were built from branches and saplings driven deep into the ground. The framework was tied together with vines and various hide strips, while the outside was covered with sheets of hide and cedar bark and bulrush mats making them more weather resistant than some of the old rugged tents that had been brought over from England. A fire could be built in the center of a wigwam, with a hole at the top to provide a chimney for the smoke. Initially, some of the settlers were opposed to living in the wigwams, seeing them as primitive or rough-hewn, but once they realized that the wigwams were closer in design to a stone house than the tents were, a dozen wigwams sat happily smoking along the flatlands of New Bristol.

During these early weeks, Patamon and Cobb forged a meaningful friendship and spent nearly all of their waking hours together. Patamon led Cobb through the dense coastal forests, sharing with him places to hunt, to fish, and to trap. As Cobb mapped the land, he and Patamon taught each other words and shared stories and legends from their cultures. Cobb began the long process of teaching Patamon English and the Nanticoke man's mind spun with visions of the European world, visions still incomprehensible to him. He was not afraid of the white-man, nor did he admire him, but he was infinitely fascinated by what world they could have possibly come from.

It was not long that Patamon's wife, Aponi, and son, Powa, joined him in New Bristol. Aponi became quick friends with Anna Stone, teenage daughter of Adam. Aponi taught Anna to weave baskets and to spin clay. Anna taught English to Aponi and Powa.

Powa, although shy at first, settled in finely to life in New Bristol. By the end of June, he and Simon and Andrew Stone were inseparable. They each carried equal fascinations for each other, in a way that only a child's limitless imagination could. For the children, this felt like an opportunity to incorporate the world of fairytales into their own lives. They littered the beach with the devices of their games. They shared clothes and toys and climbed trees upon the backs of one another. They spoke in languages unknown—unbound hybrids of their own tongues and the lawless inventions of their minds—childspeak and literary at once.

Of course the colony was not without its prevailing prejudices. Sarah Stone, wife of Adam, strongly disapproved of the inclusion of the Indians in the settlement all together. She spoke hideously of the Indians to some of the other women in New Bristol. One night, she claimed to her husband that she felt inclined to learn to use firearms for her own safety, boasting of her willingness to kill any Indian who dare cross her wrong. Adam Stone, who had his own motives for continuing a policy of peace with the hardworking and generous people, deterred her.

Thomas Stone also harbored concerns. Although he said nothing to his father, whom he knew was enjoying the benefits of befriending the Indians, he resented them. He did not trust the heathens, calling them people of the devil and succumbing to delusions that they worked under some grand plan to suddenly betray and destroy his father. He worked begrudgingly with the native men in the forest to hunt, often being out-hunted by the Indians which of course drove him mad. The Indians had attempted to advise him on tactics and help him to identify certain animals and their habits. Thomas was resistant to their help and preferred to hunt alone.

During the summer of 1599, Stone was expecting a resupply mission from London to join him in New Bristol. The expected ship would be called *The Dawnbreaker*. This ship would carry a hundred more men and plenty of supplies, wood, iron tools, horses, muskets and munitions. Stone decided that if relations with the Nanticoke continued as smoothly as they had, he wanted to teach the Indians how to hunt with firearms. He had devised a plan to trade ammunition in exchange for the pelts they scored and then to send the pelts back to England. He predicted that with the introduction of the firearm to the Nanticoke, the production of meat and pelts would increase tenfold, and he could hold ammunition hostage in exchange for the very pelts and meat they killed. The meat would feed the colony, and he would collect the entire profit from the pelts, only having to pay the hunters in musketballs, of which he had an abundance. The settlers themselves would then be able to dedicate their time to their roles as specialists, and Thomas Stone and the other men could focus on organizing a true militia.

In the light of this plan, Cobb taught Patamon how to use a musket. He demonstrated the parts and mechanics of the weapon to Patamon, who was immediately fascinated with the machine. Its perfection and symmetry amazed him. It wasn't just that it was accurate or structurally beautiful, it seemed *impossible*. He could not fathom the ability to create such uniformity in each gun, in each small piece. How each engraving and latch and loop could be so identical to that of the gun beside it. Patamon's mind grasped for understanding. He ran his thumbs up and down the smooth, graceful barrel. The *click* of cocking the hammer felt so visceral, like the drawing of a bow but with none of the effort. He felt that little *click* go from his thumb, up his arm and to the back of his head as he brought the sights to his eyes.

Cobb opened up a cartridge demonstrating the workings of the gunpowder and the musketball together for Patamon. He showed him how to pack the cartridges himself and store them properly in his bandolier. Patamon spent days loading imaginary cartridges into the rifle, shadowing a firing position, pretending to fire, and reloading his weapon. He was taught to clean and maintain a musket, to hold it properly and store it when not in use. After countless hours over several weeks of this, Patamon was allowed to fire live rounds. The two men shot targets together each day in front of a great crowd of Indians who clapped and cheered at each powerful "little thunder" that Patamon sent off. It wasn't long before they were all pleading with Adam Stone for their very own musket. For the small price of five trophies—beaver, deer, fox, or anything alike—Stone had no qualms handing out additional muskets to the eager Indians. He could already feel gold sagging his pockets.

One facet of English life that particularly astounded the Nanticoke was the domestication of the horse. Even more than the concept of the firearm, the Nanticoke were exhilarated with the possibilities of taming such a strong beast, making a companion out of a creature so uniformly utilitarian. There were only two horses in New Bristol, one being a farm nag and the other being a cavalry stallion shared by Stone and Cobb. Patamon immediately recognized the humanity in the animal. Never before had he had the opportunity to look a creature in the face so candidly. What amazed him most was that it so lucidly stared back at him, recognizing him like a friend. Before Patamon ever even rode the horse, he spent days grooming him and feeding him. He called him softly by his name and rubbed and kissed his snout, looking him in the eyes when he spoke to him. He pulled the flies from his mane and the stones from his hooves. A great fire of respect burned inside him for the creature—more respect than any European had felt for a horse in centuries. *There is a man in him,* he thought.

Patamon began to ride every day, improving little by little. Before too long, Patamon was controlling the horse at a full gallop through the labyrinth of the forest, which enthralled him to the point of boyhood joy, and Cobb even became suspicious that his steed preferred the Indian to himself.

With Patamon's ability to ride, the two men began the hardy campaign of blazing a trail between New Bristol and the Nanticoke village wide enough to fit a horse-drawn wagon. With the ability to send wagons between the two villages, they could trade much more efficiently and visit each other more often without the trouble of the two-day journey.

The first day that Cobb visited Patamon's village, he was welcomed skeptically by those who had not yet been to New Bristol—mostly women, children, and unable men. Most of the Nanticoke hid in their homes, peering out of peep holes and listening through walls at Cobb and his strange manner of speaking and moving. His shirt and coat astonished the village. The precise stitching and bright red color, made so by fine English dye, blinded their eyes in bewilderment. Some optioned to touch it, feeling the soft wool of his garment over and over.

To win their trust, John Cobb brought gifts to the village. Not only did he bring an abundance of wine, but he brought coins—metal money—with the faces of men carved into them. He also brought with him jewelry, rare stones, metal crosses, blankets of wool and a few pairs of shoes.

Patamon revealed to Cobb the acres and acres of crops that surrounded his village. The Nanticoke were incredibly proficient farmers. They had planted corn and beans, and dried them for later use. Women and children tended to gardens of squash, pumpkins, sunflowers, greens, and tobacco. They collected a variety of nuts and eggs.

The village rested on the Nanticoke River, the lifeblood of the tribe. The river's southern mouth opens at the Chesapeake Bay and the northern mouth into the Delaware Bay, cutting in half the Delmarva Peninsula. The first night John Cobb ate with the Nanticoke, they prepared clams, oysters, mussels, crabs and fish all taken from the saltwater bays. They ate in bowls made of shells and with cutlery made of bones. They decorated their dining area with the heads of bears, deer, birds and rabbits. John Cobb felt honored to know the Nanticoke and remarkably, the Nanticoke were pleased to know him.

***

On August 21, 1599 a sea vessel fast approaching the shore caught the attention of all who were milling about New Bristol. The Nanticoke stood still like cold stone admiring the sight. The brooding silhouette, a speck at the edge of the earth creeping towards them, silenced the entire colony.

Adam Stone demanded that a feast be in order to welcome the newcomers from *The Dawnbreaker*. The Stone children and some of the Indians began hauling baskets of squash and corn to the colony from the outskirts. The women began work in several different kettles over several different fires, preparing a various spread of meats with thick gravies and spices. The camp smelled of celebration. This hustle carried on for some hours and finally, the ship approached the dock. Adam Stone waited at the dock to greet the captain, a burly man with a colorful presentation, not unlike Stone himself though he was clean shaven. He had the look of a statesman, and wore his decorations and weapons with high esteem and honor. His name was Geoffrey Locke.

Locke was a man of massive stature. He resembled Adam Stone in one sense with his long black hair, colorful wardrobe, straight spine and large chest like a ship's hull. He wore a Spanish style hat, the kind that dips to one side with a feather on the other. The colors about his person made him look like a parrot or a peacock. He commanded everyone and everything in his presence with a fluttering grace. He was confident and tall, with hands like bear paws. However, he differed greatly from Adam Stone in that he was a notable statesman. He had little sympathy for piracy or the riotous life of privateering, trading, or really any seafaring in general. Nor did he care for the prospect of Indians in the colony. He spoke to Stone in a supercilious manner.

It was received that Locke was not to stay in New Bristol long; he had come to perform two exact tasks:

Firstly, to deliver supplies and people to the colony, and secondly, to summon a representative back from New Bristol to London.

Queen Elizabeth and those who directed the kingdom's pursuits of colonization requested that either Stone or Cobb return to London to personally detail the progress of the colony and to provide any maps, documents and further intelligence relating to it. Afterwards, they would be permitted to return to New Bristol aboard a brand-new ship-of-the-line, full of another round of settlers, supplies and provisions for the winter.

Naturally, by order of command, it should have been Cobb who returned to England so Stone could stay and lead the colony, but Stone could not resist the prospect of meeting with Her Majesty in person and quickly elected himself to go, leaving Cobb in charge of the colony in his absence.

***

It is unclear exactly how and why the violence commenced, but some days after Stone's departure for England, an English boy named Matthew was carried from the woods by Thomas Stone having been wounded by a series of arrows. Thomas Stone's retelling of events involved a dispute over hunting territory, and the killing of an Indian boy who would later be identified as the son of Machk, the Nanticoke chief. Matthew would live, but his wounding would initiate a blood feud that wrought terror in the hearts of the English settlers. Thomas and Sarah Stone would rally around the violence, reconceptualizing the Nanticoke as "Indian intruders," and gaining the roaring support of their fearful peers.

Cobb and Patamon both did what they could to resolve the dispute peacefully, but after days of small-scale skirmishes, the fighting culminated in a horrifying nighttime raid of New Bristol by the Nanticoke. Every man in New Bristol came forth from their homes with or without weapons to defend their families. Wigwam's stewed in flames and people poured from their burning homes, alight like birchwood, tossing themselves into the sea, emerging black and hairless like salamanders. The fighting raged for hours up and down the colony with nearly half of the population of New Bristol left dead by the time the Nanticoke disappeared back into the sleeping forest. In the predawn hush, the stench of burnt flesh and boiled blood filled the air. Pools of blood ran down the beach and into the ocean where the lip of the water was stained red. Bodies, mutilated and hacked littered the grounds so that no man could walk without stepping over the corpse of his brother or his wife or his son. Amongst the dead colonists, with three arrows through her breast and a one-inch valley through the back of her skull, was Sarah Stone.

In the subsequent days, Thomas Stone won the dispirited hearts and minds of the New Bristolites and swore revenge on the savages who butchered their families and brethren. John Cobb's pacifism was perceived as weak and sympathetic to the enemy. He was quickly impeached from his position of power under riotous conditions and replaced by the eighteen-year-old Stone boy who painted his mother as the axiomatic martyr of the colony. Cobb would find solace only in his secret meetings with Patamon.

The two men concurred that to stay in New Bristol would be to fall victim to a conflict that they did not believe in. They devised a plan of escape. On a rainy night, when New Bristol was huddled in their tents and wigwams, still mourning their dead, John Cobb kidnapped the effectively orphaned Stone children—Anna, Simon, Andrew, and the infant Christopher—and with Patamon, Aponi, and Powa, commandeered two wagons pulled by matched teams and disappeared into the west. It was September 14, 1599.

four

ON August 15, 1599, ten days before Adam Stone departed New Bristol for England aboard *The Dawnbreaker*, English forces were ambushed near the town of Boyle in western Ireland by Irish rebel forces. It was the seventh year of the Nine Years' War, a war in which the prevailing English House of Tudor was attempting a total conquest of Ireland. At this point in the war, the Spanish were supplying the Irish with weaponry and supplies, and Irish commander Hugh O'Neill's rebel forces were looking for a second decisive blow to the English after their gallant victory at the Battle of the Yellow Ford in 1598.

On the English side, Queen Elizabeth understood that to beat the persistent Irish, she must smother them. The war had already lasted far longer than she anticipated and the momentum had suddenly and starkly turned in favor of the Irish. To put an end to the conflict once and for all she sent Robert Devereux, 2nd Earl of Essex, in April of 1599 with 17,000 troops (5,000 more than were ever supplied by England to mainland Europe during the Eighty Years' War). With such daunting numbers, Elizabeth was sure to exterminate the last of the rebellion by year's end. During the summer however, there were a series of miscommunications between Devereux's camp in Ireland and his superiors in England regarding supplies and transports that were to take Devereux and his men from their location on the coast to their objective of Sligo Town.[20] An embarrassing lack of administrative efficiency denied Devereux the provisions, munitions, and requisite pack animals in time for his campaign. Time was precious and the Irish army was growing by the day; Devereux became impatient and ordered his men to set off on foot for Sligo Town undersupplied. During their march, Devereux got word of a besieged English-occupied castle, Collooney Castle, commanded by Donough O'Connor.[21] Devereux immediately sent a regiment of 1,700 men, under the command of Sir Conyers Clifford, to relieve the besieged castle.

Clifford and his English detachment marched through the Curlew Mountains and were actively closing in on a gorge called Curlew Pass. When Red Hugh O'Donnell, the Irish commander of the aforementioned siege, got word of the English troop movement, he handed command of the siege to his cousin, Niall Garbh O'Donnell[22] while he personally led 2,500 of his reserves to intercept the English march in Curlew Pass. O'Donnell spent several days fortifying the sides of the pass with downed trees, positioning archers and musketeers in the thick of the brush that surrounded the road.

In the afternoon of the 15th of August, Clifford's Englishmen were starving and exhausted, braving the undersupplied march the best they could. They trudged on with empty stomachs, demoralized for days. When they finally reached the pass, Clifford rallied his men, promising them wagons of beef once they had reached their objective. They set off for the final leg of the march at the apex of the pass when they came under intense Irish gunfire and arrow attack from both sides. They'd been ambushed. Clifford panicked and despite the ambush, pushed his men up the hill in haste where there appeared to be lightly defended Irish barricades. Little did he know, O'Donnell had hidden Irish skirmishers all along the pass, who engaged in hit-and-run attacks for the entire duration of the English advance. The English vanguard proved confident against the rebels for about ninety minutes, at some points taking up defensive positions and repelling charging infantry that poured from the thick of the forest, but as their advance continued, it became more apparent to Clifford that they were outnumbered and out-fortified. The English suffered from a severe lack of munitions, and O'Donnell became confident that he could destroy the entire English force by sunset. Several English officers went down dead and wounded as relentless Irish gunfire poured into the ranks. At this point, the English infantry began to scatter and retreat, but were met by an intimidating force of 160 fresh Gallowglass Mercenaries from the rear who halted their retreat and allowed the main Irish force to close in, resulting in fierce hand to hand combat in the center of the pass. Clifford tried to regain control over his men, rallying a small group of infantry for a counter-charge before he himself was killed by a gunshot through the chest. With the commanding officer dead, the bulk of the infantry fled, while a small group of veteran troops maintained a rearguard action, continuing to fight on to allow the remaining army to retreat. Sir Griffin Markham, commander of the 200 English cavalry present, charged heroically uphill against boulders, bodies and fallen trees, temporarily driving back the Irish regulars, buying time for the rearguard infantry to retreat before his cavalry were surrounded by Irish sharpshooters still hidden in the trees and cut down mercilessly. Markham himself was shot but not fatally.

The Irish routed the English forces down the mountainside until the English found shelter across their own lines. There, the wounded laid in unsanitary garrisons dying of typhoid and dysentery for days after the battle. Some estimates record English fatalities as high as 1,000 while the total Irish casualties were likely under 200.

Following the battle, Robert Devereux, 2nd Earl of Essex, further proved his inadequacy when he declared a truce with the Irish, unbeknownst to the Queen, and subsequently fled Ireland in cowardice. He reached London on September 28. Upon his arrival he beckoned Elizabeth to make peace. Of course at this point in the war, a defeat to the Irish not only meant a loss of all English territory in Ireland and a global embarrassment of English military prowess, but also a loss to the Spanish who had had a steady hand in informing, supplying, and puppeteering the entire Irish rebellion from Iberia. The following day, Devereux was put on trial for blatant disobedience of the Crown and for arranging a treaty for peace under no such instruction to do so. This incident became one of the greater scandals of Elizabeth's reign.

During this period in her reign, Queen Elizabeth was already facing grisly criticism. Less than ten years earlier, she had sent Sir Frances Drake and a fleet of one-hundred-fifty ships to Spain under the guise of the *English Armada*, a counter to the *Spanish Armada*, in which the English were decisively defeated. The campaign marked a beginning to Spanish rule that lasted for over a decade. Just after that in 1591 Henry IV, a Protestant, inherited the French throne. A Protestant king in Catholic France was naturally met with violent upheaval from the Catholic League, and social unrest that neared civil-war-conditions battered the landscape of France in the early 1590s. A military catastrophe occurred when Elizabeth unwisely sent men to France to support the Protestant cause and less than half of them lived to return to Britain.[23]

Just as she shook off the shame that consumed her from the failures of these two humiliating campaigns, the Irish took a stand at Curlew Pass and drove the stake deeper into her poor heart. By September of 1599, Elizabeth had gained a reputation for being weak and lacking control over her commanders. Her choices were second guessed by the English public. The costs of never-ending wars grew and grew and the country was simultaneously being hit by a series of poor harvests that ruined the economy. A huge portion of able adult men were enlisted in the military and as a result of that, domestic commerce suffered greatly. The tax burden was increasing rapidly and quality of life for the commoner in England was considered miserable. She became paranoid that her allies were betraying her or that her friends were spies, and began employing spies of her own who, all with separate interests in mind, delivered conflicting information to her which made her paranoia run even more rampant. She relied heavily on propaganda to maintain any sense of public affection, a tactic that proved relatively useless in the end. To say that Queen Elizabeth was unconcerned with Adam Stone's wellness report on New Bristol in late September of 1599 would be an understatement.

***

On the return voyage to England, Adam Stone became considerably fond of but not close to Geoffrey Locke. The two men traded war stories, tales of glory, ideas and opinions on foreign affairs, the Spanish, colonization, and the Queen herself. Locke dangled the ever-tempting prize of royalty in front of Stone's face each day as they cut across the Atlantic—the old forlorn Atlantic, now the center of the universe, abused and worn and gray like an old man's face.

Locke teased him profusely, telling him he would be in line for nobility if he was able to keep the Indians tamed and establish a consistent cash crop of some sort. Stone was delighted to detail his plan of securing and shipping pelts back to England, and even raised a discussion about the potential profit that could be accrued from that marvelous, abundant golden herb the Spanish called tobacco.

When *The Dawnbreaker* reached London, Stone was groomed, dined, and entertained for several days before meeting the Queen. He had dinner with Locke's family where he met Robert Cecil who took him to see Shakespeare on The West End. Stone was giddy to tell Sarah of the production and the dinner and all of the fine people he had met in London who were proud of him and his family.

When Stone finally did meet the Queen, she was in a fit of anxiety. It was September 28, the day Devereaux had unexpectedly returned to London, and the entire royal court was insomniac in preparation for his trial. Stone's meeting was constantly interrupted by aides and messengers pouring into the room with notes and whispers for Her Majesty. Stone sat patiently, eager to get on with demonstrating his progress.

He told her of the great success they'd achieved in the way of agriculture. He described the walls of the fort that were being constructed on the hill, overlooking the sea. He explained their contact with the Indians and the indoctrination of the Nanticoke into New Bristol. He requested a wave of masons come on the next ship; he wanted smiths and tailors and cobblers to help make the colony feel more like home. The fatigued Queen passively and quickly obliged all of his requests.

"I am quite pleased to heareth ev'rything is going as did plan, Mast'r Stone," the Queen said. "I trusteth thou shall continueth to groweth our colony acc'rding to mine own wishes. P'rhaps the title of Earl is in order upon thy furth'r successes."

And with that, she paid him something nice, left the room, and an aide entered and guided Stone to meet the captain of the ship that he would be sailing back on.

Stone set sail for New Bristol once again on October 5. The ship was called *Aquae Sanctae*, and was captained by a decidedly uninteresting man called Brown. With Stone came 108 settlers, typical provisions—guns, cattle, horses, and tools—and a personal aid of Elizabeth's to document the further progress of the colony.

The journey was painless. Stone often stood atop the bow of the *Aquae Sanctae* pointing out wave formations and bundles of clouds, seemingly recognizing corners of the ocean from his previous trips as if he were looking out at a familiar countryside. He warmed all the new travelers with tales of New Bristol. In late nights under the siren moon he told stories of the colonies to the fresh settlers. He spoke of the construction of grand houses. He talked of his family and how Sarah Stone led a team of women who cooked exotic New World meats that tasted nothing like they'd ever had before. He primed the farmers, telling them of the gloriously fertile land and ensuring them that they would be arriving in time to harvest the last of the crops. The children aboard the *Aquae Sanctae* were excited to meet Simon and Andrew and to learn from Anna who read and instructed the little ones each morning. Spirits aboard *Aquae Sanctae* were high and heroic.

The ship arrived in New Bristol on October 29. There were no fatalities on the voyage, and everybody aboard was buzzing to stand on solid ground again. It was a cold day with gray skies and a brisk fog that masked the land. When land first came into eyesight from the sea, the deck of the *Aquae Santae* erupted in cheers. Whistles and prayers lit the air. But as they rolled in closer, they saw no movement through the cracks of fog. There was no smoke or fire; seemingly nothing at all. The passengers thought that their cheers of revelry would be answered from those on the shore, but there was no answer. Crowds gathered on both sides of the ship's deck to look upon the colony. The gay energy of the deck became a muffled low whisper. Upon approaching the harbor closer and closer, it became pain-fully apparent to everybody aboard that there was nobody in New Bristol. There was no progress. It was quiet, color-less, and empty. An aura of nervousness took over the masses. Stone shouted in vain, cursing aloud for a moment before gathering himself and imploring a group of men with guns to follow him off the ship. They dropped anchor and Stone stood at the bow in shambles at what he saw amidst the fog.

They stepped onto the land and walked through the center of the settlement. Tents were collapsed, wigwams burned to ash, guns, clothes and supplies scattered and picked over by animals. Squirrels, racoons and birds ran rampant through the camp, living in the ruins of homes and inside bins and crates and bags. The most obvious horror, the horror that all of the new settlers noticed, were the bodies and their stench. Hundreds of bodies sat rotting on the beach, inside of tents and strewn across each other. Dozens of them were ratscavenged, missing limbs or completely open at their centers—entrails emptied carelessly to the salt of the high tide. Scores of fat, black, happy birds spread into the air as Stone and the men stomped through the grounds and sent them away. Most of the bodies had wounds that indicated combat. Others, mostly those that lay inside the tents, were without injury or trauma, but instead were just pale and simply dead. Stone noticed the number of Nanticoke that lay amongst the English.

It was not long after Cobb escaped New Bristol that Thomas Stone organized a counterattack on the Nanticoke village. He had convinced himself and the colony that Cobb had defected to the Indians and that Machk had ordered him to kidnap Anna and the children.

Thomas and his men struck the Nanticoke village one night, killing dozens and razing most of the village. Thomas was subsequently killed in the raid. When the remaining militia returned to New Bristol, all was quiet for some days as a cold front passed through the coast. With it, came a horrendous bout of pneumonia that swept through the colony. It killed mostly women and children at first, and it killed them quickly. There weren't enough able men to dig the number of graves that were needed to bury the dead. As the death toll rose and the morale of New

Bristol was at its most fragile, Machk struck the English once again. Anybody who had not died from pneumonia already, was slaughtered by Machk's men.

Adam Stone walked the colony alone, trying to find and recognize the remains of his brethren. He saw Richard Stuart, eyeless, split open at the stomach, bloated and blue. He saw Eda and Jean-Paul, huddled together in a tent like stone statues. There were corpses burned—bundles of bones that were once farmers, mothers, sailors, and settlers, left to anybody's best guess of who they might have been. He saw the pile of Indian bodies that were never buried. They were decomposed and rotted, half-frosted together like an iceberg of death. Horse carcasses were littered about the camp amongst the dead. The smell was so strong many of the men behind Stone vomited. They used their scarves and coats to mask their faces.

Stone looked frantically for his wife and kin like somebody does at a harbor, waiting for their loved one to emerge from the crowd of the dock. He turned over the raw bodies of women to see their faces. There were women he knew, and some that he did not. He saw children, mutilated, hairless, and unrecognizable to his eyes, that he knew in his heart could not be Simon, could not be Andrew. As his steps grew more urgent, and his throat swelled, he finally came across a wood headstone in a cul-de-sac of shallow graves on the outskirts of the ruins.

Sarah Stone
February 2, 1565-September 8, 1599
***

After having spent some days in New Bristol, recovering what he could from the rubble, Adam Stone and fifty armed men traversed to the Nanticoke village with vengeance on their mind. Stone had prepared his men to fight and to kill every last Indian of the village, but when they arrived, they found the very same scene. The village was razed, the bodies were battered and decomposing, and there were dozens of dead from apparent sickness.

The pneumonia had wiped out the Nanticoke even faster than the English. When Machk made his final strike, he himself and most of his warriors were sick. They barely had the numbers to carry out the attack at all. The survivors returned to their village and died with their families within days. Amongst the dead that Stone found in the Nanticoke village was Thomas Stone.

Adam led a funeral procession back to New Bristol and buried Thomas' body beside Sarah's. An army of flies followed him from one village to the other. He said a prayer, and added Thomas's name to the list of dead.

Sarah Stone-Dead; unknown causes
Thomas Stone-Dead; combat
Anna Stone-Dead; burned or mutilated
Simon Stone-Dead; burned or mutilated
Andrew Stone-Dead; burned or mutilated
Christopher Stone-Dead; burned or mutilated
Richard Stuart-Dead; combat
Eda Stuart-Dead; likely disease
Jean-Paul Stuart- Dead; likely disease
Henry Martin-Dead; combat
Francis Brian-Dead; burned or mutilated
Thomas Smith-Dead; unknown causes, likely disease
John Cobb-Dead; burned or mutilated
Geoffrey Lewis-Dead; combat
Elizabeth Lewis-Dead; burned or mutilated
John Pence McClaughlin-Dead; combat
Mary McClaughlin-Dead; burned or mutilated
Samuel Finn-Dead; unknown causes, likely disease
And so on and so forth…

***

When London discovered that the entire colony was lost, Elizabeth immediately discontinued the venture that was 1599's colony of New Bristol. It had suffered seemingly the same fate as Roanoke, and that fate spoke quite clearly to Elizabeth: *Do not colonize the New World*. She had officially given up.

For weeks, Stone tried to reason with her. He tried to convince her, and himself, that if given another chance and ten ships or *five ships* that he could resurrect the colony and avenge his fallen family. He begged her to send the military to the settlement and guard her borders while he re-established the colony. He asked for trust, for money, for cows, for weapons, for soldiers, all of which Elizabeth would not grant. Stone, emotionally deranged and sleepless for weeks, ceaselessly proposed that he be given one last try at saving what was once his darling, his livelihood, his little sliver of history. He attested that his success was stymied by factors outside of his control.

Not only was Elizabeth uninterested in saving New Bristol, but she was far too financially and emotionally bankrupt to even attempt it. After Devereux's trial and verdict of treason on October 1, she immediately ended the invalid treaty he had drawn with Ireland, and continued her assault on the rebellion. In November, O'Neill from the Irish Alliance sent her a document concealing terms for a peace agreement. As she attempted to navigate these negotiations, Stone persisted and continued to spin emotional tempests at her doorstep. Her hands were full as she was grievously inundated with the stress of the war and she banished Stone from her presence indefinitely.

Suffering from constant breakdowns, night terrors, tremors, and bouts of dissociation, Adam Stone was left homeless, penniless, and honorless following his banishment by Queen Elizabeth.[24]

England would not make another attempt at settling the New World until 1607 when King James I commissioned John Smith to found the settlement of Jamestown aboard the *Susan Constant*.

five

IT was late December, 1599. It may have been Christmas Day, but who was to know. John Cobb and his caravan elected to abandon one of their two wagons deep in the gully of a slow-running creek, frozen at its rims, wedged between two foam-white crests deep in the Appalachian Mountains. The whipping wind burned their faces red as they loaded the remaining wagon with the supplies of the failed one. The wood of the bad wagon was frozen and warped. The axle had cracked while navigating the wind-ripped ravine. The weight of the wagon fell upon one poor rear wheel which laid formless like kindling. There was no chance of repairing it in the storm. Cobb could hardly see his companions in front of him as the snow moved like a swarm of locusts, humming and violent between his eyes and their forms.

While the darkening earth wailed, Cobb led his party to shelter under the overhang of a cliff. It was a sort of cave with one open side which was plugged by the place-ment of the wagon. Under the cliff, Cobb built fire. The hardened travelers gathered around the trembling orange flames and slept sitting up with their blistered feet to the heat. All through the night the infant Christopher howled something abominable. He wore a fever and it was rising. His cough was ceaseless and violent and black as a coal fire. Anna Stone coddled him and cried cold tears that froze on her cheek as she watched the slow parasite of the catarrh devour her baby brother's breath from the inside. He had no way of telling them that his lungs were failing.

On the second day in the cave, Cobb slaughtered one of the horses for food. The party cooked the meat from the horse over the fire in the small cave and ate in silence. Christopher was wrapped in the hot flesh of the beast and he cried and ice froze the inlets of his small eyes while he cried and the ice dealt him a great deal of pain. The same intruding thought conquered each individual mind of the adults: *What had they done?* In their leaving New Bristol had they traded a chance at life for the sureness of death, or was it just the contrary?

When the storm passed, Cobb and Patamon packed what was salvageable of the horse meat. They set out towards the southwest on a downward slope from the high hills of the mountains. The temperature began to rise slightly, though it was still below freezing. The children walked like clumsy birds in the leather snow. Cobb rode atop one of the horses, commanding the team. Anna, Christopher, Simon, Andrew, and Powa rode in the bed of the wagon, and Patamon and Aponi rode the lone horse. After a number of days of which they'd lost count, they approached the western foothills of the range. There, Cobb spotted several stems of slithering smoke leaking from the far forest. Somebody had made fire.

***

The Shawnee village was much larger than that of the Nanticoke. There were dozens of longhouses and hundreds of people and a great sense of life that sang from the the village. As they approached, Cobb could see fires burning all over the grounds with families cooking over them. There were men talking and laughing and dragging pelts and meats throughout the streets. There were traders and small vendors on corners, some men played music with crowds of children dancing around them. The smell of fish and eggs and corn was fervent and warmed the bodies of the weary travelers who dragged themselves to the center.

There was still a purple hue in the sky from the sunrise. The thick clouds and the smoke from the fires cast a dome of lazy gray over the town that the sun couldn't penetrate. The travelers walked slowly through the fog and were met with curious eyes and speculative whispers throughout the lively town. They walked, battered and benumbed through the horde of eyes. The horses and wagon froze the Shawnee in their tracks. In the village's center, the travelers stopped and stood and allowed the eyes to assault them. Anna Stone could feel the eyes like insects crawling on her skin. It was not long before they were completely surrounded by Shawnee. Their arrival sparked a furor of mystified excitement.

The initial commotion of their arrival was remedied by Patamon. He spoke and calmed the hustling, babbling Shawnee. The great warriors of the village at first moved like goliaths through the crowd and showed their chest to the travelers, but with Patamon's word, who stood tall on the wagon, the people of the village understood immediately the dire conditions of Cobb and his party. The children looked like shriveled coral left on a sunny beach. The dark undermoon of their eyes looked like gaping holes—the skulls of exhaustion. Cobb's face was frozen in an eternal expression of sorrow. Christopher shrieked his sickened cry and Anna fell to her knees from weakness as the village gathered around. Patamon finally brought the crowd to a hush and communicated with his lifeless limbs that they were hungry.

The women cooked massive portions for the travelers, which they scarfed down gratefully. It was the most food they had eaten at one time in months. They all cleaned their plates before being led to warm beds in a longhouse.

Patamon and Aponi on the bed to his side were already in a blissful way, snoring and wrapped around each other like vines. The children too were in a heavy sleep, sunk in their hay beds in hysterical, unnatural shapes. Cobb however, laid awake, staring up at the tumbling smoke that fed the chimney. He thought of Anna Stone and Christopher who were confined to their own wigwam just across the way. He could hear the dull thunder of Christopher's moans through the walls of the two structures. He felt a helplessness inside him as he listened, a sorrow of what he had done. The infant would die, he thought. He was sure of it. But he told himself in the rebuttal of this thought that he was also sure each and every one of his party would be dead had he not left the colony. At least he hoped he was sure.

In the wigwam across the way, Anna laid with Christopher. He moaned through his teary lips. His white, bloodless ears were nearly blue. His lips were blue and hard. Anna had almost become unaware of the sounds he screamed. It was a part of her environment now; she was condemned to live in a mock of hell where the horrors of babes haunted her ears and dreams. Her life had changed. She listened to the screams. She cried in the cold. She walked now. That is what she did with her time. She listened to the screams of her brother and she walked until the blood blisters of her feet soiled her socks and froze her toes at the will of the mountain winter. She did not know where she was going, and she would never be told. Cobb would never say.

She thought about John Cobb. She watched John Cobb each day, stoic, unmoved, knowing, confident, and strong, leading her with conviction into paths no man had known, routes unseen. She cursed him some nights for what he did to her and how he had done it. She remembered the words he lured her with, telling her that her father had told him to take his kin from the colony at the first grain of danger, and that he would meet them later in the distant unknown lands. It took just a few days for her and the children to realize that this was a lie. They were not to meet their father again for the rest of their lives, and while the twin boys bellowed in sadness at this realization, Anna, having little respect for her of a father, felt conflicted in her allegiance. On the one hand, she felt that she had been bested, tricked, used. That Cobb had no right to decide her fate and pull her through a tortuous winter as such, in and out of the exotic villages of savages. She feared her brother would die. She feared that she would die. She often looked out into the nothing of the distance and dreamed that a ship had come to rescue the New Bristolites and she was sailing back to London aboard it. There she could study or marry. In fact, in the time it had taken them to cross the mountains she could have already been back and married if she'd wanted. Some days, she was sure that those other colonists were home and alive in her forgotten London.

On the other hand, she did not think of John Cobb as being of the same nature as her father. She saw goodness in his blue eyes. He was honest, he was desperate, and he was determined. She believed each word he said when he said it, even under the pretext of his initial lie. She knew he lied once so that he could tell great truths later. When he told her that she and her brothers would surely be nothing more than stone decorations on a tragic beachfront by now, she believed him. When he told her that he cared for her life and that he could not stomach the thought of leaving her behind, she believed him. When he told her that they would rest in just an hour, after they crossed the next nagging ridge, she believed him. And when he said that they would live somewhere together unseen and untouched by man, where the juvenile sins of kings and queens could not reach them, she believed him with all her sorry heart. She had grown a fondness for the sandy, boney man. She thought of the way he moved, with such admirable grace. His strong frame, his sureness of himself. His humility, his sense of humanity to the confused children, to Patamon, to Aponi, and his genuine and obvious love for Powa, that wide-open boy with a heart big enough for a thousand souls. Anna felt furious and cheated by John Cobb, but under her scorn, she thought that perhaps she did trust him. Afterall, it was of him that she was always thinking.

In the night, the Shawnee women and medicine men worked a series of oils and plants on the baby Christopher. They prayed in ceremony around him which made Anna aghast, as it all felt heathen-like. She held back tears of frustration inside the dark wigwam as the many skeletal, toothless Indian elders touched her, chanting and praying over the sound of her helpless baby brother squirming with pain. When they left her, she and Christopher cried together for what felt like hours before her sadness nulled her to sleep. She dreamed of tidal waves and crumbling mountains and siren screeches far inside the deep Hades of the oceans. She struggled in her sleep, writhing like a leper on the soil floor of her wigwam, acting out her dreams, running from everything. When she woke up in the crisp quiet of the new day, to her surprise, Christopher was not crying.

***

That morning, Powa and the brothers Stone were introduced to some of the children of the village. A sort of comfort took over Powa. He fell right into line with the Shawnee, feeling welcomed and brotherly with them. The Shawnee children were fascinated by his ability to speak English and his wearing of European clothes. He wore English boots and pants. He, Simon, and Andrew passed around their coats and shoes to let the other children examine and wear them. The language barrier certainly didn't stop them from laughing. They played ball and they wrestled and they sliced through the village in a never-ending game of tag that sent birds flying and old men cursing and parents laughing.

Patamon and Aponi had amassed a great crowd in the village center as the Shawnee turned to them for answers. They did not speak the same language as the Shawnee, but they shared stories effectively with the use of signs and some few shared words. They explained in some fleeting impression of hands and sounds, the arrival of Cobb and the origins of the white-man. They detailed the violence that had caused them to flee New Bristol. The Shawnee were captivated by the stories and treated the two Nanticoke with the respect of elders or shamans. Their journey across the mountains—well known mountains and considered to be impenetrable to the Shawnee—with the likes of the mysterious Europeans, cast them as some spiritual figures—guides, Great Spirits, or embodiments of manitou. The great theater of the two Nanticoke continued for days and nights, with their charades ranging from the dramatic, eerie arrival of *The Rose Marie,* to the distinctive legends passed down through the Nanticoke tradition. These gatherings, often marked with song, dance, food, laughter, prayer, and fellowship would be among the most unique cultural exchanges on the continent for hundreds of years to come. Not even a flicker of a thought of violence spoiled the joyous carnival.

In all, the Shawnee accommodated the travelers for three weeks. The runaways traded in much of their battered clothing for fresh blankets and pelts to get through the rest of the winter. The Shawnee women were kind enough to take some of the dilapidated wear—especially shoes—and repair them over the course of a few days. The kindness the Shawnee had shown the caravan was unconditional.

On their last evening in the village, Aponi joined the women in cooking their farewell supper. There was not much corn left over from the fall's harvest, but what was left had been dried and preserved. It was still brittle and brown as Aponi peeled it and threw the corn into the stew. She was particularly good with stews. She moved the pot about the fire, heating its contents at just the right angles to thicken or soften the base. She stirred the pot as she mastered the fire. She picked apart the turkey with her fingers, running her hard fingers up and down the bones of the bird, pushing meat into a pot over a separate fire to cook the meat thoroughly before adding it to the stew. The vegetables in the pot were thick, and an orange paste bubbled inside of it. When the turkey was cooked, she slid the tender meat into the pot and then stirred it too. Cooking with the Shawnee reminded her of her own people. She thought of the women that she cooked with in the Nanticoke village, seemingly a lifetime ago. She wondered how they were and if they thought of her often. The Shawnee women watched her as she worked.

Over supper, Cobb convened with the chief. Cobb was adamant to know everything he could about the lands beyond the village in every direction. The Shawnee chief explained that the tribe's territory extended hundreds of miles to the west. The border was defined by a mighty river—the largest in the land. The voyage to the river would take them several weeks on foot. There was an abundance of caves and caverns along the way as well as dense forests, rivers with lethal rapids, bears, coyotes, and cats. Once they reached the mighty river, however, the land would become much fairer.

The chief volunteered to guide the travelers to the edge of the Shawnee territory. He would assemble a team and act as a guide and translator for the travelers. Cobb was pink with glee.

The next morning Patamon and Aponi hoisted the children into the wagon. They squirmed and traded places for a few minutes until they'd found an orientation that made sense to their sprawled, awkward bodies. Simon and Andrew and Powa had been silent for the morning. Their imaginative wonder of the land that awaited them stunned them into a nervous rumination. Between them, the empty-armed Anna Stone could hardly be described as living as she sat with her back against the wagon wall, ignoring with the utmost apathy what was occurring around her and in turn, being quite ignored. The wagon was intentionally quiet as they got underway.

The horses pulled away from the village in a convicted, optimistic hull. Hundreds of Shawnee waved at the mysterious migrant strangers who were sent away to the west. Cobb's eye was hopeful and bright, his party had been fed and rested and warmed. He anticipated with enthusiasm the road ahead of them. In a day, the party would happily leave the Appalachian Mountains behind them, descending upon the Cumberland Plateau. In a week, Patamon would become the first man to win a horse race in the territory that would later be called "Kentucky," beating Cobb and his horse by one neck. And in a month, the group of eighteen travelers—seven New Bristolites and eleven Shawnee Indians—would safely reach the bank of the Mississippi River.

six

JOHN Cobb's contact with the Mississippi River was the first known occurrence in which a European traveled westward from the Atlantic Coast across the eastern part of the continent to meet the river. It would not be done again for nearly two-hundred years. While it was an incredible feat for its time, especially given the small size of his party and the unique circumstances surrounding his motives for travel, it was not the first time Europeans had explored the interior of what would later become the United States. In fact, it was not the first time a European had seen the Mississippi River.

By 1600, the Spanish claimed some three-million square miles of land in the New World—roughly six times more than the rest of their competitors combined. The Spanish crown ruled over nearly all of South America,[25] Central America, Mexico, the Caribbean, and the future U.S. state of Florida. Additionally, the future states of Texas, Oklahoma, Kansas, New Mexico, Arizona, and California were all entirely inside or had portions of territory that were inside an area known as New Spain, a viceroyalty of the Spanish crown that still remained largely unexplored.

The South American and Caribbean portions of the empire quickly became sources of profit with seemingly no expiration in sight. Silver, gold, precious metals, minerals, and crops were being shipped in the tons to Spain every day while thousands of soldiers, merchants, and artisans left Spain for the New World to seek glory and riches. Priests and conquistadors sought to spread Catholicism across the whole of the land. The Incan, Aztec and Mayan empires had all been wiped out by either battle or disease. Most of the indigenous peoples who survived these ailments were enslaved. However, the claimed colonial territories to the north of Mexico remained largely untouched by the Spanish for the first three decades of the 16th century.

Álvar Núñez Cabeza de Vaca was the first of a brief list of men who extensively explored interior portions of the United States before John Cobb did so in 1599. Cabeza de Vaca was second in command of an expedition led by conquistador Pánfilo de Narváez in June of 1527. Narváez and Cabeza de Vaca left Spain with five ships and 600 soldiers with orders to settle a peninsula north of Cuba known as *La Florida*—a peninsula that Juan Ponce de León had just discovered thirteen years prior in 1513. Narváez and his fleet stopped for supplies in Hispaniola for nearly six weeks. From there they made a stop in Cuba where he wished to buy more horses. While in Cuba, their departure was delayed by a hurricane that damaged several ships and killed dozens of his men and horses. The damage done to his fleet and crew was so significant, he was forced to remain in Cuba for the winter where his men repaired the remaining ships and rounded up additional volunteers to join them. Cabeza de Vaca called these initial setbacks a bad omen and pressed Narváez to delay the voyage. Ignoring the pleas of his advisor, the fleet made its way north towards Florida in February. Again, in a bout of unfavorable luck, the fleet was hit by another tropical storm which decimated the crews' supplies and morale. However, instead of turning around to resupply in Cuba, Narváez carried on and broke land around the Tampa Bay, critically undersupplied and exhausted. Immediately, Narváez sent out parties of men to make contact with the native peoples that inhabited West Florida and to scavenge for food. They came across a series of small villages, where he and his men communicated to the natives through sign language. He was made aware of a region north of their location called Apalachee that the natives claimed to be rich in food and gold. Narváez spent several months, despite the staunch protests from Cabeza de Vaca, pushing north and engaging in small skirmishes with a handful of different Indian villages, determined to find Apalachee. He kept a number of Indian men captive as guides and translators. Finally, near modern-day Tallahassee, the Spanish came across the largest village yet, which their captives identified as Apalachee. The village was seized with no resistance, and Cabeza de Vaca led a squad of men to thoroughly search the grounds for gold. They found nothing but masses of corn. The Spanish helped themselves to the corn, sacked the town and in their disappointment, decided to abandon the mission all together. They fled south to the coast of the Florida panhandle where they built five primitive watercraft and planned to sail west believing that they were near Spanish settlements in Mexico. In reality, there was over 1,500 miles of coast between them and the closest Spanish colony. On the 22nd of September, 1528, Narváez, Cabeza de Vaca and 242 men departed Florida from what is now known as the Bay of Horses.[26]

They sailed with the coast in sight until they reached the mouth of the Mississippi where they encountered yet another hurricane that wrecked three of the watercraft, killing all of their crew, including Pánfilo de Narváez himself. Cabeza de Vaca assumed command of the remaining eighty men and eventually reached Galveston Island of current-day Texas, and camped there through the winter. Fifteen of those eighty men survived the winter. These survivors then began to march westward in the spring where they encountered the Karankawa tribe, to whom they were held captive and enslaved for four years. Only four of the fifteen enslaved Spanish managed to escape. Cabeza de Vaca's exact route after his escape from the Karankawa is subject to considerable dispute, but it is generally agreed that he exited Texas by crossing the Rio Grande to the south, then, unable to penetrate the mountains, marched northwest, where he and his companions spent several years wandering the New Mexican desert in and out of the hands of several other tribes. It is thought that he then marched down the western coast adjacent to the Gulf of California to what is now Sinaloa, Mexico. This took him eight years. During these eight years, Cabeza de Vaca took to living with indigenous tribes peacefully for months or years at a time, adopting their customs, traditions, language, and eventually being named a healer amongst some of the contacted peoples. He later reported having a great infatuation and sympathy for the Indians. In 1537 he finally encountered Spaniards near modern-day Culiacán. He returned to Europe later that year. After returning to Spain, Cabeza de Vaca's tales of the immensity of the North American continent began to spread quickly. He spoke of seemingly infinite mountain ranges that at once morphed into steppes and silver plateaus that stretched for ten-thousand leagues. His reports of fighting Indians in dense forests and swamps captivated the curiosity of other explorers. He boasted of escaping coastal captivity and fleeing to the barren desert that took him several years to cross. His hardened journey to the coast of the Pacific Ocean was told and retold for generations. And of course, he repeated the legends that he had heard from the native people about cities of gold, and mountains filled with riches tucked away somewhere deep inside of the continent. This set the stage for dozens of ambitious imitators who wished to write the endings to these stories. One such imitator was Hernando de Soto, who was galvanized by the tales of Cabeza de Vaca to lead an expedition that would prove to be the largest of its kind on the east side of the Mississippi for nearly two-hundred years. It would also be remembered as one of the ugliest genocides during the Age of Discovery.

Hernando de Soto's story begins in Central America in 1520 where he had just been named the first governor of Panama. Soon after his arrival from Spain, he joined in on the conquest of Nicaragua behind Francisco Hernández de Córdoba, where he earned the reputation of a brilliant tactician, fearless warrior, and master horseman. In 1533, after years of holding office in Nicaragua and Panama, de Soto was deployed to Peru where Spain was entangled in a war with the Incan Empire. He served as a cavalry captain where he fought in the Battle of Cajamarca and led a heroic plundering of Incan camps where all of the Spanish officers made out with an abundance of gold and silver. Later that year, de Soto fought in the advance guard in a battle to conquer Cuzco, the capital of the Incan Empire. After a day of fighting, the Inca army withdrew from the city under the cover of the night and the Spanish plundered the capital, with de Soto again making out with considerable gold and silver, making him one of the wealthiest officers amongst his peers. In 1534, de Soto began service as lieutenant-governor of Cuzco while his Spanish superiors were constructing the city of Lima, the future capital of the territory known as Peru. He would serve as governor for several years.

At thirty-six years old, with riches beyond his wildest imagination, de Soto had returned to Spain and was admitted to the prestigious Order of Santiago. With his new title of nobility, the King of Spain granted him the right to conquer Florida, a task that excited him greatly on account of his admiration of both Juan Ponce de León and the now very famous Cabeza de Vaca. De Soto gathered a fleet of even greater numbers than Narváez's, sailing nine ships with 700 men consisting of soldiers, priests, farmers, engineers, families, and African slaves. There were also a great number of horses and Irish wolfhounds. His fleet landed in Tampa Bay in May of 1539. Days upon arriving at the port, de Soto stumbled upon a curious subject; a Spanish man who had taken up living with the Mosoco tribe named Poor Juan Ortiz.[27] Ortiz led de Soto and his men to the principal village of the Mocoso tribe where they received shelter and food. De Soto pressed the Mocoso people to identify "the greatest kingdom of the land" where he could find gold and riches. The Mocoso told him that he could find all that he was looking for in a land to the north called Apalachee. De Soto knew that this was exactly what they had told Narváez and Cabeza de Vaca, and had surmised that they had been tricked by the natives and that the true land of Apalachee was farther north still than where Narváez was led years prior. De Soto set off north in search of the true land of Apalachee. Ortiz was brought along as a translator.[28]

De Soto first pressed north near the western coast of Florida where he was ambushed several times by the Timucua tribe. He fought back, pillaging the villages that they encountered and seizing whatever food they could find. After a significant battle in the fall of 1539, de Soto and his men executed 200 boys and men, and raped and murdered the remaining women in what was known as the Napituca Massacre—the first documented intentional massacre of indigenous people by Europeans on future U.S. soil.

De Soto wintered near the Bay of Horses. It was during this stay on the Florida panhandle that he first heard word that distant tribes to the north were mining for gold. After the winter, he turned his attention to the northeast where he traversed the entire states of Georgia and South

Carolina before arriving deep in the Blue Ridge Mountains of western North Carolina. He spent over a month resting his men and horses while he sent sporadic search parties in all directions in hope of finding gold. After a month with no success, he set off west into Tennessee where he followed the Tennessee River south for some time, still without finding gold. He was dangerously low on supplies and turned his efforts back south where he spent another month of peaceful relations with the Tuskaloosa people. He knew that by this time, two supply ships would be waiting for him in the Gulf of Mexico, fresh from Havana with food, horses, weapons, munitions and men. Before departing the long journey due south, he demanded from the Tuskaloosa chief (also named Tuskaloosa) that he provide his men with women and servants for the march ahead. When Tuskaloosa refused, de Soto took him hostage. Fearing for his life, Tuskaloosa broke down and obliged de Soto's demands, telling him that he must go to the village of Mabila where there were plenty of women awaiting him and his men. De Soto thanked him and gifted him for his cooperation. De Soto set off for Mabila, but Tuskaloosa's men, knowing a faster route, beat him to the heavily fortified town. Upon his arrival, de Soto was ambushed. The battle lasted for nine hours and included a mass burning of the town by the Spanish. The encounter was the bloodiest fighting on North American soil up to that date and dealt almost 400 Spanish casualties and between 4,000 and 6,000 Indian casualties including mass civilian death. After the fighting, the Spanish supplies were reduced to nearly nothing, and they had lost a quarter of their horses. Several dozen men became sick, infected, and succumbed to their wounds in the following weeks. Fearing that word of such a disaster would reach Spain, de Soto rashly decided not to meet the supply ships in the Gulf. He instead marched his men farther inland, where they could rest and then carry on to Mexico on foot which he believed was much closer than it was. He found himself in Mississippi where they spent the next winter.

All of 1541 was plagued by skirmishes with Chickasaw tribes in central and western Mississippi and Arkansas. Poor Juan Ortiz had died in the harsh winter, making it increasingly difficult for de Soto to acquire supplies and directions. On May 8, 1541, they reached and crossed the Mississippi River, becoming the first Europeans to ever do so. The exact point of crossing is heavily disputed, but academically agreed to have been near modern-day Sunflower Landing, Mississippi. On the other side of the river, de Soto encountered a tribe he called the Tula. The two groups clashed in several bouts of heavy warfare near the Caddo River. Survivors of the Spanish expedition—including those who were veterans of the Incan campaigns years prior—would go on to describe the Tula as the fiercest and most skilled warriors they had ever encountered. The Tula dealt de Soto and his men several devastating blows, raiding his camps in the night and making off with what little supplies the Spanish had retained. Knowing that all was lost, de Soto often maniacally and nihilistically raided native settlements even when there was no prospect of practical gain by a victory. The entire year would be marked with this sort of senseless violence. Eventually, de Soto turned back east and returned to the Mississippi River where he died of an unknown illness at her banks on May 21, 1542. After three years in Florida, Georgia, North and South Carolina, Tennessee, Alabama, Mississippi, and Arkansas, de Soto found neither gold, treasures, or an adequate location for future colonization. Many of his surviving men were clothed in rags and animal skins, and were constantly battling illness, injury and starvation. The remaining caravan made a further attempt to reach Mexico by foot, wandering through Texas for some time before succumbing to starvation. Further survivors returned a third time to the Mississippi River, where they built rafts just as Cabeza de Vaca had done before them. It took them two weeks to sail down the Mississippi and into the Gulf of Mexico. During the two-week journey, they were constantly berated by arrow attacks from Indian canoe fleets that stalked them until they were spit out into the ocean. After fifty days, they reached the Mexican coastal town of Panuco. Of the 700 original colonists, 311 survived.

***

During this same time in the American Southwest, Francisco Vázquez de Coronado was on a similar mission. Coronado was a Mexican statesman and storied explorer who was appointed by the Viceroy of New Spain to command an expedition that would depart Mexico for the north where there were rumors of a city called Cíbola that was made entirely of gold. According to a man called Estevan,[29] the city of Cíbola sat atop a great mesa that was roughly the size of Mexico City and contained wealth unlike any that the conquistadors had ever seen before. In 1539, Fray Marcos de Niza, a Spanish missionary and friar, crossed Arizona with Estevan and returned to Mexico confirming such claims of a golden city, having "seen it from a distance."

Coronado and his party of 400 soldiers and 2,000 Indian allies set out for the north from Compostela, Mexico on February 23, 1540. In April, they crossed into modern-day Arizona through the Huachuca Mountains via the Montezuma Pass. From there they followed a "small stream"—likely the San Pedro River—northwards into the San Pedro Valley until they reached the edge of the wilderness where they finally descended upon Cíbola, wedged within the bend between the Dos Cabezas and Chiricahua mountain ranges just as Friar Marcos had described. However, the party was met with devastation when they realized that the "city" of Cíbola was actually a region of several ordinary pueblos with no extravagant riches whatsoever.

Marcos was disgraced and ostracized from the party, escorted in humiliation back to Mexico. [30]

From Cíbola, Coronado marched north until reaching the community of Hawikuh, a small pueblo controlled by the Zuni people just over the border of what is now New Mexico. After being refused food assistance, Coronado attacked the village and while victorious, he himself was injured in the battle. He and his men rested for several weeks in Hawikuh.

In the winter of 1540-1541[31] Coronado and his men were involved in a tense conflict with the Tiguex people who were based around the Rio Grande. This conflict became known as the Tiguex War. It resulted in the death of hundreds of natives and the destruction of dozens of pueblos. The fighting began as a Spanish attempt to commandeer the shelter of the Tiguex people, but were met with staunch resistance. During the fighting, the Spanish captured two slaves who would completely change the nature of Coronado's mission, one woman whom they called, "Big Eyes," and a man called "El Turco." Through these sources, Coronado was informed of a nation to the north called Quivira which—naturally—was built of pure gold and amassed a proverbial wealth, the likes of which have never been seen before. Coronado, already proving himself to be quite the fool for such a claim, set off through the Llano Estacado Steppe in northern Texas. While crossing the steppe, the Spanish witnessed the mass herding of buffalo firsthand. Later Coronado wrote, *"I found such a quantity of cows…that it is impossible to number them—for while I was journeying through these plains there was not a day I lost sight of them."*

As the Spanish entered the Great Plains, they came in contact with another indigenous community that was almost certainly the Apache Indians.[32] The Apache directed them southeast along the Red River until El Turco informed them that they had been traveling in the wrong direction of Quivira and needed to turn north. Upon receiving this news and several grueling weeks of constant redirection and foodless travel, Coronado became discouraged and decided to pursue the rest of the mission as a matter of reconnaissance rather than conquest. Any confidence that riches or fortune awaited him in the land of Quivira was shattered. He sent most of his party back to New Mexico, continuing north with only forty men. Ironically, it was after this decision that he finally came to find Quivira.

After a month of marching with his reduced unit, the party found themselves crossing the Arkansas River just east of present-day Dodge City, Kansas. It was there he found Quiviran Indians hunting buffalo and instructed one of his guides to communicate to the Quiviran. The Quiviran Indians cooperated with Coronado who showed no malice, and led him northeast for three days. Finally, Coronado reached the city of Quivira itself which was indeed a massive settlement of an estimated 10,000 Indians, however, it lacked the fabled riches that had inspired the expedition in the first place. After thoroughly searching the town, the Spanish found nothing but a single copper pendant amongst the bounds of corn, squash, beans, straw, and buffalo. After leaving Quivira,[33] Coronado ordered the execution of his guide, El Turco, and returned to Mexico in bankruptcy.[34]

***

It would take forty years before the Spanish attempted to colonize the land north of Mexico again. During these four decades, the dozens of tribes that the Spanish encountered in the middle of the 16th century worked to rebuild their villages, restabilize their economy from the constant raiding, pillaging and thieving they were victim to, and replenish their numbers as the mass slaughter and intentional genocide had killed entire villages and decimated up to sixty percent of entire tribes. The unintentional spread of disease had obliterated ninety percent of tribes along the

Mississippi River between Memphis and New Orleans, and the constant raping and sexual violence against the women left many of them infertile. These tribes developed a transgenerational hatred for the Spanish and word of their marches of terror spread incredibly quickly between regions during this period. The unstable situation in the Southwest culminated in the Acoma Massacre of 1599.

The groundwork for this massacre begins in 1581 when two Spanish explorers, El Chamuscado and Fray Agustín Rodríguez entered the land of the Pueblo Indians, being the first Europeans to do so since Coronado. The northernmost part of their journey was modern-day Pecos, New Mexico, where they found five-hundred well-built, four-story houses in a settlement of about 3,000 people. The Indians were described as "handsome" and "light-haired," indicating the consequences of probable cross-breeding with Coronado's army forty years before. The expedition was intentionally peaceful, with Chamuscado and Rodríguez agreeing to never forcibly attain what they wanted. After a brief exploration east of the Rio Grande, the party returned to the river's valley and moved west where they spotted the Acoma Pueblo high on a mesa, but were deterred from entering it due to winter storms. During the winter, Chamuscado, who was elderly and becoming sick, decided that he must return to Mexico. Rodríguez accompanied him and left several dozen soldiers and three missionaries in New Mexico to establish a small settlement and await his return. Three days after Chamuscado and Rodríguez's departure, one of the missionaries was killed by Indians. The soldiers, fearing for their safety with inadequate numbers, followed the bulk of the party south to Mexico despite the other two friars opting to remain in New Mexico with their Indian servants. The friars that were left behind were also attacked and killed with most of their servants being killed as well. Only two escaped and returned to Mexico to tell the tale.[35]

The next year in 1582, a wealthy Spanish adventurist living in Mexico named Antonio de Espejo got word of the butchered missionaries who were left behind in New Mexico and assembled and financed an expedition to either avenge or rescue the friars. He departed Mexico on November 10, 1582[36] and arrived in the land of the Pueblos three months later in February. Espejo described the valley of the Rio Grande as being populated by over 10,000 people all the way up to present-day El Paso, Texas. He then traveled north for fifteen days without encountering any sign of humans. He turned his focus to the west, where he arrived in the pueblo of Puala, the last known location of the two murdered friars. As his men approached the pueblo, the indigenous inhabitants fled to the hills where they hid from the Spanish for days. During his investigation in Puala, Espejo confirmed the deaths of the missionaries. After spending some time in the area mining for silver and gold unsuccessfully, Espejo ordered the majority of the party to return to Mexico. The eight soldiers that continued to move west with Espejo would eventually fall on the settlement of Acoma Pueblo, which Chamuscado and Rodriguez saw a year earlier. As Espejo approached the pueblo, two of his women slaves escaped his grasp and hid inside the town. Espejo and his men infiltrated the town looking for the slaves when a skirmish broke out between them and the Indian warriors of Acoma. The slaves were eventually recaptured in the midst of the firefight, and the Spanish fought their way out of the pueblo sustaining minor casualties. Luckily for them, they had an adequate number of horses and retreated eastward from the pursuing Acoma villagers. Espejo and his remaining men made it back to Mexico unharmed by the end of 1583. This incident between Espejo and the Acoma people was not the Acoma Massacre, but it would prove to be an important event in the pantheon of events that would lead to the atrocity.

A man named Juan de Oñate was hired to further explore and colonize New Mexico in 1595, twelve years after Espejo's return. Oñate claimed his primary objective was to spread Catholicism to the natives by establishing missions in New Mexico. In this process, he founded the province of Santa Fe[37] and declared himself first colonial governor. His new settlement butted up against that of the neighboring Acoma Pueblo. For almost four years, all relations were peaceful until the Acoma chief, Zutacapan, learned that Oñate was planning to push his Santa Fe territory further west into Acoma land and forcibly move the Acoma people to a new village where they would be forced to work under Spanish rule. On December 4, 1598, Oñate's nephew, Juan de Zaldívar was sent to Acoma Pueblo to meet with Zutacapan. Upon his arrival, he rudely demanded food and shelter for him and his men. At Zutacapan's denial, Zaldívar ordered his soldiers to invade the Acoma homes. The Spanish force was met with an Acoma counterattack that left Juan de Zaldívar and eleven of his men dead. Oñate learned that his nephew was killed in the engagement and ordered Juan's brother, Vincente de Zaldívar, to lead seventy men and a single small cannon to the pueblo to completely raze the village. On January 22, 1599[38] the battle began with Spanish artillery fire and light small arms fire pouring onto the mesa on which the Acoma Pueblo sat. This continued for three days, until Zaldívar and a group of men finally ascended up the mesa with the cannon, wheeled it into the street of the pueblo, and opened fire into the edifices. Massive fires broke out within the village and in the chaos, the rest of the Spanish company stormed the streets of Acoma engaging in barbaric hand to hand combat with the Indians. On numerous occasions, Acoma warriors attempted to charge the artillery but the largely reinforced cannon was too overpowering for even the largest group of warriors. Bloody melee ensued in the streets for hours and by the end of the fighting,

800 Acoma were killed in battle with hundreds more wounded. Zaldívar took over 500 prisoners and ordered that each male prisoner had his right foot cut off at the ankle. Many more people were dragged back to Santa Fe where they were enslaved for twenty years or more. Many of the women were sent to Mexico where they were held prisoner in convents and forced to study Catholicism. The entire pueblo of Acoma was deserted.

***

Just a year later, John Cobb's peaceful contact with the Shawnee in 1599 would allow him to pass through the center of the continent with ease before becoming just the second European explorer to reach the Mississippi River. Cobb's crossing point was less than two-hundred miles north of the land that de Soto died on.

Due to the incessant Spanish probing of the American landscape in the 16th century, peaceful European relations with native peoples would be much harder to establish for John Cobb as he moved westward beyond the river. Tribes along the southern part of the Mississippi River and in the Southwest were exposed to the harsh violence, unfair trading conditions, and genocidal activity of Europeans nearly one-hundred years before some tribes of the east had ever even seen a white man. By 1600, there was already deep animosity held by such western tribes.

Cobb, being well aware of the de Soto and Coronado expeditions and their tales of doing battle with the tribes of the West, intended to continue westward past the river, but to avoid any circumstance that would spoil his access to the north. He knew the Spanish were feeding into the West from its southern passage, and that the tribes that they warred with were to the south as well. He needed to keep his northern passage open in case he was confronted by the urgent need to flee. What he did not know, however, was that just before his arrival in the West, another expedition—not of a dissimilar nature to his own—would leave

Mexico and push the boundary of known Spanish activity further northeast than he could have ever anticipated.

seven

BEFORE departing England, John Cobb had sought out as many maps as he could get his hands on. There were various editions of Spanish, French, Portuguese, Italian, and English maps of the New World floating around not only England, but the maritime circuit—the world of privateers, pirates, admirals, and amateur merchants. As a sailor, Cobb had collected a small personal collection of maps—most of these were crude sketches by amateur cartographers from Cuba and Mexico. As a vassal of England however, Queen Elizabeth saw to it that Cobb was given sufficient visual and geographical context for their campaign and permitted him to view, and on some occasions copy, some of the most revolutionary maps of their time.

Cobb sat solemnly with a pipe on the floor of his tent with his maps sprawled about him—some dozen versions of the same world all with conflicting depictions of seas, mountains, rivers and borders. Amongst these relatively liable editions, Cobb did have one prized map that outlined the entire coast of the Gulf of Mexico from West Florida to East Mexico. This was an English derivative of a Spanish map called the *Carta Universal* [39] completed by Diogo Ribeiro in 1527.

From the *Carta Universal,* Cobb could see several feasible deltas that emptied into the Gulf of Mexico from the north. Taking into consideration his knowledge of the Narváez and de Soto expeditions, he decided that the river that he was presently on was the same river mentioned by both as being the largest of the land and emptying into the Gulf of Mexico. This of course was the Mississippi. How far north from the Gulf he was, he did not know, but he knew he must have been farther north than de Soto ever was. Using the *Carta Universal,* he was able to roughly estimate his position inland in relation to the east coast. What he could not tell from this map, due to the absent illustration of the actual river, was his relation to the gulf, and to the opposite coast. For this, he turned to another map.

Queen Elizabeth had allowed Cobb to study a contemporary edition of Ortelius' *Theatre of the World.*[40] He made his own crude sketch of the map of the New World presented in the atlas[41] which presented a severely distorted, but not entirely inaccurate size of the entire continent. For clues as to his present position, he turned to the mountain range.

On the *Theatre of the World* map of the New World, there is a drawn range that cuts east and west above Florida and into the center of the continent. This is almost certainly a misrepresentation of the Appalachians per de Soto's crew's tellings. De Soto indeed spent time in Appalachia, but he seemingly fell under the impression that the mountain range continued steadily west through all of Tennessee, likely until the Mississippi River. This could be because after he moved west into Tennessee from North Carolina, the mountains continued with him. After this he dipped *south* into Alabama—into the flatlands. Thus, he was never far west enough to see the mountain's end in Tennessee, therefore his reference for the direction of this mountain range was always "to the north," when in reality, the range's primary tread runs latitudinal from the Gulf of Mexico to Acadia.

Cobb understood by surveying his sketch of the atlas that he and de Soto had encountered the same mountain range and that he had encountered it farther north than de Soto had ever been. De Soto was not aware of just how far north the range extended. What Cobb did not know was whether or not the mountains that are spread west on the atlas were actually presently in front of him or not. To answer this question, he turned to the pair of rivers displayed on the atlas that run north and south into the Gulf. Logically, he figured the river farther to the east was the one he was at now, because he had only encountered one of them thus far. Seeing on the atlas that the river terminates at the mountain range, but *knowing* he must still be farther north than where de Soto traveled, he deducted that the mountain range's western existence was either inferred and not confirmed, or that de Soto never crossed it northwards or else the Mississippi River would be drawn much farther to the north on the map to demonstrate Cobb's present position. To determine his present location, he studied his own maps that he had been making all along their travels. He had sketched the northern part of the Appalachian Mountains (present-day Allegheny Range), several rivers including the Potomac, Ohio, Kanawha, and half a dozen small rivers inside of Kentucky. Additionally, he sketched the Shawnee territory, the Cumberland Plateau and cavernous landscape west of the mountains, and the dense forest all the way up to the Mississippi. He remained sleepless putting pieces together, connecting maps, and making sense of the journey they had taken thus far. After hours of puzzling several maps together, he decided that he was in the center of the continent just a shade west of the word *Canagadi* on his rendering of the Ortelius Atlas. From here, he learned that he was getting dangerously close to Spanish territory that was southwest of him in a territory known as

New Mexico. This frightened him greatly. The English by this time were well aware of the borders of Mexico and the Spanish occupation of the land directly north and west of it. Cobb also understood that in the event that this de Sotoan mountain range existed as it was described in the atlas, it would be inconceivable for his party to cross a second mountain range under the circumstances they were presently in. At once, he realized his only move was to go northwest.

eight

IN February of 1599, thirteen months prior to John Cobb crossing the Mississippi River, Juan de Oñate, the man responsible for ordering the Acoma Massacre, would come across a native Nahua man of immense interest wandering through the desert of New Mexico. His name was Jusepe Gutierrez, a former slave and at the time of his rescue by Oñate, a technical criminal. Four years earlier in 1594, two Spanish citizens named Antonio Gutiérrez de Humana and Francisco Leyva de Bonilla, made an unauthorized expedition into the Great Plains under unclear motives and elusive circumstances. The two men were not vassals of New Spain, nor were they conquistadors or men of political stature, but instead two amateur explorers who made the hazardous decision to set out with a small number of men into the greatly unexplored plains of the continent. Their journey began in New Mexico, where it briefly crossed paths with the Pueblo Indians of the Pecos River. It then ran through Texas, moved north through Oklahoma and eventually into Kansas where they encountered a metropolis that Jusepe described as "The Great Settlement;" a large congregation of Wichita Indians located along the Walnut River near modern-day Arkansas City, Kansas, roughly 140 miles southeast of the city of Quivira that Coronado had explored fifty years prior.

It was at this settlement that an argument of unknown origin erupted between Humana and Leyva de Bonilla which resulted in the stabbing of Leyva de Bonilla by Humana with a butcher knife. Humana assumed sole command of the expedition, marching north for ten days until they reached "a very large river," possibly the Missouri. Here, the unrested and irritable party fell into a state of chaos, falling victim to a number of Indian raids that would eventually seal the fate of Humana. After Humana's death, several men deserted, others fought and killed each other in power disputes, and some banded together in an attempt to return to Mexico. Jusepe Gutierrez would be the only member of the party to return to New Spain to relay this tale.

According to Jusepe's account told to Juan de Oñate in 1599, during his desertion from the expedition he and four Mexican men spent one week together traversing to the south, retracing their steps back to Mexico. The party effectively dissolved when a debate arose regarding directions, and three of the Mexicans deserted Jusepe and his companion for what they believed was the right path. The following day Jusepe's camp took on an Apache raid and Jusepe's companion was killed. Jusepe was taken prisoner and remained enslaved for over a year. He eventually escaped from the Apache where he wandered southward until finding temporary shelter near San Juan Bautista Pueblo where he was found and rescued by Oñate. After revealing his story to Oñate, the ambitious conquistador sent Vincent de Zaldívar to retrace the route described by Jusepe. On September 15, 1599,[42] Zaldívar, Jusepe and some few dozen soldiers set off north from New Spain on a reconnaissance mission. Zaldviar's journey likely traversed much of the Great Plains, just as Humana and Leyva's had, where he encountered "one-hundred-thousand buffalo" and became obsessed with driving them west to procure mass amounts of meat for Oñate's men. Zaldívar was present in the Great Plains region until November of 1599, only four months prior to John Cobb's crossing of the Mississippi River.

***

It was March 23, 1600 when in northeastern Kansas, Cobb came across what he believed to be the remains of a horse. It had a rich brown coat—not too different looking from Cobb's own horse—and it had been decapitated fairly cleanly by a sharp, European blade. Its insides had been robbed of bones, liver, heart, and meat; what laid in front of Cobb was a headless, deflated, bloody, brown, thawing horsesack. The scavengers had gotten to it, but plenty of it was well preserved by the winter. Cobb estimated its time of death to have been in the last five to six months. He examined the body carefully, stood up, and started poking around the ground that it laid on. He and his party swept the forest floor in all directions in search of arrowheads, bullets, horse tackle, remains of fire, anything that indicated recent human activity. Looking out into the flat tarpaulin of the plains, there wasn't a trace.

The last several weeks of their march was the flattest, clearest land they had seen yet. They had officially reached the Great Plains, and they greatly appreciated their plainness. To walk flat-footed in open fields under a spring sky was a blessing after the winter they had all endured. Nobody rode in the wagon by the time they had reached Kansas. The women and children were walking alongside the horses, enjoying the warming weather and softening grass. The land held pockets of concentrated forest of towering flowering walnut, elm and cottonwood trees that were just beginning to bud under the promise of a sociable sun. Outside of these meetings of trees, the majority of the land was open and forever. Of course, the wide-open spaces made the caravan prone to discovery, which nearly proved to be a problem on multiple occasions since their crossing of the Mississippi River.

A few days after crossing, Cobb and his companions were confronted by a Mississippian tribe after emerging from the deep cover of the riverbrush. The Indians swarmed the camp like wolves. They boasted weapons of all kinds. Cobb threatened them with the novelty of his firearm, the children cried like crows, huddled together on the ground underneath the clubs and spears. After several minutes of rabid shouting, Patamon and Aponi worked to settle down the Mississippians by conveying that they were not slaves, but free people from the east who came in peace with the Europeans. The Mississippians were apprehensive to believe that the Nanticoke were so friendly with the whites under their own accord. They worked further to free them, even coming close to assaulting John Cobb. After the near violence, they finally allowed the caravan to pass, but not without taking the Shawnee gifts that they carried with them. This exchange struck something inside of Cobb. He understood here that these people were different from the Indians he had encountered over the last six months; these people *had seen European's before.* There was no chance of making a good first impression—the impression had already been set. Some of these tribes had seen Coronado's soldiers torch the plains in search of gold. Some had seen their parents slaughtered in cold blood by de Soto, who took to hunting natives for sport on his perilous search for a passage back to Mexico. The Indians west of the river were not like the curious, dumbfounded Shawnee, or the friendly, amicable Nanticoke. They were skeptical and proud. They were already fighting a war of preservation—a war they had been fighting for one-hundred years. Cobb knew that he would soon become an object of vengeance and he needed to find a place to settle fast. He also knew that there was one tell-tale sign that identified a European intruder from even the greatest of distances: the horse and wagon. To the Indians of the Plains and the Southwest, carts and wagons had gained a reputation of being filled with food, water, and the ransacked supplies of native villages. The Spanish horse-drawn vehicles were often raided in an effort to take back what natives believed was rightfully theirs in the first place. Horses were thought of as war animals by the native people. The decorated officers always rode on fine, large, beautiful horses. When the Spanish plundered the native towns they usually did so by way of mass cavalry charges that left the Indian warriors defenseless and slow compared to the combat of the dragoon. In Coronado's march across the Plains, his men even began to spread the rumor to the natives that horses could be trained to eat men. In response, the more aggressive tribes such as the Comanche, Apache and Pueblo, were developing methods to ready stolen Spanish horses for their own military escapades. Cobb realized at once that he was no longer in unknown territory; he was in hostile territory.

Weeks after the confrontation with the Mississippians the land became even clearer and flatter. Often on these flatlands, when the day was cloudy, Cobb and his party became turned around on the uniform terrain as one might be at sea, with no landmarks to distinguish one direction from the other. Not as much as a misshaped stone or a uniquely tall blade of grass could be found on these plains. It was only when they encountered the bison they could reachieve their balance and westward course.

Cobb first spotted the masses of bison grazing the land of western Missouri. The cattle moved in the distance as one massive organism, but with a dizzying individualism like a swarm of bees on a beehive. The land was so flat here that one could look underneath the distant bison and see blue windows of sky through their legs, out past the herd and the earth. The herds stretched as far as Cobb could possibly see and as he got closer, he noticed the dozens—and eventually hundreds—of Osage driving them. Cobb admired with divine awe the numbers of the animal and the involved choreography of the Osage that went into leading them. He could see well that the Plains Indians worshiped the buffalo. They respected it and thanked it and never killed it in vain. Their food and housing and clothing and jewelry and tools all come from the magic of the buffalo, God's gift to them, and they refused to exploit it.

Cobb and Patamon made peaceful contact with the chief of one of the Osage clans one afternoon, overlooking a parade of buffalo under a moaning orange sun, deep in the heart of the Kansas plains.[43] The Osage people received the Europeans much more warmly than the Mississippians had. They invited Cobb and his party to stay with them in their village to the north where they celebrated the union between Cobb and Patamon—white-man and native—and the loyalty they had for each other.

While stationed and resting in the Osage settlement,[44] Cobb noticed the native acquisition of Spanish wear and weaponry—namely headwear and sabers. It was clear in conversation that this tribe had clashed with the Spanish in battle in the past, but the nature of the Spanish military expeditions was not clear to Cobb. What was clear however, was that the Osage had come into contact with colonists as recently as a few months ago. Cobb was naturally discouraged upon discovering this. He had no idea that the Spanish had ever been so far north. He knew that if the Spanish were to discover him, it would likely lead to imprisonment or even execution. He knew he could not settle in the flat open land so he asked the Osage in which direction he should continue. They directed him to the north, telling him that the Spanish had only ever come from the south and the west.

With his party rested and his horses fed, Cobb thanked the Osage on his knees for their kindness and set off in the direction they sent him. In a shocking display of civility to the Osage, Cobb and his companions stole nothing, demanded nothing, harmed nobody, and shared what they could with their hosts upon their departure.

It was after two days of walking north along the Big Blue River that Cobb was stopped at the sight of the dead horse. The dead horse was a signal to him; he had not gone far enough yet. With the finding of the horse, Cobb was forced to rethink his entire understanding of the land before him. All of his best guesses as to what territory belonged to who were useless. Any idea as to what was waiting for him on the other side of his journey had become irrelevant. He feared that an entire Spanish company could be around the next bend in the river or perhaps savage, starving deserters waited in treetops to ambush his party.

On March 28, 1600 as he led his misfit assortment of vagrants over the 40th parallel, John Cobb would become the first European to enter into what would later become the U.S. state of Nebraska, 114 years before Étienne de Veniard, sieur de Bourgmont would lay eyes on the flat, brown river he would call the *Nebraskier*—the river that would later be known as the Platte.

***

It was two weeks later just south of the Platte River when the first bad spring thunderstorm rolled in from the west. The travelers had been enjoying the sprawling plains until menacing, black clouds crawled across the sky one afternoon. Patamon was the first to suggest they stop to set up an adequate camp to keep safe from the storm. Cobb at first pushed to continue on for another hour or so, but as the thunder boomed in the distance, he agreed to cut the day's work short and set the tents.

When the storm did come, the tents were hardly adequate defenses against the raging winds and flooded grounds on which they were set. Each of the travelers were kept up all night bailing water from their tents, tying and resetting the stakes and ropes for the horses who panicked and attempted to flee at the sound of the infuriated thunder. Nobody had even attempted to sleep until noon the next day when the worst of the storm was over. Even the day after that was unsuitable for travel because the soft soil of the plains had become so flooded that the wagon sank and threatened to crack from the strain of the force deep in the grip of the mud and muck. After traversing only one mile in over two days, Cobb took up base on the south side of a stone ridge that was cut from a gently rolling hill along the countryside. They were in a stretch of wide-open land with distant forests to the north and a lovely little creek behind them. In the evening, the clouds that followed the storm passed them by and the clear sky opened up above them again. Cobb stood on the ridge looking out at the landscape of mellow brown hills, polka-dotted by the beginnings of plantgrass and pink flowers attempting their miracle of rebirth. The emptiness seemed to be a fullness to him. A distant collection of trees became brush which turned to ivy that covered a family of boulders—mysterious boulders that had rolled into the empty plains long ago from some extinct mountain that once watched over the land. The day's light began to fade and the long forgotten sound of birds filled the air.

In the aftermath of the storm, there was very little food left. The fish from the creek were small and dirty and the vegetables given to them by the Osage had been mostly eaten, save for a small sack of beans. Despite these problems, Cobb was anxious to move once more. A warm front had moved in behind the storm and the ground would surely be ready for travel tomorrow, he thought. That evening, Simon, Andrew, and Powa were asleep by sundown, shattered by the violence of the storm. Patamon and Aponi retired not long after them. John Cobb and Anna Stone stayed awake through most of the night, talking close at the fire.

In the morning the camp was packed away hastily. Cobb was roaring to move the party while the sun was high and hot. A false spring was teasing them; they were even working a sweat about the camp as they moved the crates and the tents into the wagon. Cobb and Aponi (who had become accustomed to riding a horse over the preceding months) pulled the wagon, and Patamon rode on the lone horse, drawing a slow circle around the moving travelers with a musket and his bow at the ready.

It must have been about noon when he first spotted the Pawnee. Ten warriors were moving parallel to their caravan on foot. Patamon pulled back his horse, stopped and raised his right hand high in the air and waved gently. Massive white clouds like sugar drifted overhead the Pawnee along the blue sky. The Indians were far on the flat horizon, black monoliths against the blue. They saw Patamon clearly but did not wave back. Instead, they began running towards him. It was as if they hadn't even seen him. At sixty yards, they halted in succession and drew their bows. Patamon yelled to Cobb under a barrage of arrows and the horses started off in a panic to the west. Patamon stayed behind and harassed the Pawnee from horseback as Cobb and the wagon picked up speed. For nearly a hundred yards they ran well until the wagon collapsed into a pool of soaked muck like quicksand from the flooded grounds. Anna and the children were tossed from the carriage.

Patamon joined Cobb and released the horses and flipped the wagon upside down. The women and children crawled under the makeshift bunker and the men aimed their muskets towards the Pawnee. From sixty yards they fired, hitting one Indian. The Pawnee answered with a scattered volley of arrows that missed closely. The men reloaded their muskets on horseback as the Pawnee reorganized and approached more cautiously. They fired a second set of rounds into the Indian lines, this time killing two men. Cobb and Patamon advanced on horseback towards the Pawnee. Their speed upon the fury of the horses routed the Pawnee line. Cobb drew his saber and took one Pawnee to the ground. Patamon favored the tomahawk and weaved in between stumbling enemies, driving his cold hatchet into the backs of two men. The remaining Pawnee fled in terror. All that kept Cobb from pursuing them further was the hysteric surrender of two prisoners who were shackled to one another; ghosts of men, all bones and rags. They fell to the ground and shouted blessings in Spanish through tears of joy.

***

The two Mexican slaves were devastated when they came to realize that Cobb was not Spanish and that they were not going to return to Mexico under the care of a military caravan. Despite their disappointment, they were thankful to be free from their captors and immediately pledged their allegiance to Cobb. The first order of business for John Cobb was to identify who they were and what they were doing so far north out of Spanish territory. In his sailor's Spanish, Cobb gathered that the two men, Lope and Miguel, were Nahua-Mexican farmers recruited some five years ago by two Spanish colonists to accompany them into the northern province of New Mexico in search of a fabled city of gold. Tempted by such riches, they abandoned their lives in Mexico and accepted the quest. During their travels, one of the directors of the campaign inexplicably murdered his partner which in turn tore the entire contingent apart from the inside and Lope, Miguel, and one other long-dead companion deserted the return party in search of a faster route. They were subsequently captured, enslaved, and traded several times amongst varying tribes. The colonists who approached them all those years ago were of course Antonio Gutiérrez de Humana and Francisco Leyva de Bonilla, and the only person to return to New Spain after the violence that overtook the campaign was Jusepe Gutierrez.

Lope and Miguel told Cobb all that they knew about the land. They explained the many tribes of the area, *los buenos indios, los indios malos, los ríos,* and most importantly *las montañas.* They spoke of a towering, silver body of mountains that stretched from the farthest horizon of the north to the farthest of the south. They described the peaks as unlike any they had seen before in Mexico or any other such place. Though they had been only one time—accompanying a Pawnee trade convoy—they assured Cobb that they knew how to arrive there. It was a simple task, they said. One must only follow the flat, brown river westward, then, at the fork of the river, follow it to the south. There, one would find the greatest of all mountains. There, John Cobb would find his terminus.

***

Cobb, Patamon and the Mexicans spent several days converting the totaled wagon into a two-wheeled cart. The corpse of the splintered wagonwood lay dead and drying in the grasp of the wholewarming plains like reliquiae. Inside the cart, the accommodations were as uncomfortable as they had been since leaving New Bristol. To pull the oversized load, Cobb rigged a harness and a set of traces together that would allow all three horses, manned by himself, Patamon, and Miguel, to haul it simultaneously. Anna and the children rode inside the cart. Aponi and Lope, each armed with a Pawnee hatchet, walked beside them.

The ensuing march was one of incredible hardship. The children were mostly silent for the duration of the ride. The crushing weight of death and danger sat heavy on their hearts as they rode through the bare land. Andrew combated the sick feeling with sleep. He dozed off and on throughout the days, huddled up warm between his brother and sister. When the cart hit a bump or came to a complete stop his mind jolted awake in a nightmare and he looked around before settling back into his sleep. Simon sat as still and cold as a stone with his entire head and body below the wood panels of the cart and the stacks of crates around him. He slumped down as far as he could, wide awake, watching the clouds of every color sail like ships above him as they moved west. He breathed in deep, concerned sighs like the horses. Beside him, Powa, paranoid and attentive, peeked through the cracks in the cart boards in all directions. He would spend five or ten minutes looking south and then wiggle himself to the other side of the cart where he would play watchman of the east. On one occasion he saw a family of deer jolting from one patch of trees to another and stood and shouted with so much fear and conviction that John Cobb drew his musket. Embarrassed, he sank down beneath the boards with Simon and pretended he was asleep, but when he closed his eyes he saw only the rush of Pawnee screeching like lightning across the naked plains.

On one purple evening along the genesis of the South Platte River, the sun started to dim. A fading ripeness of the day illuminated the maize brown land around them, casting a haze across the horizon. Rotting trees like bones surrounded the party as they stepped slowly into a corridor of about forty yards width. On either side of them, ravens and other dark looming birds sat and rested in their carbon oasis.

The cart breathed like a sick old man, the same agonizing ill moan with every rotation of the wheels. There was still sun in the sky, although it was behind the trees and invisible to them from their position. A deafening silence fell upon them, as if they had crossed into a vacuum. A thin, tight air grasped the forest as they slowed down the horses. Cobb's brow raised and he moved his head like an owl. Right then, as the air broke and the sound rushed back towards them, a hailstorm of arrows poured out from the trees. The shrill scream of a storm banshee ignited the woods and the Pawnee spilled out from the shadows. The cart became a chariot, proving to be a strong defense against several arrows pelting its outside. Anna squealed at the sound of the sharp stone piercing the wood. Lope was hit in the neck with an arrow and killed instantly. Cobb whipped the horses with great speed through the forest. As they carried down the trail, several more Pawnee emerged from the woodwork firing shots at the racing travelers. Cobb and Patamon lowered their bodies and tucked their heads below the neck of their horses. The cart was slow and clumsy on the forest trail as the path was full of downed branches and boulders. Cobb fired a shot from his musket that missed its target. Patamon drew his bow and answered the intruding arrows with his own. He hit two men cleanly, killing them, before he himself was hit in the chest and fell to the forest floor. Cobb and Miguel jumped from their horses. They counted eight Pawnee in all.

Aponi snatched a gun from the cart and raised it and fired a shot that found the chest of a man who rushed toward Patamon. Cobb had killed one man and was locked in a fierce melee with another. Miguel too had dispatched a man before being brought to the ground in a scrap. Patamon moved on his hands slowly with an arrow protruding from just under his right collarbone. He drew his bow and fired several hasty shots that missed their mark. As he loaded another, he was hit again by an arrow just below the first. He lost the strength to draw back his bow and fell onto his back.

Aponi rushed to her husband's side and worked to drag him to the cart but she didn't have the strength. Blood ran from Patamon's chest like a spring. He began to shed off his coat. His white European shirt was torn and stained red with blood. He tried shouting something to Cobb but his words were suffocated. Cobb and Miguel rid of the last Pawnee, each of them taking on wounds themselves. They floated like ghosts back to the cart together, stepping over arrows erect from the ground. Contorted bodies leaked rivers of blood across the ravaged, polluted pass. When they finally returned to the cart, Patamon was dead.

nine

IN the morning the travelers made their way out of the woods and Patamon was buried in the wide-open land. Aponi led a traditional Nanticoke funeral ceremony for her husband. His grave was marked with a stack of red stones, each smaller than the one below it. Cobb had dug the grave himself and for the first time since their knowing him, the company watched him cry as he laid the last of the dirt on his friend. He knelt at the mound and as if he had kept himself from crying for the last several months, he let out a wretched wail that was accompanied by a storm of tears. He took hold of the dirt that covered his friend and it fell through his hands and onto his lap.

Powa spent most of the day alone. He tried not to think of his father. A wooden, hollow numbness kept him from crying. What amazed him was the pace at which everything had changed. It seemed like yesterday that he had set off from his village for the sea with boyish anticipation prickling at his fingertips. He remembered the day he left his village with his father, and he brought with him a bow. He told him to use it if he saw something worth shooting. And then he remembered some days later when he stood on the beach and a looming, sick fear came over him as he saw *The Rose Marie,* that he, for just a moment, clenched the bow that hung at his chest, thinking that he may need it then. He remembered the words that his father had said to him, but when he recalled them, he heard them in English. He tried to remember what it was like to think in his own language. He wasn't allowed to. There was no time to think in Nanticoke. He forced himself to think in English and he felt that he was a different person than he was before the English came and colonized his tongue and his mind. He questioned the sacrifice of that. He missed his language and he missed his village and he felt his own death inside of him. As he breathed slowly and lonely, mourning the death of everything, he wished he knew if it was worth it. He wished he knew what had happened in New Bristol after his departure. He had no way of knowing if what he was going through now was worth the price he had paid or not. He had no way of knowing if the death of his father was necessary for the survival of the rest of them. He would never know. Cobb, ambitious and stubborn in his ways, would never know. Anna, who would discover her pregnancy in just a few days, would never know. Aponi, unable to walk—her heartache debilitating every last bone of her body—would never truly know.

***

When Miguel and Lope deserted the Humana and Leyva expedition in 1595, they first became friendly with a docile Wichita tribe herding bison. They spent a number of weeks peacefully living with the Wichita until there was a territory dispute with an intemperate band of Kiowa Indians. Violence broke out between the two tribes which resulted in the Kiowa taking Miguel and Lope prisoner. For nearly two years they lived as slaves to the Kiowa until they were traded to the Pawnee in exchange for Spanish horses that had been captured. For three years in the hands of the Pawnee, they were made to farm and to cook and to labor. They told the Pawnee stories of the Old World and warned them that the Spanish were coming to take their land and to drive them north. At threats such as these, they were cruelly punished. The two men had made several attempts to escape the clutches of their masters, even making it several miles south before they were caught and disciplined.

With the Pawnee, the two slaves had crossed the Plains on several occasions, reaching the foot of the Rocky Mountains on trading expeditions and bison drives to Grand Camp Creek. They trekked hundreds of miles of shining green grassland and became well acquainted with the groups that populated the western Great Plains. Miguel had become friendly enough with these groups that he decided to introduce John Cobb to the Grand Camp in 1600. He hoped there, he could paint Cobb as an enemy of the Spanish and solicit advice and supplies for his new companion. When they arrived, Miguel was greeted as an ambassador of the Nebraskan Pawnee. He introduced Cobb as a friend seeking temporary shelter as he and his caravan worked to escape the Spanish. The chiefs of the camp happily obliged. Their relations were unanimously peaceful.

Miguel became an invaluable asset to Cobb as they carried on along the foothills of the Front Range. In addition to the Grand Camp, they encountered over a dozen groups of uncontacted peoples who had still never seen a horse, a carriage, or a white man before. As Cobb worked to establish his own relations with the tribes of the Front Range, he allowed Miguel to choose his own fate: If he wished to carry on with the travelers, he was welcomed with open arms. If he wished to try his luck at returning to Mexico, he was free to leave. In the eyes of Cobb, Miguel had paid his debt by safely traversing him to the mountains. Miguel, without hesitation, chose to remain with John Cobb. They would remain friends for the rest of their lives.[45]

John Cobb knew when he first laid eyes on the magnificence of the Rocky Mountains that his path had come to an end. The sight of his Holy Land looked just as it had in his mind's eye since they departed New Bristol, and he could feel with complete confidence that he was the first explorer to ever come across such peaks. Sat at his camp along the east bank of the South Platte River, looking up at the summits of the Front Range, Cobb thought that they must be the greatest mountains he'd ever seen—these great status of the earth which made the mountains of the Shawnee look like gentle hills in a child's painting. He studied the still-white peaks that kissed the white breath of the sky where the world of man became Heaven, leaving him to guess where solid rock ended and where the dancing raindust of the clouds began. Each mountain face shone as if it were made from the finest silver, reflecting the sun's light in such divinity, such unseen and unraped Americanness that they looked as if they had stood truly and kingly in this land since before the first grain of sand moved through the glass canal of time. Cobb felt a Holiness when he saw these peaks. He knew at once he would not attempt to cross them.

A small band of passing Cheyenne tended to the travelers at the foot of the hills for some weeks. They were fed and rested, the horses groomed, and the cart repaired. Many of the Cheyenne held such a high respect for Cobb, that they even offered him and his family admittance into their tribe. He humbly declined. When the Cheyenne departed the range for their home in the north, Cobb led himself into the mountains for the first time. It was May 1, 1600.

***

That summer—just a year after his arrival in New Bristol—Cobb had finally decided on a location to build a settlement. It was on relatively flat ground about three miles inside the range along Deer Creek. The Indians had no purpose to roam the hills where Cobb had chosen to break ground; only occasionally did they mingle in the land.

He began construction with two homes. He, Miguel, and the children would venture down the creek westward and cut whatever wood they could find. There was plenty of pine, cedar, cottonwood, maple and spruce that were suitable for framing a house. The houses were not large dwellings, but they would be strong and sturdy. Stones were to be used as the walls and there was no shortage of them between the mountains. After weeks of cutting and tumbling and hauling wood, an untimely storm swept in and flooded the grounds. The runoff came down the hills in a matter of hours and overwhelmed Deer Creek which flooded Cobb's camp. He was far too close to the creek; the soil would never hold. After casting further judgment on the placement of his settlement, Cobb made the decision to move about six miles southwest where there was a smaller tributary for water and the elevation was a more stable plateau. He reached a suitable location along the North Fork of Deer Creek on August 12, 1600. It was a massive, viridescent valley tucked deep between colossal peaks and surrounded by thin clouds. The land was flat and the soil dark and fervent. He smiled something delightful through his blonde beard when he first overlooked the land.

Again, he and his companions rushed to begin simple dwellings. This time, instead of starting with two small homes, he built one larger home that all of the group would live in for the winter until he could begin on smaller dwellings in the spring. Working every day from sun-up until sundown from August until November, the first wood, cobb, and stone cabin was finished on November 23, 1600. It had a sturdy roof, a stone fireplace with a makeshift chimney, one window, and barely enough room to hold the eight of them. A feast was thrown to celebrate the erection of their first building, or more accurately, the packing away of the tents. The filthy English military tents that were waterlogged and useless were finally stashed out of sight. The travelers could recite each and every gash, hole, stain, and split on each of the tents from raw memory.

Life in the cabin would prove to have its complications, however. Three young, disorderly boys, a woman eight months into a pregnancy, a widowed native woman, and two men—one of which having almost no grasp on the common language—all shared sleeping, bathing, and dining quarters in a home that would uncomfortably house a family of four. The spring time could not come soon enough.

The first snowfall came to them in early December. The men and children had been exhausted working in the unforgiving sun every day for so many months that the winter was anticipated with excitement and relief. Even Aponi worked in the tortuous summer heat that ran through the fall, splitting her time between helping the men with building, and taking care of the blooming Anna Stone, who by August and September, had been slow moving and an object of laborious uselessness. As for the snow, Cobb's building dimensions proved triumphant as not a flake was seen inside the cabin as it fell. Outside, the children built forts and waged snow-wars between themselves. A fire burned indoors where Cobb, Anna, Aponi, and Miguel all huddled for hours, sometimes silently, and sometimes with ravishing conversation.

Finally, on December 24, John and Anna Cobb gave birth to a little girl whom they named Rose-Marie. She would be the first person of English descent born west of the Mississippi River. She was a bright cherub with gentle lips already soft as Anna's and that old undeniable Stone nose, tall and distinguished. When Anna Cobb first took grasp of her little girl in her arms, coddled and warm at her breast, she looked in her eyes—the same sea-blue eyes as her husband's—and understood, finally, her role in all of this. She understood her husband and her daughter and herself on the cosmic stage all at once in the gaze of the little love that she held beneath her. There was no room for school or for God or for London or for plays. For just a moment as she rocked Rose Marie to sleep, she understood.

Over the pensive winter, Cobb's team of horses pulled a thousand wagon's worth of firewood and lumber from the cedar-laden mountainsides to the cabin. Miguel chopped wood all winter in the biting cold to warm the home and to prepare for the spring. When the spring did come, a second dwelling was built which Aponi, Powa, and the Stone twins quickly inhabited. After the cabin, they erected a barn, an effort which occupied everybody's time for the duration of the spring and summer. Cobb and Powa hunted and trapped inside the hills and Miguel and Aponi had planted seeds of every shape and color that they had acquired from the Cheyenne the autumn before. Soon, corn and beans and greens grew from the fertile ground and made their way onto the plates of the children. Aponi began to forage fruits and herbs that ran along the eastern bend of Deer Creek. The creek was littered with mushrooms, strawberries, plums, and wild onions. By the following summer, the settlement had become completely self-sustainable.

Cobb's Valley, as it would be called, remained uncontacted for seven years after its establishment. It was not until 1607 that a small band of Tabeguache Ute Indians fell upon the settlement by accident.[46] On June 8, 1607, an eighteen-person detachment of the eastern chapter of the tribe approached John Cobb at the foot of his cabin. Their meeting was one of peace, and the two races feasted together for several days. Their relationship would prove to be one of great importance.

It was no secret that the problem of longevity had been on John Cobb's mind from the start of his settlement. He spent years procrastinating any sort of exploratory excursion outside of his valley, for the stakes were too high.

He could not risk coming across a platoon of Spanish or a band of violent Pawnee. Still, he knew he needed outside blood in his valley. With the arrival of the Ute and their display of overt kindness, he had no choice but to bend the opportunity in his favor.

It only took him a matter of days to charm the Ute into extending their stay. Soon, the two races hunted together, fished together, harvested crops together, and learned to speak together through signs and shared language. The men helped Cobb to raise new buildings and they told him of what lay over the mountains around him. Anna and Aponi were enthralled to have more women around as the spirit of the settlement had grown decidingly male over the last seven years. Finally, in the winter of 1607, Cobb received the news that he had been waiting for. A Ute woman named Ametane became pregnant with Miguel's child. A celebration between the races was held, and the couple married the following week. Miguel's own daughter, Vehoae, was born on September 29, 1608. Following this, Simon and Andrew, aged twenty, each took a bride in the summer of 1609 and expected children the following year. Even John Cobb and Anna had another child, a second little girl, Sarah, born in January, 1610. Only Aponi abstained from the agreeable fever that infected the settlement during this period. She would never wed again as long as she lived.

Cobb's Valley prevailed to be the West's best-kept secret for a number of years. Tucked away high on a plateau, hidden deep in the shoulder of the Continental Divide, out of the reach of the three European powers racing to conquer the continent, Cobb would see a prosperity in his settlement that he never thought possible during his lifetime. By 1615 the population had reached forty, and by 1640, there were 114 inhabitants. Two dozen European style homes were completed by this time, as well as a mill, a schoolhouse, and tall, strong walls around the village.

While the ancestral longevity of the settlement seemed stable, Cobb still wrestled with questions of a philosophical sort. Naturally, as these new generations grew older they sought answers to their questions of existence; the story of their origin came into question. In his old age, Cobb had become polarized in his responsibility to either found or to forgo an institution of historical preservation. On one hand, he believed that it was important and ethical for all who lived under his name to fully understand their beginnings. However, he feared that too much knowledge would entice a considerably adventurous member of his lineage to leave the valley in search for greater truths elsewhere in the world, potentially putting Cobb's life's work at risk of being discovered and destroyed. He of course sympathized greatly with this hypothetical inspired explorer, and he could not find it inside himself to mock up a sort of fabricated history to tell the unborn generation of tomorrow. Yet, something selfish and kingly possessed him. He feared the abolishment of all that he had built. The thought of his village's destruction, even long after his death, disturbed him in the night and kept him far from sleep. For years Cobb considered this problem and argued with himself late into the night. He had already observed a free, intrepid spirit in many of the young men who populated his valley.

It was Powa, a strong opponent of the withholding of knowledge, who ultimately swayed Cobb in the direction of justice. He believed that if his settlement was virtuous enough and pure enough, no man would be tempted to leave. It must remain untouched by greed, the two men concurred.

The people of Cobb's Valley would be taught world history properly, as it had happened. They would be educated on Babylon and Egypt and Atilla and Homer and Plato, just as Cobb had been when he was a boy. They would be taught of the great many European wars and the western kingdoms birthed from the belly of a suffocating

Rome. His pupils would have the right to know that they exist on a novel continent and that on this continent, Cobb attained freedom from a totalitarian England and founded his home there in the valley. In his transparency, Cobb was confident that the longevity and safety of his colony would be secured by its understood status as a fugitive state. Boys and girls were taught from a young age that the English, Spanish, and French were ruthless kingdoms ruled by self-ish kings who would sentence all of Cobb's Valley to death on grounds of treason, trespassing, or heresy if they were ever found. This narrative, not entirely untrue, succeeded in discouraging the people of the colony from exploring outside the range for over two-hundred years. Generations of families existed under the lifelong impression that the Spanish and English lurked behind each and every moun-taintop in maniacal pursuit of Cobb's lost colony. What Cobb and Powa failed to realize in their short-mindedness was that in its isolation, the colony would be dangerously unaware of the changing world around it, and they vastly underestimated just how fast it would all change.

Cobb assembled a collection of his shared volumes in-cluding histories, diaries, maps, and personal libraries and locked them inside of an oak chest, plated with iron and lined with smooth blue Italian silk. The chest was built in London in 1503 and was gifted to Cobb upon his father's death in 1588. It had since traversed half the globe with him. He laid a hide of buffalo over the chest and tucked it into a dark unassuming corner of his modest home. Six years later, mere days before his own death in 1652, John Cobb, gray-haired and gray-chinned with the same boney face and immeasurable blue eyes he'd always had, called Powa to his bedside. Powa was old with two black pony-tails that hung down his shoulders. His chin was strong and he resembled his father very much. The flesh of his face was tough like leather and a thousand brown hills rolled atop his cheeks. Cobb though, could hardly see him as the old man that he'd become. He saw the same devastating boy inside his brown face, long and perpetually hurting, seemingly in patient anticipation of its next tragedy.

Powa's torturous tenderness did not leave him after his boyhood. Nor did his unbearable quickness to feel everything there ever was to be felt, all at once. Powa had been married in 1617. He loved his wife in the way he had grown to learn to love; from watching Patamon love Aponi. Their love was consuming, unquestionable, superhuman, and forever. With his wife, Powa raised three children, one of which died at four years in an accident of rolling timber down a slick January mountainside. In an attempt to have another child the following year, Powa's wife fell ill during her pregnancy and died giving birth to a stillborn girl. In this tragedy, John and Anna Cobb concurrently suffered the loss of their first daughter, leaving the both of them distraught, or more accurately, *fervidly inconsolable,* for years. Powa's remaining two sons both grew to be quiet, peculiar men of unrealized potential. While they were intelligent and incredibly perceptive, they inherited the exhausting sensitivity of their father, leaving them untrusting of nearly everything following the death of their mother.

At Cobb's bedside, Powa kissed the man on his cheek. Their eyes met with a smile. Cobb lifted his cold, pale, dying hand across his body and set in Powa's hands, the key to his oak trunk. Powa held the key firmly and nodded his head in understanding.

"I trusteth thou shall chooseth a success'r as I has't chosen thee, bas'd on thy loyalty, goodness, and strengthe. The future of thy colony relies on thy bett'r judgment." Cobb cast a long, fleeting look at the face of his friend and sent him away with the wave of his hand.

John Cobb was buried in the pasture behind his home under a colorless summer sun. A celebration of his life was held for ten days and ten nights. Powa retold stories of their fabled adventures across the continent. Simon and

Andrew Stone toasted to his goodness and his bravery in the face of debilitating hardship. Aponi, the eighty-one-year-old sage of the colony, led a ceremony that would provide Cobb's spirit a safe passage to the next life. Anna, his widow and his world, could do nothing more than cry.

At the end of the ten days, Powa returned to the old cedar cabin. He pulled from his pocket the cold iron key that felt heavy with secrets in his soft hand. He found the oak trunk and ran his palm against the smooth hide that draped over it. The hide smelled ancient and alive. He pulled it slowly from the top of the trunk and let the key find the lock. He could feel the mechanism click with the easy turn of the key. With jarring force, the lock popped and the chest exhaled as if it had been holding its breath for a hundred years. It blew the scent of books from its lungs. The smooth oak creaked as he pushed it up and he was warmed and seduced by the fumes of the writtenword therewithin. Strewn across the silk bed of the trunk, Powa saw just what Cobb had described to him: volumes of history, hand-drawn maps of New Bristol and of the old Shawnee village and the plains where Patamon had been slain, diaries and accounts of the history of Cobb's Valley meticulously kept by month and by year. But most curious of all was an envelope that sat atop the center stack of the trunk. The envelope was stuck shut by pinegum and on its back side had in black ink, a final message from John Cobb. It was simple and read as such:

Open in the nonce of crisis.

Book III

Newbird in the West
Fall, 1836

Lineage of George, Son of Viho

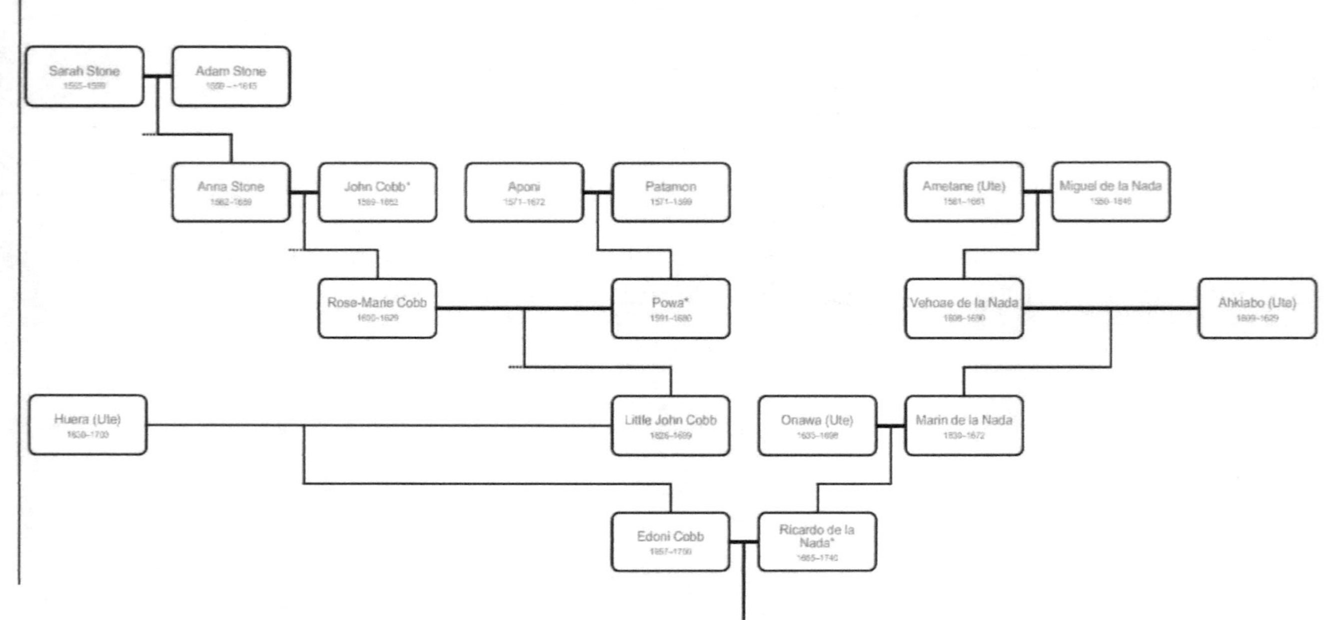

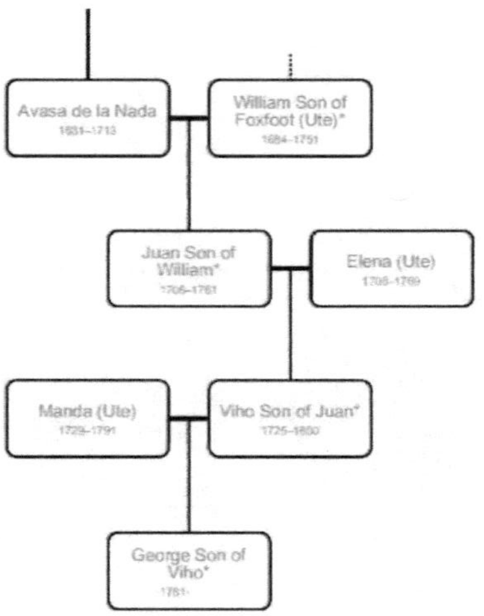

Avasa de la Nada
1631–1713
William Son of Foxfoot (Ute)*
1684–1751
Juan Son of William*
1706–1761
Elena (Ute)
1708–1769
Manda (Ute)
1729–1791
Viho Son of Juan*
1725–1800
George Son of Viho*
1761–

one

THE book of the generation of George, the son of Viho, the son of John Cobb.

John Cobb begat Rose-Marie, and Rose-Marie mothered Little John Cobb, and Little John Cobb begat Edoni, and Edoni mothered Avasa, and Avasa mothered Juan, and Juan begat Viho, and Viho begat George. So all the generations from John Cobb to George are eight generations.

George, Son of Viho, was a man of quiet conviction like his father before him. He became the keeper of Cobb's key in the wake of his father's death in 1800, and with it he inherited the scandal of his father's scrutinized tenure as patriarch.

It was in 1761 that Viho, Son of Juan, was present during a violent confrontation with Spanish hunters at the foot of the Front Range near East Plum Creek which resulted in the death of several of his men as well as the slaughter of the entire Spanish hunting party. In the wake of his contact with this growing Spanish presence near the range, he took up a strong isolationist stance, prohibiting the inhabitants of the valley from ascending into the range without a hand-appointed escort. Viho's policy to confine the population to the valley itself completely polarized the inhabitants of the land. The punishment for insubordination, Viho suggested, was imprisonment on grounds of threatening the security of the settlement. Half of the people fully supported his new stance, petrified by fear at the news of the nearing Spanish. In their eyes, any sacrifice was necessary to ensure they remain undiscovered. The men argued for the safety of the women and children—the children, who hardly understood the political ramifications of their situation, cried in anxiety at the bleak news of a looming, unseen enemy who surrounded their home. The other half of the people—trappers, hunters, fishermen and lumbermen—argued that their entire livelihood was at risk; food supplies would go bare, lumber would be nonexistent. Since the valley's inception, men had maintained regular work districts outside the village without putting the safety of the colony at risk. In the eyes of these men, Viho's policy was impetuous and would surely harm the laborers of the valley before it protected anybody else.

Forty years removed from his father's notorious encounter with the Spanish, and coming into leadership at just nineteen years old, George felt a palpable pressure from his peers urging him to end the mandate all together. George knew very well that he wanted to be a strong and admired leader. He grew up watching the trials of his father's tenure, thinking of what he would do better or how he would approach a problem differently. Even from a young age he had understood better methods to subvert the division of the settlement. He knew very well that he did not want the familiar controversy that plagued his father's tenure, nor the accusations of proposed monarchism that soiled his father's name. Lastly, he knew very well that regardless of how he navigated the political terrain under the scrutinizing eye of his colony, that the very real threat of Spanish colonization put him and his people in very real danger. What he had not realized was just how present the Spanish had been over the last two centuries. Nobody had realized how grievously close the Spanish had already come to discovering their secret.

***

Since Juan de Oñate had established Santa Fe as the first colony and capital of New Mexico in 1598, it became the origin point for at least half a dozen Spanish expeditions into the Great Plains and the Rocky Mountains in the 17th and 18th centuries. By 1761, Cobb's Valley had already been in threatening proximity of Spanish activity a number of times.

In the wake of Oñate's Acoma Massacre, the Pueblo people of New Mexico became all but enslaved to the strong, merciless hand of the Spanish Main for over eighty years. Before long, the city of Santa Fe was founded. It was anticipated to be the next great city of New Spain until a famine struck the desert in the 1670s. The Spanish and Indians alike began to starve. In response to the famine, a mysterious and ambitious Pueblo chief named Popé[47] united many villages of his tribe in a coordinated attack on the city of Santa Fe in August of 1680. Preceding the attack, the Puebloans succeeded in a coordinated thieving of Spanish horses to prevent a mass retreat. On August 10, 2,000 pugnacious Pueblo warriors rose upon the city of Santa Fe—population 2,400; men, women, and children. Over the next ten days, every trading post, mission, and small village in New Mexico had been pillaged and razed. A holdout of Spanish troops in Santa Fe barricaded themselves inside the governor's palace to repel one final attack from the Indians on August 21. Their last stand was a success, inflicting heavy casualties and forcing a Pueblo retreat. With the Pueblos off balance and temporarily regrouping outside the city, the surviving Spanish, numbering around 1,400 with another 500 slaves, fled the city in a panic. The weary Puebloans decided not to attack the retreat although they followed them all the way down to the Rio Grande at El Paso del Norte to see them off. For twelve years, New Mexico was practically barren of Spanish presence. Popé ordered that the churches were burned, and any Christian artifacts destroyed. He promised his people that with his guidance, life in Pueblo would return as it was during pre-Spanish times. The Puebloans unfortunately never saw a return to life before the white-man, as the perilous drought and famine continued in the desert for some years which left the Pueblo vulnerable to constant raids from their neighbors and archaic nemesis, the Apache. The constant warring between the two tribes prevented the Pueblo to upstart any sort of political or cultural renaissance during the Spanish absence.

Beginning in 1692, the Spanish attempted to reconquer the city of Santa Fe several times. Initially, the city was reconquered peacefully with the introduction of artillery pieces to the land which frightened the Puebloans into surrender, but the reestablished Spanish presence was soon met with repeated small uprisings by the Pueblo people which resulted in the city of Santa Fe changing hands regularly over the several years. During this period, Governor of New Spain, Diego de Vargas led a military excursion into the San Luis Valley[48] while pursuing a group of fleeing Pueblo conspirators. This would make Diego de Vargas the first confirmed Spanish man to enter into the Rocky Mountain Range, and would place him less than two-hundred miles southwest of Cobb's Valley in 1694,[49] during Ricardo de la Nada's tenure as patriarch. Santa Fe existed in a state of insecurity and instability until 1700 when the final attempted revolt by the Puebloans was put down and their population was forced to scatter into the Great Plains to the northeast.

Diego de Vargas' expedition would be the first of many explorations north of Santa Fe following Spanish reconquest of New Mexico. In 1706 the Spanish commander, Juan de Ulibarrí,[50] received a distress message from a band of Pueblo Indians who claimed they were enslaved by the Apache along the Arkansas River. These Pueblo had formerly lived in Santa Fe under Spanish rule, but escaped the Spanish in the midst of the ongoing violence ten years prior. Now, they called to the Spanish for rescue, reporting torturous conditions by their Apache captors. The Spanish and Apache were in the midst of their own violent struggles for territory and Ulibarrí saw the opportunity as a way to inflict damage on his evasive Apache enemy and to impose his will on the band of broken Pueblo who had no morale left in them to fight. Traveling north with Ulibarrí was Captain José Naranjo.[51]

Ulibarrí, Naranjo, and their party of 140 men reached an Apache settlement along the Arkansas Valley in Colorado on August 3, 1706, where they indeed found Pueblo slaves being held. Ulibarrí traded the Apache a dozen fine horses for just five slaves and immediately sent out further patrols in all directions in search of more Apache villages. To the east, he found great success with one of his captains discovering an Apache settlement along the Arkansas River in present-day Scott County, Kansas. There, he traded for additional Pueblo slaves and was told by an Apache chief that he had recently fought a skirmish with a detachment of French militia close to the Mississippi River.[52]

Ulibarrí's luck to the west was quite the opposite however, as he sent a small detachment of men up the Arkansas River for several days having not encountered any further enslaved Pueblos. They reached present-day Cañon City, Colorado where they pitched camp for one night before planning to descend back down the river and meet Ulibarrí the following day. Their camp at the mouth of Royal Gorge would place them just seventy-five miles south of Cobb's Valley.

In the middle of the night on August 22, this detachment of Spanish was held up by what they believed to be Ute Indians. The Ute demanded their guns and horses and after receiving these demands, lit the Spanish tents ablaze in their retreat. There were no casualties on either side. The next morning, these Spanish would begin their walk back eastward down the Arkansas River where they would meet Ulibarrí and return to Santa Fe on September 2. It was never discovered by the Spanish that this band of Ute thieves had not belonged to the Ute tribe at all; they were in fact citizens of Cobb's Valley led by a courageous man of Ute blood named Foxfoot. This young warrior would return from a yearlong reconnaissance voyage with fourteen young, strong horses, their cargo, and twenty-two muskets, forever immortalizing his name in the history of Cobb's Valley.

Thirteen years later in 1719, Antonio Valverde y Cosío, temporary Governor of Santa Fe, launched an expedition designed to hunt and capture Comanches along the Arkansas River who had taken to raiding Spanish camps in and around Taos, New Mexico. While he failed in his mission to capture the Indians, his expedition paved the trail for Manuel de Portillo's expedition in which he and a sizable military detachment massacred 400 Apache in the San Luis Valley in 1761. It was in the aftermath of this massacre in the fall of 1761, that fifteen civilians—traders and hunters—from Taos, New Mexico, trekked northward along the Front Range for two-hundred miles, finally pitching camp at the mouth of Stone Canyon on East Plum Creek just north of present-day Colorado Springs. These traders called the canyon home for nearly six weeks, occasionally trading with the neighboring Ute and Kiowa tribes of the plains. Their relations were unanimously peaceful and they often spent their days probing inside the walls of the range along East Plum Creek, hunting deer and trapping beaver along the creek. These hunters would conduct business just *twenty-four miles* southeast of Cobb's Valley during the tenure of Juan, Son of William as patriarch.

Juan was made patriarch suddenly, in 1751, after his father, William, suffered an untimely death of consumption. Juan was an incredibly proud man for a man of very little actual confidence. His need for constant validation in all that he did proved to be his downfall as he sought the same immortal legacy that his father and grandfather, Foxfoot, had attained in their lifetime. The only difference between them was that Foxfoot and William had never sought their fame. They had stepped into it like an aloof comet, streaking the sky with gold, unaware that a million eyes looked upon it and shouted names at its gleaming tail.

In July of 1761, Juan had begun occasionally leading wildly reckless exploratory missions under the guise of "defense operations," which in reality, were essentially offensive excursions in search of some poor lost Spanish expedition in which to rob. It was in the campsite of the fifteen hunters from Taos, New Mexico, that he found his "aggressors" and interrogated them on the morning of November 3, 1761 along East Plum Creek. Accompanying Juan, among other men, was his son Viho who documented the entire altercation and relayed it to the people of Cobb's Valley upon his return.

Juan had confronted the hunters early in the morning before they awoke, catching them unprepared and unarmed. From conversing with the leader of the group, he learned that the Spanish numbers in the territory of New Mexico had reached the thousands, and that they had been executing deep excursions into the mountains and the plains for over two-hundred years. Juan learned of the Pueblo Revolt of 1680 and the persistent trouble with the Comanche and Apache tribes in the region. The hunters made it clear to Juan that the Spanish only planned to become more present along the range in the next century and were not afraid to legislate a complete extermination of native tribes in their attempt to do so. If this wasn't frightening enough, Juan also learned of the happenings of the east coast; England's total rule and imminent defeat of France along the Atlantic seaboard. How far the Atlantic Ocean was, Juan, Son of William had no idea, but he knew that any news of permanent English and Spanish presence in any direction was unfavorable for his colony.

Under the assumed identity of northern Indians, Juan demanded that the Spanish trappers give up their guns and horses peacefully or be killed. In an attempted escape by the Spanish, Juan and his men sounded off their weapons and a firefight commenced along the creek. When the smoke cleared, three men of the valley were dead, including Juan himself. Six of the fifteen hunters survived the fight and fled to the south on foot, but were tracked down and massacred by Viho and the remaining men for fear that their story would entice an already suspicious Spanish government to come looking for the perpetrators. When Viho returned to the valley with the corpse of his fallen father, and the tales of the trappers on his tongue, the valley sprung into a panic. As a response to the hysteria, Viho instated his aforementioned mandate.

There were of course other celebrated tales of Spanish exploration in and around Colorado between 1761 and 1803, such as the forever famous Domínguez-Escalante Expedition across southwest Colorado—two-hundred miles from Cobb's Valley—that laid the blueprint for the route that would eventually become the Old Spanish Trail.[53] This excursion departed Santa Fe on July 29, 1776.[54] Additionally, there was Juan Bautista who in 1779 scored a valiant victory against the Comanche in present-day Pueblo, Colorado, ninety miles from Cobb's Valley. While these stories certainly played an important role in the development of the Rocky Mountain region, neither of these occurrences held as dire implications for Cobb's Valley as those that would come in the wake of a new player on the world's stage: The United States of America.

Luckily for the people of Cobb's Valley, as Spanish proletariat support grew for an independent Mexican government around the turn of the century, colonial intervention in the area known as Colorado practically ceased. This was, of course, until Jefferson's purchase of Louisiana in 1803.

To briefly recount the previously listed American expeditions[55] of the Rocky Mountain range: James Purcell entered the range via the South Platte River in 1803, standing only three miles away from Cobb's Valley at his closest point. In 1807 Zebulon Pike would mistakenly take the South Platte River north into South Park believing it to be the Arkansas River. He would be just forty miles from Cobb's Valley. Finally, Stephen Long's party would spend several weeks along the foot of the mountains near Platte Canyon just five miles from Cobb's Valley in 1820.

It was in 1808, after eight quiet years as the valley's leader, that Giant George ended the unpopular act of confinement that his father had instated nearly fifty years prior. The freedom to travel at will outside of the mountain valley was granted. Though people regained their right to explore the range freely, there were no officially commissioned excursions or research missions performed by the people of Cobb's Valley until 1834 when a trapper named Mohan, cousin of George, spotted the beginnings of Louis Vasquez' first fort along the foot of the hogbacks. For months following his discovery, Mohan holed up in the hogbacks night after night to document the happenings of the mysterious intruders. He finally caught his first glimpse of Franklin's Fort in late 1834. By 1835, Vasquez had moved his operation to the northeast, building his permanent residence far up the South Platte, but Jim Franklin, building his fort closer to the range, had seemed to settle in for good. Mohan told George that he was sure that the forts had to be the work of the Spanish and George, not wanting to reinstate the unpopular curfew, worked quickly to develop a solution to this problem.

His solution was precarious, but interesting nonetheless: Starting in February 1835, he began to send his stealthiest men to swindle goods from the fort in the dark of the night in an attempt to "discourage" these "Spanish" intruders from settling. It was his hope that the trappers would accuse the local Indians of the thievery, and they would engage in battle, eventually driving the settlers from the range. However, George greatly underestimated the stubbornness of his new adversaries. For over a year he got away with his petty thievery and raucous mischief at the expense of Jim Franklin, but had not seen any indication that they would leave. In the fall of 1836, when the army arrived, he foolishly deduced that he had no choice but to use violence. In hopes to lure the entire "Spanish" force into one of the canyons, he led a skirmish force of twenty men into the foothills to make themselves visible to the patrols. When Captain Jonathan Flete took the bait, George ordered his men into Platte Canyon, where he knew an easy route up the face of the walls before they became unclimbable. For hours he did exactly what Lieutenant Lockhart had surmised—stalked the infantry in the dark until they entered the narrowest ravine of the canyon and waited for them to make a mistake. During the process of stalking them along the tops of canyon walls, it became apparent to George that the men were not Spanish at all; from listening to the voices that filled the narrow space, he fell under the impression that they were English, but continued his attack as planned. Unfortunately for him, his twenty men with muzzle-loading, single-shot muskets that they had acquired in the 1760s, were not enough to completely dispatch Flete and his fifty trained soldiers. While they inflicted over half casualties, they faced diminishing returns after an hour of fighting in the dark and he decided to retreat before any of his men got hurt. Upon his return to Cobb's Valley the next morning, he ordered a team of scouts to survey each of the primary waterways that fed the plains from the mountains. When Mohan carelessly stumbled upon Russell Clark along Deer Creek and got forced into leading him back the valley, George was consumed by the disappointment of seven generations of men before him who trusted that he would keep John Cobb's secret safe.

***

When Russell Clark left Cobb's Valley, George sat alone behind a trembling candle and he thought for a long time. He felt the dusty wood of his old chair in his massive hands. He bit his bottom lip and breathed like an ape through his nose. "United States of America," he said repeatedly. "United States of America."

The next morning he called Mohan into his home and interrogated him about what information had been exchanged between himself and Clark. George was thankful that Mohan was of a relatively simple temperament, as he didn't give Clark very much to work with. He wondered to himself how much he really trusted the boy, Clark. He found the young trapper to be genuine and believed that he truly had nothing to do with the army, but the very thought of an outsider roaming the earth with his precious secret—his generational responsibility—was enough to lead him to further violence. It did not help matters that ceaselessly throughout the day a new hand pounded upon his door, all with frantic questions. People were afraid, concerned, furious, and confused. *Who was that man? What does this mean for me? For my children? What are we going to do?* George did not have these answers. His visitors became so frequent that he took to sitting outside his home in the fresh air so that the anxiety of the knocking door did not interrupt him in his rumination. He could see which neighbor was coming to encroach on his privacy from one-hundred yards away.

"Es no good, George…no sir! Never should have happened!" they said, tapping their feet. "What can be done? Oh, Lord! How did we ever get found?"

As George sat outside his home in the desperate evening he heard the faint song of a bird. It was a unique song and completely foreign to his ears. He stood to seize sight of it. He walked and walked the village with his head to the trees. He bobbed and squinted to the distance. At times he felt that he had closed in on the bird, but in an instant, it would sound off its song from the other side of the valley. Finally, just as the sun set, with the early moon already ablaze in the pale gray sky, he caught a glimpse of the feathered friend. It was a red-beaked chickadee, the likes of which George had never seen before. He studied it as it sat patiently and chirped from its tree into the night. *A peculiar little devil,* he thought. He figured it must be an eastern bird, come west with the settlers. Its mighty carelessness at the top of an evergreen in the center of his village disturbed him. The bird had no questions about where it was or who lived below him. It just sang until its next meal, overlooking the busy village in search of some bits of bread and then it sang again.

***

In the evening, with his pipe, George sat across from his fireplace in his upright chair. The chair was old, made by Ricardo de la Nada in 1730 when he was key-keeper and living in the very home that George lived in now—the home that John Cobb had built himself in 1611 to fit his growing family. The chair was large, as Ricardo was nearly as gigantic as George. It was made finely of strong oak, nearly black, with great emblems of suns and planets and flowers and deer and clouds carved into its frame and its arms. George tapped his foot absent-mindedly and he looked into the red ribbons of fire that spiraled about the fresh fuel he'd just laid in the bed of embers. He felt the four generations of men sitting in the oak chair with him.

They sat together at the fire. Ricardo was stoic and quiet and smoked a pipe as George did. William smiled his crooked-toothed smile and kissed his wife and had no time for strain or hassle. His life was good, and he knew that he would always prevail in what he did as long as he remained good. Juan sat in the chair with a temper, tired of the same walls that confined him. The fire blazed at the front of his mind, and he was ready to order off a cannonade into the forest to show each and every laughing, taunting blackbird that it was he who was in charge of this valley—no force of nature should rule him. Viho sat sad and alone, lost in the hypnosis of the fire, wondering if perhaps it would engulf his home one day as he slept, ridding his home of problems and of worry. Each of them contemplated their own complication, but none were as dire as the one that George had on his hands. He looked around his home and saw specters of John Cobb and Powa setting wood on top of wood and laying finish to the rough cedar beams above his head. They sweat and they passed him and walked through him, unaware of his existence as he sat in his chair. He desperately wished to ask Cobb for his help; to apologize that some jumpy boy from a place called Kentucky had sat at his table.

George began to think of Russell Clark. He replayed their conversation in his head over and over trying to find a moment or a word that indicated some malevolence from the boy. He wanted to trust him but had no way of doing so. George knew that he must uphold his end of the deal he struck with Clark, for the fate of his people depended on it.

He replayed their meeting in his mind ad nauseam and in some moments felt how simple a problem it was. A discovery was bound to happen, he thought. It makes great sense that Clark would be just as startled as George—that he would want to keep his own secret. Occasionally George would settle on this thought and force himself to feel resolved, but it was only a matter of minutes before it came nagging back to him. He knew he would be forced to prepare for some sort of conflict in the event that Clark lied. He had seen the blue soldiers marching in the plains with his own eyes. He knew their numbers and knew that the army had come well equipped with horses. If Clark had lied, it would only be a matter of days before he returned with the likes of the military to plunder the village.

Those final words lingered in George's mind ceaselessly with a dizzying cadence: *This country of mine, it moves fast…perhaps they will not find your children, or perhaps not even their children, but one day somebody will find this village.*

George had no way of knowing that his fate was already decided. He had no way of knowing that his discovery was imminent. His view of the world had been condemned to solace by fear, and fastened by the perilous empty hope that his generation would not be the generation that would be found. He did not know that his very existence was an obstruction to an ensuing campaign of national destiny. He did not know of the fanatical technologies that lurked on the other side of the decade. Men were to blow up mountains and send coal-powered boxcars through their rotting cavities. Immigrants from Germany and Italy and Ireland farmed leagues of corn under the same blazing sun that cooked the French balconies of New Orleans. Around the Great Lakes, an unprecedented discovery of good lumber was the catalyst for "Michigan Fever," a population boom that would ignite an industry that would turn small towns into global metropolises in a matter of years. In Texas, revolutionaries had just defeated Mexico in a grueling war that would set the stage for another conflict that would forever secure the fate of the Pacific for the victors. In New York, men escaped the punishing slums of the city to enchanting pastures where they played a game they called base-ball. It was happening everywhere. The world in which he lived was collapsing.

George had no way of knowing what it meant to live in 1836.

Something drew George out of his stupor and he stood from his chair. He fell victim to some force he was not aware of; some motive he could not explain. He stood above the flames that cackled in his fireplace, and he walked through his dark home to his lonely bedroom where no wife or woman awaited him. He lit a candle and pulled from a leather bag the long, iron key that beheld the timeless magic of Cobb's trunk. The very key that had earned him and his father, and his grandfather the very title of their name. He fell to his knees at the trunk and lifted the buffalo hide beyond the lock. When the lock clicked open, he felt the spirit of his ancestors move his very soul. Inside, it was all as he had left it last. His father's letters to him sat folded and obedient in a corner. A written draft of William, Son of Foxfoot's lauded speech of perseverance and preservation from 1719 stared back at George. It was a speech that reunited the colony during a period of near schism. George had read it several times and he read it again there, sat on the ground. The many signatures of Ricardo and Ricardo's father Marin were scattered about. Paintings of the beautiful Vehoae and her friend Rose-Marie all stacked upon each other in the trunk and sent a sensational shiver up George's spine. On top of it all of course, sealed by tree gum was Cobb's envelope.

Open in the nonce of crisis.

He held the delicate paper in his hands and apologized aloud to the man who had written it. He broke the seal of the gum and pulled out the almost translucent paper within. It was reed paper, etched with black ink. The last man to hold the note was John Cobb, old and frail, in the very room George sat now.

To whom it may conc'rn,

  If thou has't the privilege of reading mine own notation h're, thy judgment already holds mine own trust. Likewise, if't be true thou beareth the responsibility of the same action, I doth not envy thy circumstances.

  In a world untouch'd by tragedy, this letter shall never meeteth anoth'r set of eyes beyond mine own. Howev'r, I am nay daw and I knoweth yond someday, somebody shall beest forced to read it by unfav'rable luck. Let it be thee, valorous sir, fr thou art as valorous as any. Wheth'r thy calamity finds thee by accident, by misprision, 'r by unfrtunate circumstance, thou needeth not feareth. Thou needeth not to feel whey-face 'r harden'd. I didst not expecteth this anomaly of a colony to survive in a world unfit fr its ethos frev'r. Thou has't not ruin'd me. Thou art just a victim of tragedy.

  I first did step on this continent on May 12, 1599 with mine own companion of valorous mann'r and valorous shall, Adam Stone. We did found a colony togeth'r by the name of New Bristol. The colony wast with God—until it wasn't. It wast stout until it wast madeth weak by the meddling of England's greed and prejudice. Mine own companion Adam Stone wast a respectable lead.

  I did steal all but one of his children from und'r his grasp and we did flee und'r the bleak night following a h'rrific fight with Nanticoke Indians yond hath left dozens of good men, women, and children dead. The scene following the fighting wast something conjur'd only by Hades. I shall not recite it here. Accompanying myself and the Stone family were one Nanticoke family—that of Patamon. Their st'ries, I trusteth, art as well known to thee, reader, as mine own—fr our st'ries art impossible to separate. Patamon wast a great, kind, brave sir, amongst many I'd ev'r known. All who had knoweth that Indian wouldst bid thee the same. That friend wast slain und'r mine own hest in our pilgrimage to this magnificent valley. His spirit is what hast hath kept us, and thee, safe for all of these years.

  When I did found this valley, I hath felt I wast doing something chariest fr mine own family. Hadst we stayed in New

Bristol, I believeth still, we wouldst has't perish'd of certain. Escape wast all what hath seemed possible at the time; all beginnings wilt cometh at the expense of something else.

If thy gen'ration is the one of this settlement's conclusion, I am sorry. I trusteth yond thou art distress'd and sadden'd by this fact. Without prevailing dramatics, I shalt lie out two suggestions f'r how thou shouldst proceed.

If thy adv'rsary is peaceful, it is mine own belief yond this trunk at which thee standeth shouldst be burn'd with all of its contents. In the nonce yond one 'r more of the world's gov'rnments holds interest in the treasonous nature of our settlement, I wouldst giveth those folk <u>nay indication yond thou holdeth roots in New Bristol, Colony of England</u>. Burneth this trunk, and rid thy names of any Cobbs or Stones. Finally, <u>professeth yond this settlement's origins do lie in the roots of Sir Francis Drake's 1577 establishment of New Albion.</u> In the library of this trunk, I did provide a rath'r comprehensive hist'ry of Drake's life. I adviseth thee to study it, and useth the story of his contact with the west'rn coast of this American continent to thy advantage.

Alt'rnatively, if 't be true thy adv'rsary is termagant, it is of mine own proposal yond thou giveth those folk neith'r the satisfaction of battle, n'r the privilege of discov'ry in vict'ry. I regreteth to writeth yond the integrity of this colony wouldst beest bett'r suit'd completely burn'd and masterless by its keepeth'rs than defeat'd at the hands of the Spanish 'r the English. 'Twill not beest easy to p'rf'rm such a task I am acknown, but I trusteth thou agnize the reality yond und'r the completeth monarchy of eith'r of these nations, thy discov'ry and association with the New Bristol settlement shall not beest known fondly. Likely, 'twill beest hath met with sentences of death 'r life imprisonment for all who is't reside within. Thy most wondrous ambition as a people wouldst beest to leaveth behind this life, and to seek assimilation elsewh're, p'rhaps in the rampallian'rt'd tribes within the hills.

I believeth in the strength and p'rsev'rance of a people. I especially believeth in the ability of mine own kin and the kin of Patamon to ov'rcome all yond threatens it. Howev'r, if 't be true the calamity bef're thee is one of utmost destruction at the hands of a wr'ld pow'r, then p'rhaps thou shall beest bett'r suit'd to doeth as I did—to leaveth behind ev'rything thee has't known and starteth again elsewh're. Whatev'r thou doth, son, brother, friend, <u>thou art the sir to leadeth these folk.</u>

With luck from the grave,

John Cobb, 1652

two

AROUND the table at Franklin's Fort, Lockhart assaulted a poorly drawn map with his smoking hand. Ash littered about the map like gray crumbling clouds above its surface.

"It was just about here that we abandoned the creek and began the climb up the steep mountainside," he said. Captain Flete and Jim Franklin were listening intently at his side. "It was a little over an hour's march from this ridge here." He grazed his hand again over a scribbled ridgeline. "The path drawn here is not perfect, but I would be able to recite our route by heart. It will not be difficult to follow the trail of the horses."

"You are sure this was not an Indian village, Lockhart?" Franklin asked.

"There were Indians there, Mister Franklin, but this was no Indian camp. There were stone buildings and chimneys. Wood houses. I saw white men amongst the Indians. There were horses and things made of leather and cotton. Guns, iron…This was a village, I tell you. Clark can attest to this."

Clark's mouth was closed and his lips were thin inside his mouth. The points of his lips were sharp and shy. He nodded yes at the prompt of Lockhart's eyes.

"It has to be Mexicans or some lost Spanish chapter. Perhaps runaway slaves or something of the sort," said Franklin.

"I'm unsure of that. It all looked remarkably English. Not unlike Baltimore or Boston of old. *It is* old. You'll just have to see for yourself, Mister Franklin."

"Well, I'm not so sure I would venture as far from the fort as that, Lieutenant. I'm not a very strong climber. I would have to take your word for it."

"Lockhart, are you saying you wish to make contact?" Flete said. His blue hat sat on the table in front of him revealing his balding head. Thin black coils of hair stuck in all directions behind his forehead. Dark eyebrows, the size of his mustache, raised up nearly to the beginning of his thin hairline. "We should send a messenger to Leavenworth in the morning to request more men. They'd give us whatever we want given these circumstances."

"Enough with this talk about Leavenworth!" Lockhart said laughing. They'd had this conversation before. "We don't need more soldiers to make contact. If our relations are done correctly, we won't need any soldiers at all. I'll bring the cavalry down into the valley with me and we can feign our numbers of infantry by scattering them about the ridgeline. You can just as well win a battle with your tongue and your mind as you can with a sword and musket, Captain. I will simply tell these strangers that they are trespassers on United States property and are wholly surrounded. We shall prompt them to surrender to the will of the United States. They can be made citizens on behalf of their cooperation. If they do not surrender, they are fools."

"What makes you think they would surrender, Lockhart? They've already made a coordinated assault on the infantry," Flete said.

"Perhaps they can cut down the weary infantry in the darkness of night, but there is no chance they can handle the might of the Second Dragoons in the light of day."

"There mus' be two-hunerd able men in that village, Lieutenant!" shouted Clark. "Ye can't fight'em. I saw the guns!" He had kept quiet most of the night, but the prospect of any fighting rose his blood to a boil. "I saw'em wit' my own eyes. I saw the guns and the horses as well. Ain't no use in fightin'em."

"Two-hundred untrained farmers in some lost mountain village are no concern to me, boy. Where they out-man us, we have the superior equipment, training, and position." He lowered his shining eyes to Clark. "Of course, it would be expected that the young men who live here at Franklin's would join an assault if it comes to such dire straits."

Franklin and Clark peered at each other from across the table.

Lockhart spoke again, "Between my fifty dragoons, the twenty-five or so able infantry, and another twenty militia, our position would be impeccable. They would have no choice but to concede to our terms before our hand is forced into an assault."

Jim Franklin opened his mouth to speak. The center of his throat quivered as he swallowed. He looked at Clark. "Well, surely the men would help, Lieutenant."

"I 'spose we'd have to," Clark muttered.

"Very good," said Lockhart. "I imagine each of the other trappers are as good of patriots as the two of you. We have come and done what we said we would, Mister Franklin. We have stopped these so-called thieves, and we have found their so-called lair. It is only natural that your men join us in the detention of the perpetrators."

"I object to this sentiment," Flete interrupted. "These trappers are not soldiers. They are citizens. They have no obligation to join the army in any possibility of an assault."

"You must not be listening, Flete. If our job is done correctly, there should be no assault. We are to approach the valley with our entire force. The dragoons shall descend into the valley with myself, while your infantry and Franklin's men cover us from above. Intimidation alone will end negotiations promptly. These trappers would play an integral part in our enemy's peaceful surrender. Additionally, their bravery would surely be compensated by the U.S. Army to the tune of one-hundred-fifty dollars a man." Lockhart stood from the table and began to unbutton his coat. A cold fog escaped from his mouth with his breath as he spoke. "I will ready for bed now, gentleman. In the morning, we must act swiftly. Franklin, I will expect a count on willing men from your camp no later than sunrise. Their bravery and dedication to their nation will not go overlooked. Flete, alert the infantry that they will be marching."

***

In the morning the word of their departure had reached the enlisted men and they gossiped, spreading all sorts of rumors and unconfirmed speculations amongst each other. Bell, who had seen the valley with his own eyes, stayed quiet rather than join and perpetuate the tales being passed around at breakfast. Some men who were not even present on the day of the valley's discovery spoke with utmost confidence and fabricated details of the settlement and its origins.

"It's a bunch'a old Spanish from Santa Fe," one man said proudly. "Ye folk'r likely unaware o' how many Spanish colonists would go missin' in those early days. The Injuns use t' kidnap soldiers 'n farmers. Took ther' families too. A bunch'a half-breeds who took t' the mountains, that's all it is."

"I think it's more likely lost explorers," another man added. "Maybe even French from up north."

Around Franklin's Fort the smell of bacon drifted through the air in a sheeted smoke. Men cleaned their guns and polished their boots and insulated their feet with three pairs of socks to a man. Even the military looked like a militia with their layers of beaver and deer hide. There was hardly any blue at all to see on their persons. It was all fur browns and reds and blacks. Russell Clark and a contingent of seventeen young trappers dressed in tattered layers and stood together quietly with their muskets and hunting knives. They could see in the distance the tops of the mountains had frozen and a gentle snow continued to fall behind the Front Range. Lockhart trotted proudly upon his clean, black stallion firing off valiant stanzas of patriotism and duty.

"Some men encounter the prospect of glory just once in a lifetime!" he shouted. "Let your name be attached to what could go down as one of the greatest discoveries in the country's history, gentlemen. Allow yourselves to be heroic. Allow yourselves to be great!"

As he passed by Bell, he slowed his trot and then stood still for a moment overlooking the readying men. His horse breathed steam through its perfect nose and rotated its head to look at Bell. Its dark, shameless eyes seemed to pierce the shell of Bell's humanity. Bell had never felt inferior to an animal before but he knew that this warhorse could smell the pathetic scent of fear that stewed in his blood. He broke his gaze with the horse and turned his head back to his pack in front of him. The horse seemed to smirk as Lockhart pulled his reins. "Dragoons!" the officer shouted. His voice broke the noisy fraternity of the fort. Each man turned their attention to the smiling lieutenant. His long hair blew like black flames in the busy wind. "Dragoons, on me!" And he trotted outside the fort with fifty strong horses kicking dust into the faces of the goggling infantry.

A steady snow soaked the men on their march up Deer Creek. Two squadrons of infantry led the march in a column two men wide. Flete and Lockhart walked at the head of the column. The entire cavalry marched behind them, two men wide when possible, but usually single file along the thin mountain trails. Their own carbines were drawn and held with one hand as the other held the reins of their vehicle. Riding on their own horses with the cavalry column were nine of the seventeen trappers, including Russell Clark. They held an assortment of motley weaponry from varmint rifles to old British muskets to Spanish carbines to the brand new Hawkens rifles that were even better than what the army had. And as if the insufferable self-satisfaction of the cavalry was contagious, even the mounted trappers felt something of a pride sitting on their horses marching in column with the cavalry, high above the poor-legged infantry.

Behind them, were the rest of the trappers—eight men—who walked in line on foot with the rest of the infantry as a rearguard. Bell was one of these men. He was near the back of the entire march, watching snow fall off the brim of his hat, sometimes soaking his chin. He thought about how easy it would be for him to slip out from the column into a hoard of trees completely unnoticed. Of course he would not defect, but the mere possibility tickled him—nearly taunted him—as he walked. Bell had been consumed with thoughts of leaving the army perpetually since the massacre in Platte Canyon. He figured after this mission, it would be a month's march back to Jefferson Barracks. From that point he would only have three months of his service left. He would be given at least one month's rest at the barracks once he returned from the West, giving him only a two-month window to be reassigned to another mission. As long as the soldiers of the east kept up against the Seminoles, Bell imagined his remaining months of military service to be spent at the barracks. The prospect that this march along Deer Creek would be his final assignment provided some motivation to see it through. He hoisted himself upon white rock without complaint. He cut himself on thorns and pines without quarrel. He stepped in the ever-present droppings of the horses before him, unirritated and accepting of his duty, for after this, he would be free.

Along the frosted ridgelines the snow fell harder. The tips of the mustaches worn by the dragoons began to freeze. The infantry combatted the numbness of their hands by hammering them upon their thighs to stir the nerves awake. Deer Creek, usually humming a steady song, was reduced to a gentle chime as ice had already begun to take hold of its banks.

Halfway up the mountain, the party lost its first casualty; a horse. The terrain had become difficult and the snow very thick. The horses slipped and slid as they walked upon rocks that were slick with ice. One poor steed misstepped into a snowtrap and curled its ankle on a stone that hid beneath the white. He teetered and fell towards the ledge. The dragoon that mounted him bailed off to the side towards the column and watched as his steed kicked for a moment at the slippery snowdust trying to stand again. It rolled under its own weight to the ridge where it fell a lethal distance and met the snow below with a dull *thunk*. The poor dragoon was left to walk on foot.

The army reached the overlook onto Cobb's Valley in the early afternoon. For a moment, as the officers looked on, the column broke and the heads of the soldiers bobbed and peaked out over the ridge until Flete ordered them back into formation. Everybody wanted to see what all the fuss had been about. The onlookers were not disappointed as what they saw was exactly what they had been sold: A thriving, sizable community in the style of Old England wedged between western peaks of the Rocky Mountains.

The snow had covered the valley considerably and dozens of chimneys coughed out sweet smoke that floated onto the hills and warmed the army. Below, horses walked happily, men cut wood and pulled sleds of lumber. Some children had built a snow fort and played on top of it in the fairgrounds. As unordinary as it was, it was nothing out of the ordinary at its essence.

From behind the lip of the ridge, Lockhart began to order the men into position. He spread the infantry and the militia of trappers out along the easy hills above the valley. They surrounded the valley in a half-moon, looking down their barrels at the center of the fort. In some areas barren of trees, he stuck a cluster of men to appear as though the ranks were thicker than they really were. High in the trees however, he stationed lone sharpshooters—trappers and infantry who were known to waste no shot.

Together and triumphant at the head of the trail that descends into Cobb's Valley—the same trail by which John Cobb first entered his valley—stood the entirety of the 2nd Dragoons. As he readied his descent, Lockhart called to Flete and Clark. They assembled at his side.

"Somebody of some authority should be joining me in the valley. In my humble opinion, it should be Clark."

"Well, sir—" Clark started.

"You are Franklin's representative on this mission, Clark. What happens here affects you and yours more than anyone else. Franklin would be with me if the old gollumpus could have made the climb. He would hope that you'd be the one to make contact."

Clark's swollen eyes stared back at the lieutenant. There was no escape from the fate presented to him.

Lockhart spoke again. "Flete needs to stay here and direct the infantry. Besides, he's already blown his chance to negotiate with these people. Come boy, you will ride with us."

Lockhart led Clark and the rest of the cavalry down the hill in a slow trot. The boy's mind spun with nerves. He could not imagine the prospect of facing George. Equally, this was no time to inform Lockhart that he had been down these valley steps before. He hoped that time would freeze, that God would grant him one miracle and that he could leave while the others were imprisoned by the shackles of phenomenon. He even thought perhaps the moment of inertia would never come, that they would descend the valley forever and he would never actually confront George. He believed he would have a solution to his problem at any holy minute, that all would solve itself with patience, though he did not feel patient. He felt empty and very sad. By the time the villagers caught wind of their descent, he had accepted his fate.

A crowd began to gather at the northern wall of the fort. Lockhart waved his gloved right hand high in the air. Fifty horses crunched through the hard snow behind him. At the gate, Lockhart was greeted by a group of armed guards. They looked him over in his bright uniform. Lockhart held the rest of the cavalry behind him with a motion of his hand and looked down at the head guard. "Lieutenant Samuel James Lockhart, 2nd Dragoons, U.S. Army at your service, good sir. He beside me is Russell Clark, just a boy-citizen, but an expert trapper and involved party in this urgent matter. We request a council with whom may be the authoritative body in this fine land."

The guard looked at Clark and recognized him. Clark avoided contact with his eyes, instead looking only at Lockhart.

"I can escort thee to George," said the guard, "but thy soldiers here must remain outside the walls."

Lockhart's face fell long in amazement. He had not expected the guard to reply in perfect English.

"Very well," said Lockhart laughing, "let us be introduced to this George and perhaps we will get a clue as to what in blazing Hades is happening here."

At George's door, Clark began to cycle through each and every possibility of escape. He considered denying his name and insisting that they'd never met before. For a moment, he nearly came clean to Lockhart there at the foot of the cabin, telling him the truth and that he was sworn to secrecy by death. Before he could settle on any one delusional solution, the door creaked open and the giant man with the dark unnerving face smiled to see the two Americans.

"Mister Clark," George said, "I see thou has't brought thy friends. I had a notion thou would introduce us."

three

FOR hours as Lockhart and George spoke, Clark made himself small at the table. The two diplomats wouldn't as much allow a cough let alone a comment from the boy. He was left to stew with fear as the two distinguished men spoke of serious matters; the nature of nationdom and law. In his silence, he sweat like a weeping urchin. A tempest of dread moved through him. Lockhart and George had silently agreed at their introductions to let Clark suffer in his rumination. He was to be dealt with later, after the adults had finished their business.

George, who wore dull grays and browns, animal hides and starry stones like marble around his meaty neck, was happy to speak with Lockhart, who in a way, was exactly his foil. The officer was muscular and strong and spoke confidently with shiny words through provoking smiles. He was used to receiving what he wanted. He was a sort of master at the art of exactly that. George on the other hand, was strong because he was of great mass. His shoulders mirrored the width of the table. His jaw was that of an ox, and his hands were deep like buckets. He too was accustomed to achieving nearly everything he set out to achieve, not for his charm—of which he had none—but for his dark urgency, his sureness of himself. His physical intimidation and his sharp, clear mind settled every score with every enemy he'd ever known before. To play mental chess with a man who had never been told no, was exciting for him. He spoke slowly and at one single pitch.

"We have always known we were close to the Spanish," George said plainly. He rolled up his sleeves revealing his dark forearms, large like logs. "Especially with all the horses around. Mine own father always told that there were Spanish south of here, but we never actually witnessed any soldiers so it was impossible to place their colonies."

"Yes, I understand," said Lockhart. He tapped his fingers against the pine table, thinking.

"We have not seen anybody. We have not needed to. We have everything here."

"It is the most interesting thing I think I've ever heard," remarked Lockhart. "Now tell me, George, after abandoning the Drake Expedition, did your ancestors come straight here? Or did they live on the coast for some time?"

"We do not know for certain. I place the date of our origins in this valley near 1580. That is an estimate. Our ancestors left us very little literature to reference. Our only history is oral. I learned from mine own father the story I told thee. He had been told by his father."

"And to recount this tale if I may, sir, three men of English origin were separated from Sir Francis Drake's landing party in New Albion, 1577. They took Indian wives and traveled east until they finally settled here in this valley. Stop me if I am wrong, sir. Some years after that, a lost band of Ute Indians joined them. Your people have been happily hidden ever since. Your only visitors have been the wandering horses."

"That is correct." George's eyes were dead and his mouth hardly moved as he confirmed his fable. He tried to not speak more than he must, lest he make a mistake.

"What fortitude it must have taken these men to not feel the natural desire to...to...to conquer! To explore!" Lockhart said excitedly. "Forgive me, sir, but I just find it so impossible to believe that your forefathers felt no lust for glory. No passion for campaign."

"They were surely a disciplined lot," George said.

"And yourself, sir. Disciplined indeed."

"I am proud of it."

"Now, George," Lockhart leaned in closely as if to whisper. He took a quick look at Clark who he had momentarily forgotten was present. "George, I have to know then, what drives a people such as you to steal from the poor trappers on the plains? And why for heaven's sake, did you lay an assault on the U.S. Army?"

The giant looked blankly at the lieutenant. His eyes widened but he said nothing.

"George, in the world I exist in, an unprompted assault on military forces is synonymous with a declaration of war. And I must tell you sir, my superiors took your assault as such. I will tell you the truth. Surrounding this village right now, I have over five-hundred men along the ridges and the treelines, well-armed and enraged. That is in addition to the fifty cavalry that are held at your gates, and the fifty more that are on the other side of the north ridge. We have enough men here now to put an end to your Atlantis and make it nothing more than another fairytale. However, I am a man of an open mind and open heart. I am always willing to negotiate."

George's blue eyes began to wander inside the deep wells of their sockets. He took a sharp look at Clark. He stared at him with the mad wickedness of a brute.

"If you would like, George," Lockhart continued, "I could be inclined to arrange for you and your little town to be incorporated officially into the United States. I would stay here for a little while and govern matters as I saw them while we sent for an official representative to come and conduct a sort of census in the valley. We would properly identify these people and set them up to pay taxes and such—legal matters. They would have names, occupations and *stories*. They would *be somebody* in the eyes of a government. As of now they exist as fleeting ghosts in the winds of history. That is no way to live and die, George. With citizenship, they could go on to become prominent people. They could properly exist. Let me assure you that our magnificent new country breeds geniuses and men of stature from all fields; our cities excel in global sciences, craftsmanship, arts, military studies, religion, and agriculture. Think about your children, George.

"My government would draw you a formal contract, and even though this is already American soil, you will still be paid handsomely for your land possessions because of the…let us call it, misunderstanding. You would remain in a position of relative power, I will personally see to that. Perhaps you will be made councilman, assistant to the governor. With your utmost cooperation, you could someday become governor yourself. You would only have to cede military control, and seeing as we know each other now, I will insist that military operations be ceded directly to me so that you and I could work hand in hand in developing and protecting this land. I want to be a friend to you, George. What you have here is special, sir. Your lovely secret is generations ahead of every settlement two-hundred miles in any direction! Think of the possibilities, if you will. All you must do is shake my hand and surrender what weapons you may have. No man will suffer. You may even keep your horses. It is what's good for your family."

George's anxious hands began to come alive. They sweat and squirmed atop the table. He had no answer for Lockhart. He felt deep in his gut, like the pit of a peach, 236 years of travail by all the good men that came before him to preserve and to nurture what he possessed now. He looked at the cedar beams of John Cobb's cabin. He looked at Ricardo's oak chair, alone and ancient across the room. He looked at the insolent face of Lockhart, opposite him, blinking in the pale white sunlight that bled through the wide window. Finally, he looked at Clark sitting beside him, defeated and stirred. He thought of his words one month ago that had haunted him in the night, kept him from sleep, and foretold this moment: *"Somebody will find this village."*

"Rat!" he shouted in his rage. His voice boomed in the small cabin and shook its walls. "Deplorable vermin! Thou shouldst be killed!" The boy jumped in his seat. A sweat soaked his flushed face. His blonde hair fell before his eyes but he hadn't noticed.

"Ah yes," Lockhart added, "it is high time we address your quarrel with the trapper boy."

"There is no quarrel. He dishonored me. We had arranged a covenant and he broke it."

"He seems to be quite gifted at that."

Clark finally burst to his own defense, "I upheld my end, George! I never told nobody!"

"Do not try and falsify your ways now, boy. You will only look like a fool," Lockhart said. He turned to George. "Clark here could not wait to tell me of his discovery. He led us here every step of the way. He's been insisting on being rewarded for it, which I would have happily obliged had I not recently discovered his thieving of army supplies. He is a sinner and shark. It is your own fault, George, for believing he possessed any such honor."

"Bastard!" Clark shouted.

"Your pleading won't save you now, child," Lockhart said dismissively. He pulled from his pocket his pipe and a small pouch of tobacco. He packed it leisurely and looked at George. The large man was taut like a tightrope. His skin looked like it was on the verge of tearing at the strain of his big bones. He stared down at his hands that sat atop the table.

"Have either of yee no understanding of goodness? Of virtue?" George said.

Lockhart lit his pipe and lifted his chin, intrigued by George's prompt.

George spoke again, "This valley was birthed and maintained for over two-hundred years not by men who succumbed to the temptation of what was facile, nor by men who laid down their arms when challenged by crisis, but by men who dreamed to escape the likes of men like thee, Lieutenant Lockhart. We have been a stout and peaceful people for over two centennial moments by living in accordance with one simple sentiment: to be valorous. I maintain a responsibility to mine own fathers before me. I maintain a responsibility to myself and my brothers. For the rest of mine own life I would have to live in the solemn shadow of shame if I was the man—in eight generations—to relinquish control of the anomaly that was built here inside these mountains. There is no place like this land here, sire. The virtuous man inside of me, and the spirits of those who died before me, will not allow me to turn this land over to your government, sire. With that, I ask thee to leave my home."

Lockhart blew smoke that laid across the table like a living fog. He sat quietly for a moment rolling his eyes in their beds thinking, quite deeply, about George's words. His legs were crossed and he swung one foot steadily as he thought. The ornaments of his uniform swayed gently with the movement of his foot.

"You certainly are a peculiar man, George," he mustered. "I am shocked by your genuine aspirations of decency. Your commitment to the integrity and deranged sentimentality of your home is as forthright as that of the Indians. Sadly, I tell the Indians just what I shall tell you: I have no respect for your position. For in your ignorance, you are resisting the very quiddity of the ideals that you champion. In your pride you resist change. Progress. You are like the Gaul who believes you will fare against the Roman. You are the fish who thinks it can outswim the bear. You are David, sir, and I am Goliath—not because I am any stronger than you, but because I am tomorrow. My ally is the sureness of time, the inevitable, the crisis of now. I carry with me a promise; a story already written, ready to be read. And no stone you can muster to sling could ever knock me down, for I have already won. I might as well be the harrowed reaper to your tried ways. You call your little valley an anomaly, but you have not known an anomaly until you have seen my United States, dear George. In your refusal to comply, you relinquish your chance to know the true anomaly of democracy. We are a kingless country, we are a Godly country. It is a great irony—a great irony indeed!—that you, George, would make a fabulous American with your untethered pursuit of freedom and virtue and legacy. I regret that you will be unable to see the global phenomenon of your very ideals at work. You have decided to forgo a chance to know New York City and all of its brick castles and the cunning genius that can be pulled right from its air. You will never see the majesty of the Mississippi River flow from the heart of our nation down the golden kingdoms of corn to the swampy delirium of New Orleans. You have neglected your chance to join a brotherhood of equally virtuous men who fought and died for seven long years to free themselves from the old tyranny of England. They fought to establish the world's first nation that bore no king. Their graves litter the streets of Boston, of Philadelphia, the banks of the Hudson, the orchards of Georgia, and woodlands of New Jersey. And most tragically, I regret to inform you that with your rejection of a peaceful integration, you consent to a violent occupation. Good day, dearest George, I will see you on the field." Lockhart placed his hat on his head, stood from the table and turned towards the door. He heard the sigh of Clark's chair behind him as the boy stood to follow him. "Oh, and

George," Lockhart turned and said, "have your way with the boy. I've gotten all I've needed from him."

***

From his window, George could see the smoke. He conquered his incessant pacing for moments at a time to stand still at the window and count again and again the number of fires that he saw burning upon the ridgeline in the darkness. How many men had Lockhart said he had? Five-hundred? More?

Behind George, three of his companions were deep in discussion. They were all dark men with Indian eyes and throats that spoke in commanding, flat words. They held guns on their laps. The light in the cabin was dim and the conversation was dire. George listened selectively as he gazed out his window.

"As long as we keep their horses from breaching the walls, I do believe that we could repel an initial attack," said one man.

"I heartily disagree!" spoke another. "The infantry could swarm us—one-hundred on each of our four sides and climb the bloody walls if they wanted to. We're doomed, there is no option but to surrender."

"Damn me if I surrender. I'll be the first to die before I surrender," spoke a third.

"Or thou will just live long enough to watch the rest of us get skinned alive."

George offered nothing. He just stared into the blue night, his head turning cartwheels as to what he should do.

In the valley, even in the late hour, men stood awake and alert with guns and bows, peering up at the glowing treeline on the ridge. They walked in haste about the pathways carrying torches and arrows and supplies to be used for the impending fortifications. They were joined by young schoolboys who ran these supplies and carried messages all about the valley. Some of the boys held bows and guns. Their long hair on top of their small round heads bobbed like apples on water as they rushed from corner to corner. The women and youngest children sat deep in their dark homes, unsettled and unasleep. George breathed in long, intentional breaths as he watched the scene unfold before him. Outside of his home, lying flat on his stomach with his face to the soil was Clark.

Clark shivered on the ground under the cold moonlight. A frozen wind seemed to breathe off of the silver surface of the moon. His coldness was helpless. His hands were cuffed and his feet were chained to a tall deep stake that loomed over him—not unlike one made for a beaver trap. He could feel his heartbeat inside his face—his swollen face, bloodied and black with bruises. He wished that George had used a mallet instead of his cannonball hands. The side of his beaten face laid flat and he looked up at the ridgeline where he too could see the smoke of the fires where the army had pitched camp. His body convulsed on the ground stiffly as he laid. He wished to cry, but wasn't sure that the muscles would work. It hurt to blink; it hurt to do anything.

Clark could calm himself occasionally, letting himself breathe and almost go numb in the biting cold until he remembered his fate before him. He knew that Lockhart was proud enough to attack. Lockhart's bluff had missed, but he was not about to allow himself to be perceived as a fool. The lieutenant was sure that he could inflict enough damage on the village to entice a surrender. In the night, he had convinced Flete that the battle was already won—at dawn he would attack. It had been decided. With that, Clark knew that in the chaos of the ensuing fighting, he would almost surely be killed. Both sides had casted him as an enemy and a traitor. Lockhart had already filled the camp with rumors that Clark had been an accomplice of George all along, organizing the raids in the night and keeping a hardy slice of the loot. It would take just a single man, enthralled with the passions of war, to end his life. What would stop such a man from putting his saber through his back, or his muzzle to his head in an act of indulgent vengeance? Clark decided that his only hope—and it was a slight one—was that Bill Bell would discover him first, and find it in his forgiving heart to free him. As he thought of innocent Bill Bell, he drifted off into a cold, spiraling sleep, and he cried.

***

Clark awoke to a hundred stomping feet passing him in what sounded like the deep earthy roar of a buffalo herd. The first shard of sun had snuck out from underneath the heavy clouds of the east. The lone beam tore through the fog and lit the ridge where Lockhart's cavalry stood in formation. Each of them held a torch with a furious flame of red fire like fox fur that burst from its body. A bugle sounded off and echoed at the stone walls of the valley and then the horses raced down the ridge at speed. A crack of muskets poured down from all sides of the valley. With the first volley, a few men within the walls fell. Around Clark's head, dirt spit from the stray rounds that found the earth beside him. To answer, the defenders fired a scattered volley into the charging cavalry but to little avail. Halfway down the drift of the hill, the cavalry split into two groups, sending off into opposite directions. The Americans above began to fire at will and a hailstorm of lead pestered the fort. George's men began to scatter and run from wall to wall but they could hardly get any eyes at all on the foot soldiers who were hidden in the trees and the rocks of the ridges. They began to fire sporadically into the mountain side and into the masses of horse, occasionally hitting one man or his horse and causing them to fall together. George began to shout, attempting to coordinate and concentrate the fire of his men, but as the horses got closer, his men fell victim to the fast, dizzying maneuvers of the cavalry and wasted round after round into the dirt.

Lockhart, who had been smiling since his descent from the ridge, gave the order to toss the torches. Dozens of fireballs poured onto the walls and deep into the village, some landing on the roofs of houses and woodpiles. Sections of the walled fortress began to smoke and burn and the men who ushered to put out the flames were cut down by the patient infantry who were still at work in the trees above. Lockhart's men each drew their carbines from their horses and in unison fired a volley that devastated the front row of heads that poked out from behind the fortress walls. With the leveling of his initial defenses, George ordered his own cavalry—a mere thirty-six common men on horseback armed with old Spanish muskets and dull swords—out into the field to pursue the dragoons.

Clark could hear the two cavalries crash in battle for what seemed like a lifetime. The moaning of swords and the ignoble squeals of slain horses filled the foreground of his senses—the clanking machinery of war. Inside the fort, men fell from their wounds and crawled to the cabin walls, painted with bullets. Black smoke from the fires slithered like snakes between the houses and blinded the men as they flailed about the village in panic.

George expected another wave of cavalry to emerge from the ridgeline. He stationed forty of his best sharpshooters along the wall facing the camp and ordered them to concentrate their entire fire onto the next cavalry charge. He paced in his courtyard and waited patiently for the additional cavalry. Still, they had not come. Outside the walls, his own horsemen were fighting honorably against the domineering dragoons, but were close to breaking as their horses were unfit for such combat. One by one, the twenty remaining horsemen came leaping back into the fort, bloody and wounded, their horses bucking in confusion. Lockhart's men dared not chase them into the depths of George's reserves.

George was not unconfident. He still worked with a surplus of men, heavily fortified and encouraged. He watched as his brothers and cousins and friends manned the fences in shifts; one man would fire off into the mountainside and run low across the ground to reload as another took his place. A constant retaliation of fire answered the rounds that poured in from above. He watched these men fall dead to the savage winds of war.

George tried to gauge the number of men that were hidden along the ridge. For several minutes he counted the constant reports. Looking out into the land around the fort, he counted only thirty remaining dragoons. The man beside him was suddenly hit and fell without sound. His eyes looked to the sky and blood leaked from beneath his garment. Immediately he was lost. George ducked and guided himself to the center of the fort near his home. He took stock of the positions around him.

"George," a faint voice snuck up on him in a whisper. It was a soft and pale voice that seemed like it may have been a product of his own mind between the commotion of the fighting. He paused to ensure that he had actually heard it. "George, listen…" it said again. He turned and saw Russell Clark pinned to the ground. His voice was broken from his beating and it sounded like the hiss of a cat. "George," Clark said again, now that he had the giant's attention.

George stepped toward his prisoner.

"They're finished, George. Lockhart is outta' men. He's beginnin' to panic. Look." George gazed up and saw Lockhart's cavalry regrouping on the mountainside. They began to retreat up the hill back to behind the rocks. The horses were wild and fought their commands. "That's all there is, George. He lied to ye. There was only fifty horses and another forty infantry. That's all he had. This is all they got left."

From the ground, George looked like a towering Douglas fir, wide and tall above Clark. His two legs looked like two round trunks. Smoke from the burning homes poured through the crotch of his legs and covered Clark in a black blanket. He coughed and with his cough he howled from the pain. He felt his broken ribs press against his lungs.

George bent over the young man and moved his mouth to speak but nothing came. He unchained his feet from the stake. He freed his hands from their shackles and Clark's numb limbs spilled onto the ground helplessly. "If thou art able, go," he said.

Another volley came down onto the fort. Every single able man under Lockhart's command let off a round. A dozen of George's men fell. The dragoons appeared re-formed at the ridgeline once again. They held another set of torches. The bugler was dead so Lockhart screamed in a hoarse voice and what was left of the troop charged ahead racing under scattered fire from the fort. Just after them, the whole of the infantry followed from the sides. It was a full-scale charge. George's men scrambled to brace the frontal assault.

"George," Clark called, but he had left to join his men.

"Hold your ground!" George yelled. A bombing of torches came over the walls and into the fort, some landing at the feet of the defenders and propelling flames up their legs and onto their bodies, lighting them whole as they danced an evil jig for their lives. The dragoons burst through the crumbling walls and the infantry began to fight in melee over the tops of the fort against the defenders. Slowly the American forces slipped through the burning posts or hacked down new doors of their own. Horses ran amuck through the village as houses were set to flames and Lockhart strode handsomely through the corridors of chaos cutting down men with such awesome grace one might have believed he was holy and invincible. The rattled defenders began to break and retreat under the illusion of the vast charge.

"Hold!" shouted George. "There are no more! This is all they have!" His commands were in vain as the roar of the fighting filled the air. George himself became caught dueling swords with a young trapper.

Finally in the dust of battle, Clark rose to his feet and began to limp to the walls. His eyes were swollen nearly shut, and his legs moved only of sheer will. He cut through the crowd, unarmed, and nearly unrecognizable as the fighting became merciless around him. He watched men's faces become eggs, trampled by horses. Others found death more intimately, by the slow seduction of the bayonet. Ahead of him he saw Bill Bell, fighting fiercely with a man. Bill's face was ragged and sore. It looked as though it had aged one-hundred years since the last time Clark had seen it, just the evening before. His eyes were deep and ceaseless and very sad. His lips were folded into his terrified mouth as he swung the butt of his gun towards his strong enemy with no poise at all. He was clumsy and afraid. In an ill-timed lunge, his enemy misstepped and fell to one knee, catching himself from tumbling completely with his weapon. Before he could rise, Bell's bayonet met him below the chin and he fell with a bawl. Clark squawked at the sight and tried to call for Bell, but before he could speak, he fell, hit by a stray arrow in the back. He could feel the arrow poke at his stomach like a cat clawing at his insides. He cursed and felt the wet wound. His hand emerged painted in blood. Already, his vision began to blur. Bell had not seen him.

The fighting men turned into a melted and molten gray that swirled around him without definition, featureless and chaotic. On the ground he felt the cold grass and it felt good to lay his warm head upon it again. The cold grass cooled his fever and he opened his mouth to breath and his tongue fell from his face and laid in the grass. He tasted the earth. "Bell," he said into the grass. "Bell." Men rushed by him as if he were already dead. He blinked at the sky and heard the voice of Captain Flete.

"Retreat!" it called. He screamed it like a comet and the word bounced in Clark's empty head like iron. *Retreat.* The field before him became sparse. The noise of the feet began to spread out as the men dispersed outside the fort. Even George's men fell back to their own defensive positions towards the center of the village. They had no interest in chasing the routed Americans. They had no will to carry on.

Clark laid in the field and he felt the omniscient time-swell of a dream in his mind. He felt that he had always been on the field, that he was born from this field and at certain points in his fading vision, that he existed inside the earth below the field. In front of his eyes he saw the wet leather of two black boots. He turned onto his back, engaging the arrow even further. He breathed in but felt air leave his lungs. He saw Lockhart, bloody and crazed above him. The lieutenant was missing his hat. His sword was black with blood. His eyes looked like black holes in a soulless skull.

"Lockhart," Clark began to sputter, "Lockhart, ye haffta take me. Take me, please. Take me with ye. Please, I'm sorry. I was 'fraid. It was an innocent mistake. Please."

"You betrayed your country, young man."

"Please sir, will ye forgive me? I need help, sir. I should have told ye." Clark began to spit as he spoke. Blood leaked from his mouth. He grasped with his hand at the earth and pulled grass from it. "Sir, please, I was so 'fraid. Ye b'leeve me, yes? Ye forgive me? Take me with you, sir."

Lockhart smiled down at Clark. "You poor boy. You should have told me the truth all along. We could have avoided such a tragedy. Nonetheless, I am known to be a forgiving man and I do forgive you for your sins, no matter how heinous they may be."

Clark began to cry. As he heaved, his bruises tortured him. He could feel the feeling go. His heart slowed and his head panged. He wasn't able to find air. He could hardly see Lockhart for the blinding light. "Would ye find me a doctor, sir? Please? Would ye find a doctor?"

Lockhart tapped his tongue to the tip of his mouth and shook his head slowly. "Unfortunately, there is no use, boy. You're not going to make it anyway."

four

A gentle floating snow began to blow along the Missouri countryside as Lockhart stood at the cold window. He watched columns of men march in blue, stepping perfectly in formation and turning in time on the other side of the white glass. Crackling bonfires leaked smoke all along the barracks and the red hearts of the fires blinked and waved like flags in the dark afternoon. Stews of meat and beans and corn cooked above the banners of flame.

Beside the window, taking up most of the wall was a portrait of Jefferson. The former president's eyes seemed to follow Lockhart as he stepped from the window and walked slowly about the room. Jefferson's face was solemn but dutiful, as if he had grown tired of hanging there. Lockhart tried not to look back at him. Other portraits surrounded the dark wood room. Knotty pine boards enclosed Lockhart while he gandered at each and every decoration on the walls. Medals and deeds and written honors were framed and encased in glass alongside the paintings. The stuffed head of a wild boar breathed out at him adding an intensity to the aura of the room. As he stepped lightly and politely, the door spoke and Colonel Poole walked commandingly to his desk. Lockhart stood at salute.

"Please, sit Lieutenant," Poole said with the wave of a hand. Lockhart sat himself slowly with a muffled groan into the simple chair across from the colonel. The colonel turned to him at the sound of his ailment. "How are you? Are you wounded?"

"With mere aches, sire. Nothing serious." Under Lockhart's coat, the screaming stitches from an arrow wound were pulling themselves apart with each breath he took.

"You made it better off than most of your troop then."

"Yes, that is right, sire."

Poole was an old man with a white mustache and thin white tufts of hair atop his jaundice head. He was between muscular and fat with a round chest and strong, long arms that hung like vines down his tall body. He stood at over six feet and he knew it. A bulbous pink nose held his face together like an anchor as he spoke animatedly. He hardly looked Lockhart in the eyes as he spoke, manufacturing busyness.

"I'm happy to see you back here alive, Lieutenant, but I'd be happier to see the rest of the men I sent you with. Is this report correct that just eight of your fifty dragoons have returned with you?"

"That is correct, sire. And for the infantry—"

"Ten men."

"That is correct, sire."

"And it is my understanding that even the dead have not returned with you. A shameful detail to be responsible for, Lieutenant."

"I am aware, sire. There was no way to recover the dead given the critical circumstances of our retreat. I swear an oath to you that in time, these fallen heroes will certainly be recovered and properly honored and buried for their sacrifice."

Poole was looking down at a sheet of paper. He pulled a pair of spectacles from his front pocket and rested them atop his mountainous nose. His eyes glided along the paper for a few moments before he set it down and turned his leisurely attention back to his guest.

"Lieutenant, as you are aware, our relationship with the American frontiersman is of the utmost importance to us here at Jefferson Barracks. For the citizens of our nation who brave the tumultuous elements of the plains and take the first step across the great Mississippi River into the infinite unknown, we are their only sense of security. Given our location, our ambitious jurisdiction is quite literally the entire plot between here and Mexico. It is our duty to protect and encourage American expansion even at the level of the individual citizen. When we fail to carry out such a duty, the public's respect and confidence in the United States military to act accordingly in hazardous scenarios deteriorates. As an officer, it is crucial that you uphold the standards of the officers around you and before you to maintain the suggestion that we are in complete control of our western border. With the spreading of news like your failed attempt to remedy Mister Franklin's Indian problem, a sense of lawlessness spreads like wildfire amongst the next generation of settlers who wish to enterprise the West. They will in turn, distrust our helping hand and attempt to tackle the unpredictable frontier by themselves, likely resulting in further tragedy. You understand the sequence of events that shall arise due to such failure, Lieutenant?"

"I do, sire."

"If there are two things that we must keep from manifesting in our conquering of the West, they are tragedy and lawlessness. Let the West not be branded by such marks."

"I agree, sire."

"We must seem as though we are in control of our situation, even if perhaps, we are not. With that said, your report has piqued my interest." The colonel leaned over his desk with wide, curious eyes.

"I imagined it would, sire."

"I would like to hear, from your own mouth, your account of the events."

Colonel George Poole had spent nearly his entire career in administrative roles in Washington. He had seen combat in the Chesapeake Campaign of the War of 1812, commanding a force of mounted infantry for over two months, repelling British forces all over the peninsula until their eventual invasion of the nation's capital forced his retreat. Following the war, his poor respiratory health and untreatable limp sentenced him to a desk job for the remainder of his career. His days were spent sifting through documents, writing letters, putting pins on maps, and acting as a middleman between his superiors and his inferiors. For his loyalty to his country and his rank, he was put in charge of Jefferson Barracks in 1830.

Poole listened as Lockhart offered his account diligently. He withheld no facts as to the nature of his enemy. He told Colonel Poole of Flete's journey into Platte Canyon and the ambush that followed. With considerable detail, he conveyed Russell Clark's knowledge of the valley and his betrayal of the military per his withholding of information. He accurately depicted the dozens of native tribes that he encountered along the foothills and presented maps and names for each of the many rivers, creeks, streams and brooks that were subject to his ceaseless excursions. However, it was in the telling of the final engagement between his own men and the valley people that Lockhart felt inclined to modify his tale.

"When I first encountered them, I spoke with the leader peacefully," Lockhart said. "I sat in a humble home—a low, cedar cabin lit by candles and decorated in pelts and Indian arts. The man I spoke with was called George. He was of great stature, larger than you, sire, and had attributes of both white-man and savage. He spoke old English with an odd accent I could not recognize. He was well spoken, though, and educated. We spoke of history and he had considerable knowledge of such matters as the Egyptians, Rome, and even Columbus. However, he seemingly had no reference whatever for our current place. For instance, he had initially taken us for Spanish and was startled completely at the news that the Spanish had no claim on our continent any longer. He had never heard of a nation called Mexico and certainly had not considered the existence of the United States."

"And you are sure that this George was of European descent?" asked Poole, completely engaged.

"I am sure, sire. Hardly any of the people amongst the village were full Indian. Some were plainly white with blonde hair and blue eyes. Some were as such but with Indian features. I heard people speaking English and Spanish, as well as native languages I had never encountered before."

"Extraordinary."

"Indeed, sire."

"Did you speak with George of his origin?"

"I did, sire, allow me to continue."

Lockhart spoke for some time relaying George's fable about the Drake Expedition. Poole was smiling, practically licking his lips with enchantment at the tale. Lockhart performed duly for his audience of one. "And it was at this meeting that I discovered that the Clark boy was working for George."

"He was one of them?" Poole blurted.

"Unlikely. I believe he had come across George under his own accord and struck some pact with the valley people that benefited him in some way."

"And what happened to the Clark boy?" asked Poole.

"I left him to George as I departed the cabin. After our council, I presented George with an option to surrender his weapons—as nearly all of his men were armed upon my arrival—allowing my men to peacefully commandeer the settlement until I could send for proper government acquaintances to legitimize the village and incorporate it into our nation. At this point George became disgruntled and refused my offer and demanded that I leave the premises. I left the Clark boy in George's hands. I did not see Clark again after that."

"I see."

"It was as I ascended the mountainside with the Second Dragoons that we came under fire. Immediately, I lost ten men as a storm of bullets and arrows followed our tails. Flete answered the attack with some covering fire but it had not come soon enough as George had already sent his own cavalry up the hill to follow us."

"They had horses?"

"Yes, sire. As my cavalry engaged theirs, I signaled for Flete and his men to come to our rescue as we were overwhelmed. The infantry joined us in a melee. We fought valiantly, repelling the first wave of the attack, but before we could find our way back up the steep mountainside, we were becoming surrounded by George's own infantry, outnumbered three to one. Each and every one of Franklin's volunteer trappers were slain in the fighting. Captain Flete, fought and died a hero as you know." Lockhart was growing passionate in his seat. His face began to redden and spit flew from his tongue as he spoke. "It is my humble opinion, sire, that we return to George's valley with sufficient numbers—perhaps an entire company of men, including artillery—and kill or capture each and every one of these half-breeds! I would love for you to lay your eyes on the valley yourself."

The two men were interrupted by the entrance of a servant who held a tray of tea that the colonel had forgotten he'd ordered. The man, lanky and young, stepped like a dancer with long, careful steps through the room as the two men retreated to the backs of their chairs. Two steaming glasses of tea were set on the table in front of them and as the door behind the servant shut. The men stared quietly at their respective cups. Lockhart sat still and watched the colonel as he rocked slowly in his chair in a pensive state. He seemed to have words in his lungs, trapped by his closed lips. It would only take the softest crack of the mouth to say what he wished to say. He reached for his tea and brought the hot cup to his face. He opened that cavernous mouth to take a sip and finally the words came.

"I'm going to share with you something that I shouldn't, Lieutenant."

Lockhart perked up like a curious dog and smiled. The corners of his mouth bent as he attempted to hide his eagerness. He was a sure bitch to the inclusivity of military intelligence. His strong, commanding demeanor only ever coiled under the pressure of a senior officer.

"You own my trust, sire," Lockhart said.

"Lieutenant Lockhart, there is a record that goes seldom touched in Washington. It has existed since colonial times and has been preserved by generations of men who have long studied it and confronted its innate problem with inconclusive results. It has long been thought to contain a quite *insolvable* problem due to a lack of tangible evidence and gaping holes in information. By the time the record had piqued any initial interest in the authority that held it, all parties involved were surely dead.

"During my stint working in intelligence, I became quite familiar with this record. It has been only recently, since our conquering of the West, that it has come to hold any importance again. What follows is to stay between you and I, Lieutenant." Poole's steady hand held the hot tea above his lap. He blinked at Lockhart who nodded his head. "In 1671 three Englishman by the names of Thomas Wood, Thomas Batts, and Robert Fallam led an early colonial expedition from the Colony of Virginia into the

Appalachian Mountains. Their excursion into the Appalachians was one of pure reconnaissance. It was debatably the first time Europeans had crossed these mountains. England's claims in Virginia and up and down the Atlantic Coast had grown to a sustainable volume and a growing curiosity began to drive men deeper into the unknown to begin to take stock of what elements and resources lay ahead. Their journey was one of great success as they eventually crossed the tallest crests of the mountains and wound up descending westward into northern Virginia."

"A marvelous tale," Lockhart remarked.

"Indeed. When they returned to the colony, they brought back maps and news of strong rivers full of freshwater and fat fish. They spoke of grounds for hunting and for building and the potential for silver and gold and precious rocks deep in the mountainous terrain, as far as the eye could see. They had achieved unanimously peaceful relations with the natives of the mountains. This inspired a great lot of settlers to push westward and found many of the important Virginia mining communities we know today. In short, the journey was an astounding success. However, the men brought back with them one peculiar finding. In the high, jagged peaks of the mountains, they found a wagon. It was a well built, English style wagon whose wheel and axle had cracked. It had apparently been abandoned. The vehicle wasn't in any riding shape as the men approximated it had been sitting for some fifty years. They reported their findings to their superior, Abraham Wood. Wood was a sort of catch-all character in his day—he began as an ordinary trapper but finished his life with a variety of military and government positions to speak of. At this time, he was working for the Governor of Virginia. The following spring, Wood followed the three explorers into the mountains himself and laid his own eyes upon the wagon. The men disassembled the thing and brought scraps of it back to the coast where it was presented to the governor and eventually linked to another wagon dating back to 1599—a wagon left behind in a failed English settlement in present-day Delaware called New Bristol. I trust you are familiar with the famous failed colony."

"I am aware of the story of New Bristol, sire."

"Surely not all of it, Lieutenant." Colonel Poole finally brought the now trembling glass of tea to his eager lips and enjoyed its warmth for a moment. He closed his eyes as he drank and set the cup down on the table. "Are you familiar with the plight of Adam Stone?"

"Perhaps not fully, sire."

"During the formative days of the colony, Stone was called to England to meet Elizabeth and then to lead a subsequent resupply mission back to New Bristol. When he returned to his colony, he found it abandoned. When he returned to England once more, he had with him a report of the dead. Nearly all of the colony's inhabitants were accounted for in some way or another—some had been killed by Indians, others dead by disease—but for those who were burned, they were deemed unrecognizable by Stone and his crew, and remained unidentified. Now, follow me here, Lieutenant. Even taking into account the mutilations, some remains were never found all together, leaving the report with fewer numbers of corpses then there were known inhabitants. This discrepancy was initially thought to be negligible. It was chalked up to the taking of English prisoners by the savages in their retreat. There were no objections to this theory which was widely believed until the discovery and identification of the wagon in 1671. It was then that Stone's record was reexamined and it was noted that only five of the eight recorded horses were present at the time of his report. Six other horses had been reported missing. There was no mention of wagons in either of his reports. In 1672, after a full reexamination of Stones records in light of the finding of the wagon, the Governor of Virginia wrote—in no tone of accusation or suspicion—that the lumber and build of the wagon found in Virginia matched that of a wagon from the lost New Bristol settlement. What is more curious, is that there were horse reins attached to the wagon found in Virginia. I trust you can see where I am going with this."

"With ease, sire."

"This case puzzled the minds of dozens of men for decades before it was decided that there was no conclusive explanation for the found wagon and the mystery reached a dead end. In the meantime, of course there were more important matters to attend to regarding the birth of this nation. This file again remained untouched, though talked about in some circles, for over one-hundred years until 1803 when the few remains of another wagon were found in a Pawnee village in southern Nebraska by U.S. scouts. When confronted about the origins of the parts, the Pawnee claimed that it had been in their village for as long as they remembered. At first, it was considered to be the parts of a Spanish wagon until the lumber was examined. Now, the Spanish had been making their New World vehicles in Mexico by this time; it was determined that this particular lumber was European—and not just that—the wheels bore markings that were synonymous with a 16th century wheelmaker from England. It was later discovered that the wheels of the wagon found in Virginia bore identical markings. As did the wagon in New Bristol."

"Sire, are you suggesting—"

"The chances are not great, Lieutenant. In fact, they are quite poor. But each stone follows the other quite magnificently, you must admit." Poole finished his tea and breathed a heavy breath. "It is of my opinion, Lieutenant, that the men you have just done battle with are the lost descendants of Adam Stone, founder of New Bristol, 1599."

✳✳✳

The horses cursed like sailors pulling the guns up the snow covered ridge. A single day's march had taken the company three because of the inclusion of the guns, and it was only a matter of hours before night fell on the freezing soldiers. The artillery officer was a small mustachioed man with a face like a rabbit and a voice like a frog. He hardly stood taller than the guns that he commanded. Repeatedly throughout the day he had dismounted his horse and personally shoveled the snow that had sunk the wheels of his 12-pounders. His men pushed from behind the guns as the horses were whipped to lashes.

"Blasted snow!" the little man kept shouting.

"Just a ways further," Lockhart ensured. Lockhart may have been the only man on the march who had not felt the cold. All of his senses were inside himself. He thought nothing of the gusting snow or of the struggling artillery. His mind was with George already. He had prepared himself for weeks to either capture or destroy the man that had dealt him his wound. Though it was not his stitched torso he wished to avenge, it was the wound he had accrued on his name. It was the blemish on his perfect record. His overconfidence and ill preparation had led to not only his first defeat, but the utter annihilation of his assault. Word had spread throughout Jefferson Barracks, and even as far as Washington, that Lockhart's men had been wiped out entirely by an untrained force. The gossip that floated between certain officer's circles was made of several vague pieces of chatter and misinformation. Some spreaders of the story identified the assailants as lost Mexicans. Others had gone as far to believe that it was Franklin's own men who ambushed Lockhart and Flete in the valley. Moreover, there was a great misunderstanding about the Clark boy who became interpreted as either the leader of the antagonists or the great martyr of Franklin's party who Lockhart was inspired to avenge. However, the most popular story among all of the differing accounts, was the mundane and embarrassing narrative that Lockhart's men had been ambushed and exterminated by a small band of Indians. For nights Lockhart laid awake in bed with hot blood and curled lips, agonized by the lies that were spread about him. He was, of course, under oath to Colonel Poole not to relay any information whatsoever about the true account of events to the public. Additionally, the men who survived the engagement were isolated in Washington—interrogated by an intelligence team and were not to be released until the matter was resolved.

While suffering the public scrutiny of a thousand eyes and the onslaught of questions from his peers, Lockhart, cold and determined, trained his body and mind to exist completely within itself. His ears had gone deaf, his eyes had gone blind. He ate only so he would not die. The entirety of his existing energy was focused on interning the giant George, and laying waste to the valley that he resided in.

Beside Lockhart on top of an equally regal and valiant steed was Colonel Poole, whose gloved hands quacked with cold. The colonel was calm and hopeful. His mustache was frozen with the drippings from his nose, and his black eyebrows—the only dark hair left on his head—were turned white with frost. He turned his head behind him to see the infantry stacked like waddling penguins behind the six guns. The horses skated on the ice of the ridge and the guns nearly rolled backwards in what would have been a lethal accident.

"Why don't we leave the damned guns behind!" yelled the colonel. "It will be another week before we get them up this mountain."

"We are close, sire," snapped Lockhart. He turned his dead face to his commander. "It's just on the other end of this ridge. It's less than an hour's march."

At the head of the infantry column stood Captain Web Wilson, who had replaced the late Captain Flete. He led one-hundred men in slick, black boots up the glazed hill. They coughed and shivered. Wilson himself had lost the feeling in his fingers and toes. "This is all a mess," he continued to say to his lieutenant. "Lockhart has us wrapped up in a lunatic's game of vengeance."

When they finally reached the top of the ridge the four officers—Poole, Lockhart, Wilson, and the mustachioed artilleryman whose German name nobody could remember— commanded their columns to halt, and they stepped through the underpass of white pines slowly at Lockhart's lead. Behind them, horses snorted and many of the men bent over and hurled into the snow.

Lockhart had preemptively planned the assault. "We will call the guns to follow us to the edge of this ridge. Just ahead, we'll be able to gaze down into the valley. We can place the entire battery there and cushion it with infantry. They should start their barrage immediately. The cavalry will split into two groups on either flank and another platoon of infantry will make a frontal assault. I'll show you just what I mean when we approach the valley. Keep yourselves low."

The four men walked, crouched, in a silly looking side-step. The curtains of their long uniforms dragged along the ground across the blue ice. Colonel Poole, massive and round and with a bad leg, was crouched taller than the artillery officer standing. He kept a hand on his saber.

"It's just here," Lockhart said as they approached the dirt lip at the edge of the overlook. The four men stood shoulder to shoulder as they approached the valley. The gray sky was still and ugly. Purple clouds formed behind the mountains towards the unseen horizon. An iridescent hum seemed to protrude from the mountains ahead. Those massive stone towers loomed over the men like Olympus; like Zeus, and Lockhart recognized them and removed his hat as he looked to the frozen faces of the palisades before him. They had watched all of it from the beginning and they knew the sorry, tragic truth about the whole affair. They had seen the arrival of John Cobb and the death of Powa and the birth of Foxfoot and the trials of George. Lockhart nearly thought of praying, asking them for their wisdom and their mercy before he peaked over the ridge and into the valley, but the mountains would be silent and he knew it. They were sworn to secrecy some hundreds of millions of years ago—the secrets of eternity. To know everything and to say nothing, Lockhart thought, must either be spiritual bliss, or the price paid for eternal life.

The men approached the overlook and peered down at the vast, wide valley. Its creek was frozen.

"Oh my," Colonel Poole uttered. "What has happened here?"

Lockhart blinked mindlessly at the scene. He wished to speak but the muscle laid flat at his teeth.

"Lieutenant?" Wilson asked.

The rabbit-faced artillery officer cursed in German under his breath.

"They've gone," Lockhart finally mustered. His eyes hadn't blinked and they began to hurt inside their sockets. "They've up and gone."

Inside the valley, the land was flat. There were no buildings. There was no wall surrounding any such town. A few lonely witness trees stood with gaping space between them. Frozen mounds of ash where houses used to stand were scattered all about the land.

The men descended with a platoon of infantry into the land. Lockhart went all around its perimeter detailing with his waving hands where they had fought and where the buildings stood and where the stables had been. He pointed along the fence line, where the deep holes of the wood beams that formed the walls were uncovered from beneath the snow. Ash and fine chips of wood filled the cavities. Some dozens of bodies laid frozen underneath the white blankets. The soldiers uncovered the bodies from under the frozen snow. They chipped away at the hard snow with their bayonets and shovels. The transparent blue faces of the dead threw horrid looks of fear at the officers. They were frozen by cold, but looked molten like wax. Ice froze over each eye so that the sockets were formless and shone like cicles. Some men gathered the bodies in one line and identified the husks of the former men.

"It seems that everyone is accounted for except for Private William Bell, sir," said one sergeant to Lockhart.

"Bell?" Lockhart snuffed. "Which was he?"

"One of Flete's men. Skittish private from New York. He was listed amongst the dead but he is not here."

"Nonsense! Of course he is here, keep searching."

Where George's cabin had once stood, a loan cedar log rested, charred and dead, chopped by the hand of John Cobb all of those years ago. The iron lock of his father's old English chest laid like a shell on a hill of ash; the cremated history of his life and his family. Poking around the ash on frozen feet was a red-beaked chickadee, lost and looking for food. It shivered in the cold and at the sight of Lockhart's tormented stride it dashed into the air and sailed to the tall pines that enclosed the valley to the west. It sang its song from beyond the valley clouds.

"They've burned it all down," said Lockhart. "Where on earth have they gone?"

Poole placed his hands on his broad hips. His eyebrows were high and he spoke with the peaceful tone of admitted defeat, "Well, there's a lot of country out there."

THE END

Maps and Notes

Carta Universal

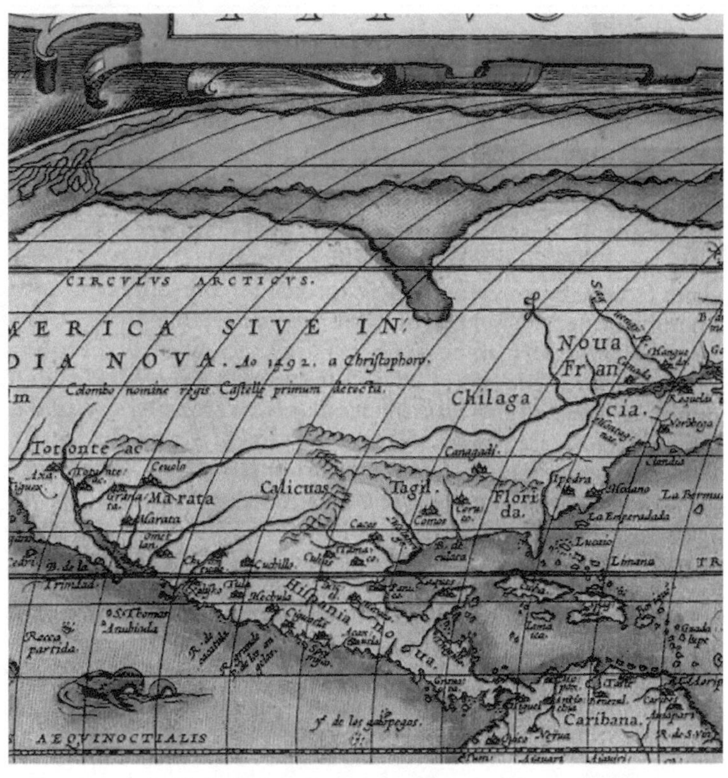

Theatre of the World

<u>Notes</u>

[1] Before this in 1702, Spanish scout, Captain José Naranjo, is said to have made contact with the South Platte River on a voyage from New Mexico. He called the South Platte, *Rio Jesus Maria.* He could be considered the first explorer to make contact with any of the three Platte Rivers, though he was not of European descent whatsoever, being a Pueblo Indian with allegiance to the Spanish.

[2] Villasur believed that his scout, the aforementioned Captain José Naranjo, had reached the Platte River several times by 1714. It is more likely that Naranjo, having reached the South Platte, had not realized that the South Platte River and the Platte River were not the same river.

[3] Fatalities included that of Captain José Naranjo, who was staunchly opposed to the mission to begin with.

[4] The only known French activity of this period were French-Canadian brothers Pierre and Paul Mallet following the Platte River to the South Platte River on a trade voyage from Kaskaskia, Illinois to Santa Fe in 1739.

[5] The two men would look for the burned and abandoned ruins of Étienne de Veniard, sieur de Bourgmont's Fort Orleans along the banks of the Missouri River, but to no avail.

[6] LeLande was a trader who was sent to Santa Fe to establish commercial relations with the Spanish, but upon his arrival to the city in 1804 he was arrested and held prisoner until 1806 when he agreed to accompany the Spanish on their mission to the Pawnee settlement.

[7] Fifty years later during the first Colorado Gold Rush, gold was indeed discovered in South Park as Purcell had said.

[8] La Ramee was a French trapper known for his unanimously peaceful relations with native tribes during his time in the West in the early part of the 19th century. He held a popular trading rendezvous along the North Platte River, settling there permanently in 1815. After his mysterious death in 1821, his land would be adopted by William Sublette in 1834 under the name "Fort William." Later, the fort would fall into the hands of the U.S. military and be renamed "Fort Laramie," serving as an invaluable position, and hotbed for violence during the United States' long-running and controversial conflicts with the Sioux.

[9] Hunt and Stuart had just established Fort Astoria on the Pacific mouth of the Columbia River in present-day Oregon in 1810 for John Jacob Astor's Pacific Fur Company. On their route back to St. Louis, they chose to avoid their previous northern route of the Missouri River due to increasingly violent activity from native tribes in the area. After crossing the mountains of Idaho, they instead dipped southeast into Wyoming and marched for several days before discovering what one member of the party described as "the celebrated South Pass" in the month of November, 1812. The South Pass is essentially a broad prairie of level elevation at the lowest point of the Continental Divide that allows a natural crossing point through the Rocky Mountains. Before its discovery, explorers were forced to either climb and cross the range itself, or to go completely around it by way of the Missouri River. The option to now pass straight through the mountains along the South Pass plateau with relatively no trouble at all completely changed the way Americans thought about trade and navigation in the West. From South Pass, Hunt and Stuart followed the Sweetwater River eastward to the North Platte River and traversed its entirety (being the first white men to do so) until its convergence with the Platte River in Nebraska which eventually led them back to their faithful Missouri. After the failure of the Pacific Fur Company in 1814, the South Pass route would go widely unused until it was discovered again in 1824.

[10] Jedediah Smith and Robert Campbell were trading fur with Crow Indians along the North Platte River when they came across South Pass. Smith immediately sent a member of his party to St. Louis to relay the news of the new shortcut to General William H. Ashley (the man for whom he was doing business). His findings were soon published by the U.S. Secretary of War which sparked a massive influx in traffic along the North Platte in the coming years. It should also be noted that Smith's publishing of his discovery would directly lead to the founding of the Oregon Trail which was forged right through the Pass and provided over 400,000 new settlers with a practical route across the Rockies for several decades.

[11] The other being a very brief visit by French trappers Auguste Pierre Chouteau and Jules de Munn who traded horses with a group of Apache.

12 Long had been on several western expeditions before, including manning the helm of a scientific contingent in Yellowstone the previous year.

13 Spain's hoarding of land and their desire for a limitless empire would eventually be their hubris, later resulting in the outbreak of more concurrent revolutions than they could afford to fight.

14 From here he sailed the coast of Long Island and found himself in the Hudson River, where he encountered thirty canoes of Lenape Indians. This would make him the first European to see what is now New York City.

15 Six months after Verrazzano's initial voyage, a Portuguese-born explorer and former member of Magellan's crew named Esteban Gómez, would roughly follow Verrazzano's route up the North American East Coast. Unlike Verrazzano, Gómez's crew thoroughly and accurately mapped this coast; their findings were reported to the famed cartographer, Diogo Ribeiro, who used them to compose a 1525 map—the first map to depict a single uninterrupted North American East Coast. These findings would make a laughing stock out of Verrazzano's claims that he saw China.

16 It must be mentioned that around this same time French explorer, Jacques Cartier, was arriving back in France from his final of three voyages (the first beginning in 1534) along the St. Lawrence River and upon the land that would later be known as Quebec.

[17] The first settlement in what would become the United States was a small Spanish colony called San Miguel de Gualdape in present-day Georgia in 1526. The settlement has roots in an exploration commissioned by Lucas Vázquez de Ayllón in 1521 which took place along the coast of Georgia and South Carolina before finally settling along what is generally accepted to be the Sapelo Sound about forty miles south of Savannah. San Miguel de Gualdape was abandoned in a matter of months due to harsh winter conditions, starvation, and violent relations with the native tribes. Peculiarly enough, the second and third attempts at a permanent settlement in the modern-day United States would come in the form of French colonies—not in the northeast, but in the southeast. In 1562 the French would attempt to build a fort they called Charlesfort on Parris Island, South Carolina. Charlesfort would succumb to the prototypical struggles of an early colony and last only a matter of months. The same colonists who established Charlesfort would go on to found a Fort Caroline near present-day Jacksonville, Florida in 1564. Though better equipped than Charlesfort, it would eventually perish after a series of armed bouts with Spanish St. Augustine in 1565.

[18] Years after his return to England, Drake fought valiantly against the Spanish Armada as a head Admiral of the English fleet, defending the country from the greatest attempted full-scale invasion in the history of warfare up to that point. He died in Puerto Rico of dysentery in 1596 after a failed attempt to conquer the city of San Juan.

[19] An island in present-day North Carolina deemed "suitable for colonization" by two English scouts, Phillip Amadas and Arthur Barlowe, who are responsible for the first use of the name *Virginia*.

[20] A strategic advance-base not far from the principal western passage that led to an area of Irish controlled territory that London had been pressing Devereux to capture for the bulk of the war.

[21] O'Connor was an Irishman fighting for the English cause and one of the only Gaelic chieftains that London could count on for support.

[22] O'Neill, O'Connor, O'Donnell, O'My!

[23] Coincidentally, or perhaps not, Robert Devereux, 2nd Earl of Essex was also the commander of this campaign in France preceding his time in Ireland.

[24] Adam Stone fell into relative obscurity, spending time as a vagabond, sometimes working odd jobs in and around London. It is believed that he joined a crew of pirates sometime in 1606. After this year, there are no official records of his existence, although there is reason to believe that the particular crew he was associated with landed in Bermuda in 1611 and picked up a group of young men that had been stranded on the island after the Sea Venture was shipwrecked there in 1609. The Sea Venture was an English vessel led by Sir Thomas Gates in 1609 that was bound for Jamestown, Virginia from England. Gates led a fleet of seven ships that carried a total of 600 people and a year's worth of supplies. This journey is historically known as, The Third Supply Mission. It was a resupply mission for the imminently failing Jamestown colony. On the 24th of July, the fleet braved a series of hurricanes and Sea Venture became separated from the other ships and veered south, blown by the storm. The other six ships made it to Jamestown together, but Sea Venture found herself battered and her crew exhausted, off the coast of Bermuda. Once on the island, Gates ordered that two new ships be built from the scraps of Sea Venture and the plentiful Bermuda cedar that was seemingly as strong as oak. Gates proposed that once the ships were built, they would set sail for Jamestown, meeting the rest of the fleet. However, rebellion stirred as most of the crew stated that the hurricane and shipwreck had freed them from their contracts and they were permitted to either stay in Bermuda or to return to England. Such rebellions were met with staunch executions by Gates and his loyalists. Gates instated prison-like conditions on the colonists, threatening them with starvation and execution if they did not comply with the building of the ships. One sailor who escaped the wrath of gates was one Christopher Carter, who sailed aboard Aquae Sanctae with Stone in 1599 upon his infamous return to New Bristol. After returning to England from New Bristol, Carter spent several years as a London blacksmith until attempting for a second time to fulfill his dream to travel to the New World aboard Sea Venture. Carter and a few other escapees survived on Bermuda on local food for about a year until a crew of pirates arrived to rest and service their ship. Little is known about this meeting, but it has been said that a man named Stone Graves, believed to have been Adam Stone, was on this crew. It is said that Graves often spoke about his days exploring the coast of the North American continent and living with Indians, trading spice, and doing battle with the Spanish—all things consistent with the character of Adam Stone. By the unofficial account of other crew members onboard this pirate vessel, Christopher Carter and Graves recognized each other immediately in Bermuda, and Carter happily joined him aboard the vessel. The two men were inseparable for years, as if they were father and son. Unfortunately, both men were killed on waters outside of Santo Domingo in October of 1615 after their ship became engaged in combat with a Spanish fleet.

25 Brazil's eastern coast was colonized by the Portuguese and her northern and western boundaries were impossible to penetrate on account of the Amazon Rainforest.

26 Named as such in reference to the dozen or so horses that were slaughtered there for meat. Additionally, the soldiers used the iron from melted horse tackle to forge tools and nails in construction of the rafts.

27 Poor Juan Ortiz had ended up in Florida in 1528 when he was aboard a ship that was searching for the lost Narváez expedition. Upon Narváez's disappearance, several Spanish search parties were sent to patrol the west coast of Florida in search of any sign of the campaign. During one of these rescue missions Ortiz and his companions were lured ashore by Uzita Indians who tricked them into believing that they carried a message from Narváez. Upon engaging with the natives, Ortiz and his companions were captured and all of the crew were executed by the Uzita tribe. Ortiz was spared only at the insistence of the chief's daughter, who begged her father in hysterics not to kill the man. Ortiz was enslaved for several years until a rivaling tribe, the Mocoso, attacked the Uzita village, burning most of it down in the process. The Uzita were forced to relocate and the chief demanded that Ortiz be sacrificed in a religious ritual. The night before the sacrifice, the chief's daughter smuggled Ortiz out of the camp where he was told to escape to seek refuge with the Mocoso tribe. The Mocoso allowed Ortiz to live among them and valued his skills and diverse cultural knowledge. By the time he was found by de Soto, he had become fluent in both Mocoso and Uzita.

27 De Soto's men would later claim that they *rescued* Ortiz, even though he refused to dress in the proper Spanish hidalgo garb that was provided for him, instead choosing to dress and live amongst the Mocoso that accompanied them north.

[29] One of the three men who wandered the southwest with Cabeza de Vaca in the 1530s.

[30] He sent Melchor Diaz, a governor and companion, to escort the friar south and then to meet the maritime leg of the exploration at the confluence of the Colorado and Gila Rivers. The maritime expedition was led by a man named Hernando de Alarcón and was coordinated to resupply the Coronado expedition en transit. By the time Melchor Diaz reached the assigned meeting point, de Alarcón had already come and gone, proven by the letter that he left in a bottle under a tree for Diaz, detailing the location of the buried supplies. From here, Melchor Diaz would cross the Colorado River and conduct the first intentional and meaningful exploration of California's interior, going as far as the Imperial Valley before dying in a freak-accident on his way back to Coronado's camp. De Alarcón would go on to sail further up the Colorado, being the first European to conduct such a deep excursion of the river. He would also explore the entire northern terminus of the Gulf of California, disproving the long-standing misbelief that California was an island.

[31] The very same winter de Soto and his men were nearing the Mississippi River as they fled Mabila.

[32] One man whom Coronado encountered was old and blind. The man could hear the Spanish from the lips of the colonists and told Coronado, with the help of translators, that many years ago, he had met "four others like you," likely a reference to Cabeza de Vaca, Estevan and their two companions six years earlier.

[33] While in Kansas in 1541, Coronado was only about five-hundred miles northwest of de Soto whose party was under constant ambush from the Tula people in central Arkansas at the same time.

[34] For a time it was believed that Coronado had traveled as far north as present-day Nebraska, but more modern studies suggest there is no evidence to prove he did so. It is far more widely believed today that Coronado made it as far north as the Kansas River.

[35] The survivors who chronicled the expedition counted a total of sixty-one pueblos visited over the course of their one year in New Mexico and Texas with an estimated combined population of 56,000 Indians.

[36] The exact date of Anna Stone's birth.

[37] His initial settlement in the province of Santa Fe would be north of what we would consider modern-day Santa Fe. The city of Santa Fe would be established in 1610.

[38] On this day in London, John Cobb met the family of Adam Stone for the first time as he had just accepted Stone's proposal to join him as second in command on a voyage to the New World.

[39] The *Carta Universal* (see page #250) contained elements of a previous Ribeiro map entitled *Mapa de América* from 1525 (see endnote #15). It also would be an important element in the creation of a larger, amended map titled *Padrón Real* in 1529. The *Padrón Real* was an ongoing project map constructed by the likes of over a dozen Spanish explorers and cartographers over the course of several decades with significant contributions by Diogo Ribeiro. The *Real* would go on to be the master-map for all future Spanish explorations and the template for future amended maps.

[40] *Theatrum Orbis Terrarum* (see page #251) is an atlas of the world made up of fifty-three different maps and published in 1570. It had been improved and reissued widely by 1598. It was the first atlas of its kind to depict a completed pair of New World continents alongside long-standing maps of the Old World.

[41] This map shared elements of both Giacomo Gastaldi's 1546 *Universale*, and Gerardus Mercator's 1569 *World Map*. Interestingly, the former depicts a more *accurately shaped* New World, while the latter's erroneously obtuse continent contains *better detail* regarding interior geography. The map featured in the *Theatre of the World* is a favorable melding of both.

[42] One day after John Cobb and his party escaped New Bristol.

[43] This meeting was near present-day Coffeyville, Kansas.

[44] Near present-day Junction City, Kansas.

[45] Ironically, just over a year later in the fall of 1601, Miguel's old companion from the Humana and Leyva Expedition, Jusepe Gutierrez, would return to the Great Plains leading Juan de Oñate along the same route that he had taken during the expedition in 1595. This would put Gutierrez and a commissioned Spanish military expedition less than one-hundred miles from where Cobb first rescued Miguel in the spring of 1600. Unsurprisingly, Oñate would end up fighting several bloody battles with the Wichita and Apache tribes on his return route to New Mexico after an attempt to kidnap native children for the purpose of Catholic conversion turned violent. This absolute failure of reconnaissance would mark the end of Spanish intervention in the Great Plains for multiple generations.

46 The Tabeguache band of the Ute tribe were a widely nomadic band of hunters who relocated with the migration and natural movement of deer and elk several times a year.

47 Alleged father of the Indigenous-Spanish scout, José Naranjo, who would go on to be the first confirmed explorer to reach the South Platte River in 1702. See endnote #1.

48 The San Luis Valley lies just on the western side of the Continental Divide and just one-hundred miles south of the South Platte River.

49 De Vargas' entry into Colorado was preceded only by a voyage by Juan de Archuleta who was also on the hunt for slaves in 1664, some decades before the Pueblo Revolt. It is likely that de Archuleta was the first European to step foot in what is today Colorado. Though he did not travel far enough west to see the mountains, Juan de Archuleta would be about 120 miles from Cobb's Valley at his closest.

50 Who had just surveyed the land that would later become the city of Albuquerque, calling it a *superb location to settle a new town*.

51 Who would later die along the Platte River on the disastrous Villasur Expedition of 1720. See endnote #3.

52 This news paired with reports of French activity along the Platte River (Étienne de Veniard, sieur de Bourgmont), would lead to the aforementioned Villasur Expedition.

53 A trade passage that would link Santa Fe to Los Angeles beginning in the early 19th century.

54 Just twenty-five days following the signing of the United States' Declaration of Independence.

55 Detailed in Book I, Chapter II.

9 7989 9943 97008